"Am I a cowboy now?" Charlie asked.

Ash ruffled the kid's hair, then pushed off the bed. "You're a novice cowboy. How's that?"

"That means beginner?"

"Right. Smart boy."

"Sometimes I'm not." He ducked his head.

"Well, that's why you're seven. You still have a lot of growing to do."

"Mom says so, too."

"I'd listen to your mom."

"And you." The boy's smile healed a spot in Ash's heart.

"On this ranch, that's a given. Your mom in her room?"

"Uh-uh. She's right behind you."

Ash struggled around. Rachel leaned in the doorway, hands tucked under her arms. Defensive and a little wary. He'd done that. Kissing her had not been clever. But he couldn't stay away. One look from those blue cat eyes, one word from that expressive mouth, and he was as lost as her son was with his boots on the wrong feet....

Dear Reader,

As a child growing up on a large farm, I adored the freedom country life grants—its wonderful clear-lined skies, the big-mooned harvest nights, and winter days cold enough to make your cheeks ache. And in the midst of this pristine beauty were the animals: horses, cows, dogs, cats—creatures with personalities all their own.

We always had a herd of horses running in the pasture and, throughout the summer, cattle grazing on leased land. Each season brought about specific events. February and March meant calving season and watchful nights. Summer meant haying. And fall signified harvest and the time to "bring the cows home" again. Winter, of course, lent to slower and colder days, but certainly not without chores!

Is it any wonder that a story about a cowboy would evolve in my mind?

While Ash and Rachel and the journey they undertake are entirely fictional, the magic of hearing coyotes yap deep in the night and feeling the sting of winter winds against the skin are experiences of the heart.

May you enjoy this tale about a stoic rancher from Montana and the woman who breaks past the fences he's erected around his life.

Mary J. Forbes

THE MAN FROM MONTANA

MONTANA

MARY J. FORBES

Silhouette®

SPECIAL EDITION®

Published by Silhouette Books

America's Publisher of Contemporary Romance

SILHOUETTE BOOKS

ISBN-13: 978-0-373-24800-1
ISBN-10:   0-373-24800-8

THE MAN FROM MONTANA

Copyright © 2006 by Mary J. Forbes

Visit Silhouette Books at www.eHarlequin.com

Printed in U.S.A.

Books by Mary J. Forbes

Silhouette Special Edition

A Forever Family #1625
A Father, Again #1661
Everything She's Ever Wanted #1702
Twice Her Husband #1755
The Man from Montana #1800

MARY J. FORBES

grew up on a farm amidst horses, cattle, crisp hay and broad blue skies. As a child, she drew and wrote of her surroundings, and in sixth grade composed her first story about a little lame pony. Years later, she worked as an accountant, then as a reporter-photographer for a small-town newspaper, before attaining an honors degree in education to become a teacher. She has also written and published short fiction stories.

A romantic by nature, Mary loves walking along the ocean shoreline, sitting by the fire on snowy or rainy evenings and two-stepping around the dance floor to a good country song—all with her own real-life hero, of course. Mary would love to hear from her readers at www.maryjforbes.com.

To my editor, Stacy Boyd—
for believing in me

Chapter One

She could smell the story. Feel it in her veins.

A hot, pulsing thing that would procure the career she'd vied for these past ten years.

Will you finally be proud, Daddy? Will you think my journalistic skills are comparable to Mama's?

God, she hoped so.

At the crossroads Old Joe the baker had described, Rachel Brant stopped her rusty Sunburst and scanned the three desolate directions vanishing into the rolling Montana countryside: ahead toward the south, left going east, right westward-ho. Each road as long and gray as the next. Each banked in dirty plowed snow and flanked by fields covered in icy white quilts.

The Flying Bar T lay west, toward the Rocky Mountains.

Carefully, she picked up the curled, yellowed photograph on the passenger seat. Tom McKee in army green with his Vietnam platoon, a giant man dependent on a wheelchair since 1970.

Tom, Purple Heart recipient, had lost his legs and left arm saving the ragtag remainder of his men from Hells Field. A battle that had been swept under the military's carpet for over three decades. She wanted to beat the dust from that carpet, make her dad proud.

But according to the locals, Tom rarely came into town. His son was the McKee they knew. Midthirties and widowed, Ashford McKee ran the Flying Bar T and guarded his family's privacy like a jackal on a fresh kill.

Ash. The man she had to get through to get to Tom. They said he resembled his father. Tall as a pine, silent as a forest.

And keeper of the Flying Bar T gates.

Tossing down the photograph, Rachel took a slow breath. *We'll see.*

Stepping on the accelerator, she headed for the snowy peaks shimmering with sunlight, for the pine and forest man.

She would get her story, come hell or Ash McKee.

Beyond the fence lines, fields undulated over hill and knoll and into gullies. "I hope you're worth it, Sergeant Tom," she muttered. "I hope you're worth every shivering second Charlie and I have had to endure in this backwater hole."

Ten days she and her seven-year-old son had been in Sweet Creek, Montana. Ten days in this godforsaken land of snow and bone-freezing temperatures. And in this final week of January, with spring still a couple months away, the warmth of her previous job in Arizona was a frosty memory.

But all would be worthwhile if she got this story. Tom would be the last of seven vets she had interviewed over the years, Sweet Creek the conclusion to the no-name towns she and her little boy would have to pretend was home.

Was it too much to hope Tom McKee would rent out his guesthouse as Old Joe said? Maybe. She had been living on hopes and wishes for years; might as well add one more.

In a fenced pasture, she saw cows huddling around piles of hay on the frozen ground, while long-haired horses munched from bins in lean-to shelters. Evidently, the sunlight belied the eight below temperature.

She turned onto the last stretch of road and saw a dark, writhing mass a quarter mile in the distance. Soon, the mass became a herd of Black Angus flanked by a pair of horses with riders: a man wearing a quilted navy coat and a deep brown Stetson, and a young woman bundled in a red parka and wool hat. Two black-and-white border collies swept back and forth across the road, instinctively herding any animal selecting a different direction.

Rachel pulled behind the riders and tooted her horn; the herd's stragglers broke into a trot, tails aloft.

The man scowled at her car. The woman—no, *teenager*— smiled. Rachel recognized the girl from their meet last Monday. Eager to write a weekly high school column for the *Rocky Times,* Daisy McKee had come to the newspaper during the girl's forty-minute lunch break. A few words about her proposed column and she was out the door, rushing back to school.

A nice kid and Ashford McKee's daughter.

Rachel looked back at the man astride a mammoth horse the color of dense fog. *Ash McKee.* Big and commanding as the far-reaching, pristine landscape on which he lived. Four days after her arrival, she had noticed him at the feed and-seed, intent on getting whatever it was he was buying into the bed of his truck.

Darby at the coffee shop had pointed him out. A coup for Rachel, who, as a reporter, needed to know her town, and right now Sweet Creek was that town. Most essentially, she needed to ferret out details about the McKees; they were her reason for securing the position at the *Rocky Times,* a twenty-page weekly aptly named during the Depression Years, and now reaching conservative ruralists throughout Park County.

The herd trotted toward the ranch's wide-spanning iron gates, neither McKee nor Daisy making an effort to move the cattle aside. Rachel rolled down the window. "Excuse me," she called to the man.

He whistled between his teeth at one of the dogs.

"Excuse me," she called again. "Mr. McKee? Could I get by?"

Cold, dark eyes turned her way. "Can you wait? We're a hundred yards from the pasture gate."

Yes, she could wait. If he'd ask nicely.

"I'm looking for Tom McKee," she said to the broad rump and ground-reaching charcoal tail of his horse. "Would you know if he's home?"

The man reined the beast around on its hind legs, its tail swinging like a banner on a battle field. Two leaps and the animal danced beside her car.

"Who wants to know?" McKee demanded.

He was cowboy through and through, down to the scuffed, worn brown boots he wore. She shivered. A modern-day Clint Eastwood in *Pale Rider*. All he needed was the six-shooter.

"Rachel Brant. I'd like to talk to him."

The horse was magnificently male and powerful, crowding her spot on the road. Safety inside her vehicle seemed trivial in lieu of those commanding legs, that mighty chest. And she wasn't just thinking of the horse.

"What about?" McKee snapped.

"That would be between me and Mr. *Tom* McKee, sir," she said, her tone friendly but firm.

"Not when it comes to reporters."

Surprise struck. "How did—" Had he recognized her in Sweet Creek on a given moment, watched her as she'd watched him?

"Entire town knows," he said, reading her perplexity.

Of course. She'd experienced enough of small-town America to know how the grapevine worked with six-hundred-and-ninety-two souls. New face arrives, phone lines hum, coffee klatchers drain buckets of dark roast—and tongues waggle.

From her position in the car, she had a clear view under his low-brimmed Stetson. Down a smooth, elegant nose the man's aloof eyes bored into hers.

Perhaps if she got out of the car.

She looked at the powerhouse horse shifting its lethal hooves. *Come on, Rachel. You've dealt with difficult situations all your life.*

Opening the door, she climbed out. The wind blew her short hair into her eyes, flapped her coat hem around her tall boots. The scent of horse, cow and leather rivered across her nose.

McKee's willful jaw was dark with overnight stubble. His scowl deepened. "Go report somewhere else, Ms. Brant. You're not welcome here."

Beneath its rider the huge stallion pranced, the saddle creaking with the man's weight, the animal's energy. Frothy clouds gusted from red nostrils and long white teeth champed the bit. Headgear metal jingled. A knight's horse. A *rogue* knight's horse.

Along with her fanciful imagination a thrill traced Rachel's skin. "I'll let Tom make that decision."

"His decision's no different than mine."

She clutched the panels of her coat. "According to you, maybe. But I'd like to hear him say it."

"Tom doesn't like reporters."

No, you *don't like reporters.* So she had heard in town. Could she blame him? She knew about his wife dying in a car accident five years ago. A reporter chasing a mad-cow story in the community. A *Rocky Times* reporter. Driving too hard, too fast, taking a curve like the reckless kid he was. The impact had killed McKee's wife instantly. The reporter walked away.

McKee's eyes were tough, remote and held her in a vice.

Hugging herself against the cold, she looked up at him, a man of dominion in an expanse of blue. Somehow, she had to win over this warden of the Flying Bar T.

"Please. I'm looking for a temporary place to live until I can find something in town. I understand your ranch has a guesthouse for rent. I'm willing to pay summer rates." Anything to get Charlie out of that seedy Dream On Motel.

McKee leaned forward, arm on the saddle horn, and her skin flushed under his stern survey of her body. "The cottage is closed," he said, then slowly straightened in the saddle. Under him, the big horse spot-danced like a Lipizzan, its mane swaying a foot below its neck while McKee controlled the reins with one large, gloved hand.

Rachel kept her stance, swallowed hard. Instinctively, she knew he would not let the animal step on her. Squinting into the bright Montana sky, she offered, "I'll pay peak season rates." For the story, but mostly for Charlie. *Two birds with one stone.*

McKee studied the herd trotting ahead of them; several cows lowed. The Stetson's brim shadowed his eyes, and that obscurity sent a tingle across her arms.

"Go back where you came from, Ms. Brant." His voice was low and without mercy. Spurring his mount forward, he left her staring after the cattle now rushing through the pasture's gates.

An animal broke free and the black-and-white dogs darted out, piloting it back to the herd in seconds. Daisy jumped from her chocolate-colored horse—half the size of the gray—to close the gate. When her eyes caught Rachel's across fifty feet of road, she sent a two-fingered wave, then climbed into the saddle before following McKee to the barns.

Go back where you came from.

He hadn't meant Sweet Creek.

* * *

Ash led Northwind, his prize Andalusian stallion, into the big box stall at the rear of the horse stable.

She had nerve, that woman.

Last time newshounds swarmed the ranch was five years ago, chasing that goddamn stupid mad-cow story. A bunch of bull that cost Susie her life.

But this one didn't want a story, just a roof over her pretty head.

Pretty. No damn way would he think a hack pretty.

Except she was. That bob of hair the color of his mother's antique cherrywood sideboard, those eyes that tilted slightly at the outer corners. Cat eyes in Siamese-blue.

They always sent the pretty ones on a story hunt.

Did you not hear what she said? She wants to rent a room.

Right. That he would believe in another life.

He yanked the saddle off Northwind hard enough to make the horse sidestep. "Easy, boy. Don't mean to take it out on you." Hauling the gear into the tack room across the corridor, Ash clamped his teeth. Yeah, that was all he needed, a word wizard living on his ranch. A word wizard with media broadcasting power. And her power—if she chose to use it—could be a thousand times worse than the taunts and gossip he'd endured in school.

Well, dammit, this ranch was his life, and though he held its paperwork together through the eyes and smarts of his family—they paid the bills, did the ordering, worked e-mail and the Net—those bills and orders came through his direction, his guidance, his *knowledge* of the land and the animals. Still, the fact he wasn't college educated sat like chain mail on his shoulders.

And while he couldn't put the onus of that fact on the head of a woman he had met for three minutes, newsperson or not, neither could he trust her.

His family had seen its share of run-ins with the *Rocky Times*. The year Ash turned sixteen, Shaw Hanson, Senior, had sent his team to the Flying Bar T after Tom was accused of not feeding his stock properly due to his disability.

Ash snorted. All of it drivel. Still, the newshounds had fed like a wolf pack on the ASPCA's investigation. Yet, to this day the person or persons who'd pointed the finger at Tom remained a mystery.

And then there was Susie's death….

The memory twisted a knot in Ash's gut. Now a *Rocky Times* reporter wanted to rent the little cottage she'd designed and he'd built? Never.

"Dad?"

He turned from retrieving a currycomb off the tack room wall to his fifteen-year-old daughter standing in the doorway. A sprite like her mother with big green eyes, a mop of long red curls. But strong enough to lift the saddle she carried to a loop hanging from the ceiling rafters.

His heart bumped. "Hey, Daiz. Need some fresh bedding for Areo?"

"Already did that this morning."

He crossed the room and wove the loop into the hole on the pommel and around the horn.

"Thanks." She tossed the blanket over a wooden drying rack in a corner. "What did Mi—that woman want?"

"Nothing important."

Daisy reached for a second currycomb. "You chased her off."

"She works for the *Times*." And that should explain it. He went into Northwind's stall. "You know how I feel about them." About Shaw Hanson, Junior, and *his* crew of sleazy reporters.

"Yeah," she said slowly. "I know."

He glanced over his shoulder. Her expression sent a shaft of pain across his chest. She still missed her mother, missed their girl chats, Susie's laughter, her hugs. Hell, *he* missed those hugs. He combed Northwind's powerful withers. "I won't let her hurt you, honey. And I won't let her come near your grandpa." *Or this ranch.*

"Oh, Dad." She sighed and turned into the corridor.

What the hell?

"Daisy?" He peered around the door as she disappeared into Areo's stall. For a moment, he stood wondering if he'd heard right. Her voice had held resignation, not sorrow. Had he disappointed her by chasing off that journalist? He shook his head. No. She knew how their family felt about the Hansons and their editorial finesse. It had to be something else. Well, she'd tell him in time.

Back in Northwind's stall, he brushed down the big dapple-gray stallion, then filled his water bucket and manger. As Ash finished, Daisy exited Areo's stall. "All done, pint?" He strode down the aisle toward his daughter. The dogs, Jinx and Pedro, trotted ahead.

"Yep."

"All right. Let's see what Grandpa's got for lunch."

They headed from the warmth of the barn into clear cold air. Hoof and boot prints pockmarked last night's snow. Ash slowed his stride for his daughter. They walked in silence toward the two-story yellow Craftsman house that Tom's great-grandfather, an immigrant from Ireland, had built in 1912.

Ash set a hand on Daisy's shoulder. "Good thing your teachers had that in-service today. Don't know if I could've moved those steers without you."

"Oh, Dad. You and Ethan do it all the time when I'm at school."

Ethan Red Wolf, their foreman. A good man. "You know Wednesday is Eth's day off. Anyway, things go ten times faster with you helping."

"You always say that."

"And I mean it."

A grunt. "What did the reporter want?"

Back to that. His pixie-girl, forever the little dog with an old shoe when she focused on some particular subject. While her tenacity baffled the heck out of him at times, he was damned proud when she brought home her straight-*A* report card. "She wanted to talk to Grandpa about renting the guest cottage."

"Are you gonna let her?"

"No."

"Why not? We could use the money."

He rubbed Daisy's shoulder. "We're not so hard up, honey, that we need to rent to a reporter." Never mind that the woman in question had him thinking about things he hadn't thought of in a long time. Like how pretty a female could be and how feminine her voice sounded on the cold morning air—even though she pushed with her words.

"Got any homework that needs doing?" he asked, veering off the thought of Rachel Brant and her attributes.

"Some social studies and English."

The thought of Shakespeare and essays had him sweating. "Better get at it after lunch."

"I need Grandpa's help. We're doing this project in socials." A small sigh. "I have to ask him some questions."

"What kind of project?" They walked up the wheelchair ramp to the mudroom door at the side of the house. Tom was good at English, good at reading and writing. If his blood had run in Ash's veins maybe—

"We're supposed to pretend we're journalists." Shrugging off her coat, Daisy trudged into the mudroom ahead of Ash. Her eyes wouldn't meet his. "And…and we're supposed to interview a veteran, so I was thinking of asking Grandpa."

Speak of the devil. First a real reporter and now a make-believe one in the guise of his daughter. No wonder he had hated school. Teachers were always pushing kids into role-playing and projects, pretending they were real life. Just last week, John Reynolds's eleventh grader brought home an egg and said it was a baby. Ash snorted. What the hell was the world coming to anyway? Eggs as babies? Kids playing war correspondents?

Ash closed the door, hooked the heel of his left boot on a jack. "You know Gramps won't talk, Daiz."

Holding back her long, thick hair, Daisy removed her own boots. "Well, dammit, maybe it's time, y'know?"

Ash glowered down at his child. "Watch your language, girl."

A tolerant sigh. "Dad, it's been, like, thirty-six *years*. Why won't Grandpa talk about his tours? I mean, *jeez*. It's not like they happened yesterday. He even got the Purple *Heart*." Frustrated, she kicked her boots onto the mat with a "Get over it already" and flounced into the kitchen.

Ash watched her go. They had been over this subject two dozen times in the past three years, the instant she reached puberty. She wanted to know episodes of her heritage, about her mother, about him, about Tom.

Ash had no intention of talking about Susie or her death. Too damn painful, that topic. What if he accidentally let out the truth, that his wife was as much to blame for the accident as that two-bit journalist?

He shook his head. No, he couldn't chance it. Hell, *thinking* about it gave him hives.

Maybe one day he would tell Daisy, but not during her "hormone phase," as Tom put it.

As for Tom…Vietnam was the old man's business.

Ash entered the quaint country kitchen. "Hey, Pops."

His stepfather, bound to a wheelchair for three-and-a-half decades, swung around the island, a loaf of multigrain bread in his lap. "Daisy in a mood?" On the counter lay an array of butter, cheese, tomatoes and ham slices ready for Tom's specialty: grilled sandwiches.

Ash walked to the sink to wash his hands. "In a mood" was the old man's reference to Daisy's monthlies. "She's upset about a couple things, yeah."

"What things?"

"Wants us to rent out the cottage to a reporter."

Tom snorted. "You're kidding, right?"

"New one hired on with the *Times*. Drove out here this morning while we were moving the yearlings."

"You tell him we're not interested?" The chair whined behind Ash. In his mind's eye, he saw his stepfather pressing a lever, raising the seat so he could maneuver his stump legs into the open slot Ash had constructed under the counter years ago.

"Not him. Her." *A sassy-mouthed woman with big eyes.*

"Her?"

Ash leaned against the sink and crossed his arms. The reporter splashing the ASPCA story across the front of the *Rocky Times* twenty years ago had been a woman and Hanson Senior's wife.

Tom slapped cheese and ham onto a slice of bread, cut the tomatoes deftly with his right hand.

"What'd you tell this reporter?"

"That she's not welcome." He glanced toward the stairs, warned, "Daiz sees it differently. Figures we need the money."

"Huh." Right hand and left prosthesis worked in sync over the sandwiches. "What's her name?"

"Rachel Brant."

Silence. Then, "Brant, huh?" More slicing and buttering. "Suppose we could use the extra cash."

Ash straightened. "You crazy?"

Tom shrugged. "Why not? Place is sitting empty. Might as well burn it down if we ain't gonna use it. Besides, with calving season starting, Inez'll be feeding extra hands over the next couple months."

Inez, their housekeeper and Tom's caretaker, was in Sweet Creek at the moment, buying two weeks' worth of groceries. "We'll get by," Ash grumbled. "We always do." He did not need the Brant woman here, within walking distance, *within sight.* She was a journalist and he would bet a nosy one, prying until she got a barrel of tidbits to create a stir with her words. "Stories," they called those reports. He knew why. More fiction than fact.

And with her working at the *Times,* talking to publisher–owner Shaw Hanson Jr.... Hell, Hanson probably sent her to the Flying Bar T as a dig on the McKees. After all, Ash had gone after Hanson for sending Marty Philips to sniff out that mad-cow scare. Two days following Susie's death because of that cocky young kid, Ash walked into the newspaper and kicked ass.

And where did that get you, Ash?

Tossed in the hoosegow for three days.

Tom buttered six additional slices, cut another two tomatoes, assembling enough for a soup kitchen. "You said Daisy was in a snit over a couple things. What's the other thing?"

"Social studies project."

Across the counter, his stepfather eyed Ash under a line of bushy gray brows. "You wanted it done yesterday."

"No. I don't want her bugging you."

That narrowed Tom's eyes. "Me?"

"She's supposed to interview a vet for war facts."

"Huh. Don't they have textbooks for that?"

"They do, but this time the kids are supposed to get it from the horse's mouth. So to speak."

"Well, this old horse ain't talking." The chair hummed as Tom wheeled around to the range. "Same reason you don't talk about Susie," he muttered.

Same reason? Hell, there were things Ash would never share with his family. Like the day he'd buried Susie. How he'd gone back at dusk and sat where he'd put her ashes and cried until he puked. How he pounded his fists against the sun-dried earth, cussing that she'd known better than to drive after drinking, a fact he found out from the coroner four days later.

Alcohol at three in the afternoon.

Alcohol affecting her competence.

No seat belt. Busted windshield. Busted brain.

God help him, but Susie's disregard was his secret. Not Tom's, and never, *never* Daisy's.

His pain. His *business.* Like Tom with Nam.

Ash pushed away from the counter. Patting the old man's shoulder, he said, "I'll tell Daiz to wash up."

At her computer in the cramped newsroom of the *Rocky Times,* Rachel put her face into her hands and took a long, deep breath. Yesterday she had gone about it wrong, driving out to the Flying Bar T, trying to get past Ash McKee and his warhorse.

God, when she thought of the rancher and that animal… They exuded a beauty and authority that kept her enthralled for twenty-four hours. McKee's pole-erect back, his muscular thighs controlling the animal whose charcoal forelock shrouded its eyes. The man himself blocking the sunlit sky with his mountain-wide shoulders, his Stetson.

She rose and went to the window beside her desk, drew up the dusty blinds, welcoming the sunlight. Shaw had swept the sidewalk clear of snow. On this last day of January, the sky promoted a bank of gray snow clouds to the north, which meant that before midnight February would be whistling its way over the landscape.

Several pickups drove down Cardinal Avenue, their wheels churning the previous night's snowfall into a crusted brown blend. Across the street, a two-tone green crew-cab angle-parked in front of Toole's Ranch Supplies.

Ash McKee stepped down into the crystalized mush. As he closed the door of his vehicle, his gaze collided with hers across the street. Rachel drew a sharp breath. Again, she saw him on that sweat-flanked horse, smelled the steamy hide of animal, the leather of the saddle as the rancher leaned down toward her....

He turned and disappeared inside Toole's.

Ash. Here in town. Tom, alone on the ranch.

Rachel snatched up the phone on her desk. In the face of what she wanted, Ash McKee was a massive problem. Local lore, gleaned at Old Joe's Bakery and Darby's coffee shop down the street, said he was not a man to take lightly. *And when did that stop you, Rachel? You've met men far more daunting than this one. Case in point, your father and Floyd Stephens.*

This was her chance. Phone Tom while his son was twenty miles away, talk to the old soldier about the guesthouse first, give him a reason to speak with her. Later, she could bring up the story.

"At all costs, get the story." Her father's mantra.

Nerves and guilt lifted the hair on her nape. *Don't think. Do.* Her fingers shook, but she punched the number without stumbling. At the other end the phone rang twice, three times, six times.

"Come on, pick up or at least get an answering machine."

Eight rings... "'Lo."

"Mr. McKee?"

"Yeah?"

"My name is Rachel Brant." She glanced toward the window. No Ash. "I was out your way yesterday to see you, but—" she couldn't stop the edgy chuckle "—your cattle were in the way, so I wasn't able to—"

"You the reporter?"

"I, uh—yes, that's right. I work at the *Rocky Times.*"

Silence.

"I'd like to talk to you, sir, if you have a moment."

"You're looking to rent the cottage."

So Ash had relayed the information. "If possible."

"Ain't my deal. It's Ash's. Convince him and you'll have a place to hang your hat."

"I thought you owned the ranch."

"I do. But the cottage is his venture."

"Actually, I'd like to talk to you, too."

"Like I said the cottage is—"

"I know, Ash's business. But I'd like to talk to you about something else."

Pause. "This got to do with some damned story?"

"In a way, yes, it does. I—"

Dial tone. He'd hung up. *Damn.* Now what? Should she phone back? Go out anyway while Ash was in town? No, she couldn't trust how long he'd be. The last thing she needed was to get caught out in the boonies with a fire-breathing dragon on her heels.

She should have left it with renting the guesthouse, waited until she was out there to talk to Tom face-to-face.

She sat and fumed at her desk. Almost two weeks of planning gone down the drain. Two weeks of schmoozing with the townsfolk, getting to know them on a first-name basis, cracking smiles she didn't feel, pushing her little boy into yet another school with strange kids. Living in a moth-eaten motel.

All for what? Fame and glory?

So her father—an editor with the *Washington Post*—would recognize she was as capable of meritorious reporting as her mother had been? Qualified to make the big leagues, to one day write her way to a possible Pulitzer?

Worth loving just a little?

The thought left a barb. Bill Brant had loved no one but his long-dead wife, Grace. Times like these, Rachel wished, *wished* her mother still lived. But she had died of cancer twenty-four years ago, on Rachel's eighth birthday. A day branded in her mind. Not only had she lost her mother forever, but her daddy had set the blame at his daughter's feet. Stupid, Rachel knew. But still.

She had to try. *Had to.* For her own sake as well as her father's.

But, oh, she was tired. Of the lying, the pushing, the shoving. Of living in seven different backwater towns in seven states, soliciting local newspapers for a job—just so she could have the time to gain the trust of their wary resident Hells Field veteran. God, what she wouldn't give to find her own niche and have Bill Brant be happy for *her.* Just once.

"You don't give up, do you?"

She jerked around. Ashford McKee stood five feet away, big and tough as the land he owned. *A pine and forest man.*

Hands buried in a sheepskin jacket, Stetson pulled low as always, he stared down at her with dark, unfriendly eyes. Slowly he removed a cell phone from his pocket and lifted one smooth black brow. "We McKee's keep in touch."

She should have known. A fly speck couldn't get past him without that speck becoming a mountain.

Rachel rose. At five-ten, she was no slouch, but beside him she felt gnome short. "I'm sorry," she said, "but as I mentioned yesterday my issue is with your father—who I understand owns the Flying Bar T?"

Annoyance flickered in those dark eyes, then vanished. "Issue? The only *issue* I see here is *you*—harassing my family."

"Making one phone call is hardly harassment, Mr. McKee."

He studied her a moment with eyes that might have offered warmth because of their clear-tea color. Not today. Today they were frozen as the earth outside. "What do you want with him?"

"To ask about the guesthouse." She pinched back her guilt at the omission of the story.

"And he told you to talk to me. What else?"

On a sustaining breath, she said, "I'm writing a freelance series about Vietnam's Hells Field." She let that settle. His eyes remained steady, unreadable. She pressed on, "I've been working on the story for several years. Your father is the last of seven surviving veterans and the key to the series. I'd like—" she swallowed when McKee's eyes narrowed "—a chance to talk to him. Please."

"Why? There've been three decades and two wars in the interim."

"Because in an already controversial war, Hells Field was a battle that was undisclosed."

His pupils pinpricked. He understood. A battle fought, facts swept by the wayside, one soldier the fall guy.

"Leave him alone, Ms. Brant."

"I can't. At least not until he tells me no."

McKee stepped into her space. Crowding her. She smelled his skin and the soap he'd washed with this morning. And hay, a whiff of hay. "We don't need old war wounds opened. Go back to reporting the *weekly* news."

"Look," she said, desperate. "You can read what I've written about the other vets so far. I'm a *good* reporter."

His jaw remained inflexible. "Tom doesn't want you hanging around him any more than I do."

Except, the heat in those dark eyes when they settled on her mouth indicated differently. A zing shot through her belly.

"I understand," she said slowly. And she did. Newspeople were too often an unwelcome lot. "You don't like reporters."

She turned back to her desk. Dismissing him, dismissing the entire conversation, her entire mission. God, why was she so needy when it came to pleasing her dad—*oh, face it—*

when it came to men in general? Men like foreign correspondent Floyd Stephens, pontificating how a kid—*his son!*—would dump her career in the toilet. Men, valuing her according to some parameter.

Rats, all of them. Shuffling several pages of notes, she muttered, "If I had somewhere else to go I would."

Which was, in itself, a paradox. If it hadn't been for her need to make her father proud, to prove to him—and all men for that matter, maybe even to herself—that she was a capable and creditable career woman, she would not be in these sticks.

She would not be begging Ash McKee to understand.

A movement from behind reeled her around. He still stood by her cubicle.

"I thought you'd left," she said, vexed. Why didn't he just go?

Under the hat, his tea eyes were pekoe dark. "Where are you staying?"

A tiny hope-flame. "The Dream On Motel." She thought of Charlie sleeping in that dingy room, the lumpy bed, inhaling smoke-stagnated air into his young lungs. When it came right down to it, his welfare was more important than any story. God, she should just get out of this town and go back to Arizona. At least there it was warm and Charlie had a little friend.

She pushed a wing of hair behind her ear. "I have a child, Mr. McKee. A boy. That's why I need a place. Somewhere clean and—and welcoming. I know," she rushed on, "you said I'm not welcome on the Flying Bar T, but you won't know I'm there. I won't come near your house without permission. And if your father doesn't want the interview, that's fine. Scout's honor."

She hated pleading with him, this man with his invisible iron wall surrounding his people.

"How old is he?"

"My son? Seven."

Again, those unyielding eyes. "I'll talk to Tom."

She couldn't help sagging against her desk. "Thank you. Thank you so much. You won't be sorry."

He didn't answer. Simply looked at her. Into her. *Through her.* Then turned and strode from the newsroom, out the squeaky door, into the street.

Chapter Two

Ash jaywalked to his truck. A light snow had begun to fall again, fat flakes that caught on his hat and shoulders.

What the hell happened back there in that newspaper office?

How could he even consider renting the cottage to her? She with the fine-boned cheeks that he damn near touched when she looked up at him with those cat eyes.

He climbed into the pickup, backed from the parking slot and drove out of town.

Of course, the kid had done it. Picturing her boy—with her July-blue eyes and burnt-brown hair, probably minus a front tooth—in that dump of a motel where Ash had sown his oats at eighteen, splintered the stone around his heart.

Why hadn't she told him about the boy before? Was she using him to get closer to Tom? No, her eyes when she mentioned the boy's name said different.

She loved her kid. The way he loved Daisy.

Shoving a hand through his hair, Ash sighed. Sucker, that's what he was. Sucker for kids with sad stories.

He'd been one himself once. He and his sister, Meggie, living in that ramshackle house on the edge of town, their mom trying to put bread on the table and decent clothes on their backs. Until Tom entered their lives. Tom, changing lives with the Flying Bar T.

Ash had to give Rachel credit. She'd woven herself right under his skin in five blasted minutes, persuaded him to let her rent Susie's cottage. Oh, the bit about talking to Tom was only a formality. He knew it, she knew it.

Hell. Here he was, managing nine hundred head of Black Angus and fifty-five hundred acres of land and he'd been bamboozled by a woman—and a seven-year-old kid he had yet to meet.

She'd been daydreaming about him striding across the street with snow on his big shoulders when her desk phone rang the next morning.

"Rachel?" His voice rumbled in her ear.

Her breath stopped. The way he said her *name*... "Yes?"

"You want to look at the cottage, it'll be open Sunday."

In two days. "Thank you for letting me know, Ash."

"Welcome. What time?"

A civil conversation. "Can I come in the morning, say, ten?"

"See you then." The phone clicked.

For the first time in forty-eight hours, she smiled. McKee hang-ups were becoming a tradition.

At nine-thirty on Sunday, she drove out with Charlie strapped into the backseat and hope in her heart. Snow continued to fall in intervals, spit flakes on a brisk, cold wind the wipers scraped up in narrow, inch-high drifts on each side of the windshield.

Ahead, the road lay in stainless splendor while behind, the car left a single pair of tracks. Beyond the barbed wire fences, field and hill faded to a duvet of white.

She'd be seeing him again. Ash McKee. *You're not there for him, Rachel. It's the guesthouse, remember? And Tom.*

Still, her heart quickened. She had to admit Ash was an attractive man—in a cowboy sort of way.

"Are we there yet?" Charlie fisted fog off his window.

"Five minutes, honey bun. After the turn ahead, we'll be there."

He sat straighter, trying to peer over the passenger seat, his eyes round blue discs behind his glasses. "I can't see."

"Trust me, it isn't far. Warm enough back there?"

"Uh-huh." He settled back and began *vrooming* his red Hot Wheels Corvette across his little thighs. The car had been one of her presents on his sixth birthday and his favorite, it seemed. Rarely did the toy escape his sight. Her little man, no different than most little boys his age and no different than an adult male salivating over the real machine.

You lost out, Floyd. You lost out when you walked away from our baby.

"Are we going to be living on a ranch with horses and cows and stuff?" Charlie asked.

"If Mr. McKee will rent his guesthouse to us."

"I don't like living in that motel. It stinks."

"Can't agree with you more, champ. Let's keep our fingers crossed that Mr. Ash will say yes."

More vrooming. "Is he the guy for your soldier story?"

She glanced into the rearview mirror. "His daddy is. Which might cause a problem when it comes to renting from him."

"Why?"

"Because Mr. Tom might not want me on his property when he finds out I also want to interview him."

Another quarter mile passed. Charlie vroomed, then said, "Maybe he has nightmares about wars like Grandpa."

Her jaw fell. "How do you know that?" Bill Brant would die before he admitted any weakness to his daughter.

"Sometimes he sleeps in the chair. Y'know that one that goes back like a bed? And once he started hollering about killing somebody. I think the guy had a gun."

"That doesn't mean he was dreaming about war, Charlie. Sometimes people dream about violence."

"I asked him when he got awake. I asked him what a gook was."

She cringed at the ancient epithet. "Son, that's a very unkind word. Did Grandpa explain it to you?" Unbelievable.

"Well, kinda. And then he said I shouldn't make up stories."

She squinted into the mirror. "Were you?"

A hard head shake. "Grandpa was snoring, then he started yelling. And making faces like he was hurt or something."

She kept her hands steady on the wheel. "When was that?"

"Last time we went to visit in the summer."

Last August. They'd traveled to the coast of Maryland and stayed in the vacation cottage her father purchased fifteen years ago. Rachel loved the ocean—its smells and sounds, how the salt breeze tasted.

"Is that the only time he talked in his sleep?" She slowed for the last turn as the Flying Bar T came into view—and fancied Ash McKee thundering up the road on his Crusader steed.

"Uh-huh. He never slept in the chair again."

Of course he wouldn't. Not with an alert, intelligent little boy within hearing distance.

The weathered two-story Craftsman home she'd glimpsed over the backs of the cattle last Wednesday now loomed through the snow.

Driving closer, she noticed the house inhabited a timbered horseshoe with the corrals and outbuildings, including three massive barns, scattered several hundred yards westward. Today's snowfall hid the Rockies from sight, but four days ago their great, hulking, cotton-capped shoulders were cloaked in a mantle of blue sky.

Ash McKee lived amidst poster-inspiring beauty.

Not Ash. Tom. She was here for Tom. And Charlie.

The black-and-white herding dogs rushed out from under the porch as she pulled up beside the green pickup Ash drove to town.

"Will they bite, Mom?" Charlie's voice trembled.

"I don't think so. They're border collies and like to herd sheep and cows. They're not mean." She hoped. But who knew how Ash McKee trained his animals? The warhorse had ground at its bridle bit with long, strong teeth.

She shut off the car, grabbed her purse. Today she simply wanted introductions. No note taking. No pushy reporter manners. Just smiles and a possible welcome to rent.

"Come on. Let's see if Mr. McKee is home."

Snowflakes speckled her wool coat and Charlie's blond hair. Cautious of the dogs, Rachel walked with her son up the steps next to a wheelchair ramp. The animals crept back under the wooden deck. So much for guarding the place. Quite possibly Ash, himself, had the watchdog scenario in hand.

The door swung open. The eager high school columnist and Ash's companion from last Wednesday offered a smile full of braces. "Hey, Ms. Brant." She winked when she spotted Charlie.

The boy ducked shyly behind Rachel.

"Hello, Daisy."

Petite and red-haired, the teenager wore low-rise jeans and a bust-fitting knit top that exposed her navel. If Rachel had a daughter her age, such revealing clothes would not enter her closet. Oh, who was she kidding? Fifteen years ago, she wore tight tops and leggings, much to Bill Brant's irritation. In the succeeding years, her tastes had tempered to conservatism, like the warm black dress slacks and aqua sweater she'd dug from the motel closet this morning. Bill would label the clothes plain classy, pun intended.

"I'm here to see your dad and your grandfather."

"I know." Daisy leaned forward and whispered, "Dad doesn't know about my column, okay?"

Before Rachel could respond, Ash McKee stepped into the entryway. His dark eyes locked on her, then swept over Charlie. "Bringing reinforcements?"

Without the Stetson, she saw he had beautiful hair. Thick and black and linear and scraped back in a style that pronounced his weather-toughened cheekbones, his long, graceful nose.

"Hello again, Ash." She set a hand on her child for comfort. "This is my son, Charlie. I couldn't get a babysitter so he's with me today." She tried a smile, failed as those eyes riveted on her face.

Daisy saved the moment. "Dad says you'll be renting the guest cottage."

"We haven't decided yet, Daiz," Ash interjected, shutting the door behind Rachel.

"But I thought you said—"

"Not yet." While his eyes gentled on his daughter, his tone was resolute.

"What's to decide?" she argued.

"So. Our company's arrived." A gray-haired, craggy-faced cowboy in a pearl-buttoned shirt rode around a corner in a motorized chair.

Tom McKee. The key to Rachel's series.

A second, a blink, then his pale blue eyes widened, as if he recognized her, his pupils rounding to the outer edges of their irises before his surprise vanished. Puzzled and certain they had never met, Rachel stepped forward, held out her hand. She was here for the guesthouse.

"Rachel Brant, Mr. McKee. Pleased to meet you."

"You the one phoned the other day?" he asked, giving her hand a light shake.

"Yes." A knot formed in her throat at the sight of the strong, brave man. In that instant, she vowed to make him proud with her words.

"What story you digging for, Ms. Brant?"

Her cheeks warmed. "Today, we're just looking for a place to live, sir."

The old man stared at her with an intensity that had her shifting on her feet. Then he nodded. "Ash will show you around back of the house." Decision settled, he glanced at his son, though Rachel knew it wasn't, not entirely. Not from the line of the younger man's shoulders beneath that denim shirt. She could have skipped pebbles across them.

"Come with me," Ash ordered, and left the room without checking to see if she followed.

With a smile for Tom McKee, she and Charlie followed Daisy through the house to the kitchen. The girl murmured, "I'm so glad you'll be staying here."

Rachel wanted to ask about the whisper at the front door. About Ash not knowing of Daisy's column.

They entered a deep kitchen sporting a horde of knotty pine cupboards, an ample work island in its center and a Sub-Zero refrigerator. To the right, a rectangular oak table stood gleaming with light flooding in from floor-to-ceiling windows that faced snowy evergreens. And everywhere, photographs of a red-haired woman. Upon the antique phone table, upon whatever wall space remained unclaimed by cupboards.

Susie, the wife who left Ash McKee widowed.

Without a coat or hat, he waited by a back door sheltered in a small alcove next to the pantry. On his feet, his work boots remained unlaced.

He held open the door as Rachel and Charlie stepped into the cold morning. The wind stung their faces while they followed Ash down a wooden walkway toward a tiny cottage looming thirty yards ahead amidst a snowy stand of pine and birch.

Opening the guesthouse door, Ash waited for her and Charlie to step inside.

It was a dollhouse. Three miniature rooms with lace curtains pulled back with bows, a tiny state-of-the-art kitchen. Cozy living room with a round rug and cushiony furniture in earthy tones. Santa Fe prints on the walls. Dried hydrangeas in a tall vase on the coffee table. Above the stone fireplace hung a wooden, hand-painted sign: Welcome to Flying Bar T Ranch.

No portraits of red-haired women.

Ash wiped his boots on the welcome mat, then walked toward the kitchen situated in the far right corner. "The stove is gas." He slanted her a look. "Ever cooked with gas?"

"Yes. The place is lovely, Ash. Thank you." She meant it.

"Not me you should thank, it's Tom."

She understood. It was Tom's ranch, after all. If Ash had his way, she wouldn't be here. "I will. And thank you for not mentioning the series I'm writing."

"How do you know I haven't?"

"Because I doubt he would've let us in the door, and he wouldn't have invited me to see this house."

"You're right. He wouldn't."

Ruefully, she turned away, surveyed the room again. No matter that the McKees lived solitary lives. They were good people. She did not want to hurt them, if she could help it in any way. Her father was wrong when he'd told her to "do anything to get a story."

Ash said, "Upstairs are a couple bedrooms and the bathroom. If you want to use the fireplace I'll haul in a few logs from the main house."

"Thanks. This is…fine. We won't need the fireplace." She didn't want him doing anything extra, not when his cold eyes and implacable jaw said he would rather she lived someplace else. Like the North Pole. Still, she couldn't help wondering, "Do you usually rent out the guesthouse in the winter months?"

In town, she'd heard about his wife's trail riding business— the one he'd packed away after she died.

Suddenly, his eyes changed, gentled, and she wondered how it would feel to see them soften because of her. Then the emotion retreated and the dark, icy stare settled back in place. "This is a working ranch. We don't have time for tourists and the like during our busy months."

And the like. City folk, out for a quick joyride on a ranch. Curiosity seekers. People of her ilk.

She tried blunt honesty. "Ash…I know you wish I hadn't come into your life, but—"

"You know nothing of what I wish, lady."

"Rachel," she said quietly. "My name is Rachel. Can we call a truce? At least until I talk to Tom again about the interviews?"

"When do you plan on telling him? Or are you hoping to move in here first?"

In other words, execute a con job.

She lifted her chin. She may be a newswoman but, whether he believed it or not, she had a smidgen of propriety, of decency. She was not entirely her father's daughter, but her mother's child. "I'll explain the minute we return to the main house."

"It's cold in here, Mom," Charlie whispered, swinging her attention away from the man across the room. "Is it gonna be freezing when we live here?"

"No, baby." She righted his eyewear perched at the end of his pug nose. "There's a heating system same as in the other places we've lived."

Ash strode to a gauge on the wall beside the coat closet. A

flick of his finger and she heard the furnace kick in. A couple more adjustments and he'd set the daily program. Done, he walked back to where she and Charlie stood on the welcome mat.

"Trail riding," he said, "was my wife's business."

In other words, apart from the ranch.

"She decorated this building, did the booking." He looked around. "No one's stayed here in fifty-five months."

Since she died. Rachel would be the first. A woman he didn't want on his ranch, a woman he certainly didn't want sleeping in his wife's dollhouse.

Rachel wanted to say "I'm sorry" but in light of why she was here, the words felt phony. Story be damned, this cottage was exactly what her son needed. "Charlie," she said, "wait for me at the main house, okay?"

"Why?"

"Because I need to speak with Mr. Ash a moment."

Her son darted a look at the man, worry in his blue eyes. "You gonna be long?"

"No." She fiddled with his wool hat, tucked the tiny 'Vette into his pocket. "A minute. Now go on. I'll be right behind you."

She waited until her son slipped out the door, then turned to the man with his hands on his hips. "I don't know what happened in the accident that took your wife's life and I can only imagine the loss you suffered. But I assure you I won't change or damage anything in this building or on your ranch. And I will continue looking in town for a more permanent place. As soon as I find one, we'll be gone."

"Don't you mean once you've finished interviewing Tom?"

For a moment, silence. "Why *didn't* you warn him?"

"That you're here because of a Vietnam kick?"

"I'm here because my son needs a decent place to live."

One brow rose slowly. "You going maternal on me, Ms. Brant?"

"It's the truth."

He laughed softly. "Now there's an interesting word coming from a reporter."

She wouldn't back down. "You haven't answered my question."

"Tom handles his own battles."

In other words, handicaps did not make a man less a man.

She sighed. "I'm unsure why you dislike me so much. Is it because I work for a newspaper, or is it me personally?"

"Who said I dislike you?"

His hot tea eyes speared her heart, ran a current down her thighs. She saw his desire, saw him fight the emotion.

Her nerves smoothed. Whether *he* liked it or not, his attraction to her was as true as the air they breathed.

Linear brows lowering, he moved closer. "Cat got your tongue?"

She stepped back. "I think I should go."

Remaining alone with him hadn't been a good idea. Rough Montana terrain, fifteen-hundred-pound horses and thousand-pound cows had crafted his body.

But she had observed his expression with his daughter, when he thought of his wife.

Something in her eyes had him suddenly turning for the door. "Inez, our housekeeper, will clean the place over the next few days. I'll call you when it's ready."

"Ash…"

Head down, back to her, he waited. In that second, she wanted to touch him. Just a touch. A palm to his spine, easing the stress she sensed churning under his skin.

"You're a kind man. I'm very—Thank you. For everything."

His shoulders heaved a sigh. "Best get back to your boy." Opening the door, he strode into a thick, lazy snowfall.

* * *

Tom was at the kitchen table with Daisy and Charlie, drinking hot cocoa, when Ash returned from the cottage, Rachel in tow. Seeing his stepfather in that chair, so mangled…and then for her to head back to town without a hint, without honesty…. Ash frowned. It wasn't right.

He shot Rachel a look. *Honesty is best up front.*

Clever woman read his thoughts. Directly to Tom, she said, "Mr. McKee, as I mentioned on the phone the other day, renting the guesthouse isn't the only reason I'm here."

On her forehead sweat poked from her skin as if she'd sat for an hour in a sauna. "I'm freelancing for a magazine on the East Coast, as well as working at the town paper."

"A magazine?"

"Yes, *American Pie*. It's like *The New Yorker*. I'm doing a series. It's about…"

She was nervous, Ash realized. A journalist nervous about a story. Interesting.

"It's about survivors. From Hells Field."

Tom scrutinized the woman for a long moment, eyes and face rigid as stone. Deep in the house, the cuckoo clock chimed the half hour. "What for?"

She leveled her shoulders. "Because it was one of the most controversial battles in that war. And you—you were the leader of a platoon of nineteen Marines of which only seven survived."

A hush fell. Ash imagined angsty commotion in her mind as she waited: Tom would tell her to leave. He'd sic those cattle dogs on her the minute she and Charlie stepped outside. And Ash, family defender, would chase her car on his horse all the way down the road.

Tom's lips pulled tight. "Old news. Fact is, the more years between, the more people forget. Better that way."

She glanced at Ash, looking, he suspected, for support. For a split second his heart skipped and he almost stepped beside her. Then he saw Daisy, transfixed at the table, and he moved, instead, within reach of his daughter. Damn straight he was the defender of his family.

His positioning wasn't lost on Rachel. Her gaze wove from one to the next, finally settling on Tom. "Wouldn't you like something good to come out of all you've lost, Mr. McKee?"

The old man snorted. "You're barking up the wrong tree, Missy. Ain't got nothing to say about Nam." The chair hummed backward before he spun around and headed toward the hallway that led to his private rooms.

"Grandpa, wait!" Daisy jumped up from the table. "*I* want to know about Hells Field."

Ash moved around Rachel, blocking her view with his back. "Daisy, let it be."

"No," she cried. "God. You'd think that war was garbage we should throw out. People died, Dad. Over fifty thousand of them. Grandpa was there and he was wounded, and I don't even know why or how. This isn't just our country's history, it's *our* history. *Mine!*" Her tiny nostrils flared. "Just like Mom is."

Tom wheeled down the hall. Conversation over.

"Argh," Daisy muttered. "Stubborn old man."

"Daisy." Ash gentled his voice, touched her shoulder.

She shrugged him off. "You're as bad as him. You don't want to talk about Mom any more than he does about Vietnam. It's like every time something bad happens, we put a lid on it. Like that's gonna make it go away. It's not. And neither is Mom's death no matter how many pictures you hang."

"Daisy Anne—" *Dammit to hell.*

"It's the truth." Tears shone in her eyes and his heart broke. "Thanks for trying, Ms. Brant. At least you got them to admit there *was* a Hells Field."

Ash glared at Rachel. *You hurt my family.* For that, he could not forgive her.

But she surprised him again. "Sometimes—" she turned to his daughter "—it's better to let history and the past fade. It softens the pain."

Not an hour here and she was peering into places he'd nailed shut for years. He started for the door. "I think you should take your son and go."

"Why this war?" Tom spoke from the hallway, surprising Ash. Though his stepfather had returned, severity thinned his lips. "Why Vietnam?"

"Because my dad was in it," Rachel replied, giving the old man her full attention. Tom's pupils pinpricked.

"My grampa calls it the black hole," her son piped up.

"Hush, Charlie."

Tom zeroed in on the kid. "Why's that, boy?"

"Cuz a bunch of people went in it and never got out."

"Charlie," Rachel whispered. Her gaze scooted from Tom to Ash like a creature trapped by wolves. "We'll be getting back to town. It's been a pleasure, Tom. Daisy." She refused to look at Ash.

Feeling's mutual, lady. He reached for the door but his nose caught her perfume, a wisp of springtime.

Oh, yeah. He wanted her gone.

"Just a minute," Tom said, halting them all. "I'll make you a deal, Ms. Brant." He looked at Daisy. Under grizzled gray brows, his eyes eased. "My granddaughter wants to know about the war for a school project. You help her write that story and I'll do your interview."

Ash gaped. "Pops—"

Tom held up a hand. "However, my son and I will read your work when it's done, and you'll fax it from this house so there's no chance of changes." His jaw was resolute, his eyes strict. "Ash can decide if he wants to rent the cottage."

"Thank you." Relief washed over her face.

Before Ash could interject, Tom spun his chair toward the kitchen, Daisy in tow.

God almighty, Ash thought. Was the old man losing it? Less than a week ago, he'd been resolute about his secrets. Now *this?*

Determined to dig out his father's motives later, he waited by the door, watched Rachel help her son with his coat. The scene conjured up Susie with Daisy at seven and Daisy batting her mother's hands, declaring, "I can put my coat on, Mom. I can *do* it." Charlie held out his thin arms for his mother's help.

At the top of the porch steps, she faced Ash. Her brows were dark and sweeping. A swallow's wings.

He fisted his hands in the pockets of his jeans when the breeze caught a strand of her hair against that lilting mouth.

"I'm sorry," she said, "for upsetting your family."

If he pulled her against him, her head would rest against his collarbone. "Apology accepted."

"Well." She pulled on her gloves. "Goodbye, Ash."

He could tell she didn't expect to hear from him again.

"See ya."

She walked through the snowfall to her car where Charlie petted Jinx and Pedro. A minute later, her Sunburst drove from the Flying Bar T and the dogs crept back under the porch.

From the office window, Tom watched Ash stride across the snowy yard. The dogs rushed from their hole to tag his heels. He was a good man, his stepson. A devoted father, a dedicated rancher. A proud man.

And upset with Tom's decision about the interview.

Why? Ash had asked once Rachel had driven back to Sweet Creek. Why, after all these years, would Tom spill his guts to a journalist? Why not simply write it down—if he wanted Daisy to know?

What Ash didn't understand, Tom mused, was that Rachel Brant held the key. She would unlock the past. Tom's, Ash's and, most of all, her own.

Tom could take it all to the grave. But she'd come, *she'd come* and—God help him—he could not pass up the opportunity.

Thirty-six years was long enough to live in silence. Hell, the *five* years following Susie was long enough.

Ash hadn't liked Tom's saying they needed to move on. Sure, moving on from Susie was his son's decision to make, like moving on from Hells Field was Tom's, but sometimes a man had to give his kid a push. Tom didn't want Ash boarding up the pain for decades, or having it fester the way it could.

He hoped Ash rented the cottage to Rachel. For Daisy's sake—and the boy's—he hoped, even though Rachel's questions would dredge up heartbreak like sludge out of a Texan oil well.

The snow fell harder. Every day Ash cleaned the walkways so Tom could wheel to the barns, see the new calves. And, dammit, that held a pain all its own.

He remembered a past he wanted to forget.

He dreamed a past he wanted to forget.

They had lived long enough in a house of mourning. Susie's pictures everywhere collecting dust. The cottage sitting empty and cold. The summer trail riding business lying fallow.

A half decade of walking around in silence, fearing that one word, *one name* would break a heart again and again.

Silence couldn't mend anguish. It couldn't sew shattered legs and arms back onto a body. It couldn't erase memory.

Tom knew.

Rachel Brant would change their lives and in doing so

change her own. Ah, but she had her mother's height, her eyes. And her father's mouth and hair.

Yes, Miss Brant would discover the truth with these interviews. They'd all come to understand the truth.

Tom felt it in his gut.

Like when the VC waited in the trees above their trail.

The time had come.

Chapter Three

Oh, yeah, Ash thought. He got the old man's meaning loud and clear. *Tom's* past. Like the Flying Bar T was *Tom's* ranch. And Ash, the stepson aka hired foreman. *Stop being an ass. Tom was there when your mother didn't have two nickels to her name.*

Ash had been two, his sister Meggie one, when their biological dad died in a chopper crash in some Vietnam swamp toward the end of the war. Six months later, their mother became Tom's nurse. A soft-spoken woman with a broken heart that Ash couldn't heal, no matter how hard he tried.

Yes, Tom had given his name as well as his heart to Ash and his sister. He loved them as he'd loved their mother, God rest her soul.

But not enough.

Not enough to change the deed of the land into a partnership with Ash when he turned twenty, twenty-five, thirty. Not even on his last and thirty-seventh birthday.

And now here was Tom again, deciding to give interviews o Rachel Brant, pushing Daisy into the "moving on" mix. Daisy was Ash's daughter, not Tom's.

And what the hell was the old man up to prodding Ash to rent Susie's cottage to Rachel Brant? Not that he hadn't thought t over, but still. That guest cottage was his. *His* money, his time had gone into its construction.

Tom might have final say in matters of the Flying Bar T, but not on the cottage. The thought rankled. *Why, Pops? Why haven't you changed the deed? Afraid I might cause a financial disaster with my nonexistent reading skills?*

In school, Ash had endured countless methods designed to interpret the printed word. A few strategies had helped somewhat, others caused more confusion, and later there had been an adult support group in Billings.

In his midtwenties, because Susie had wheedled him to take a course, he'd worked daily with a tutor specializing in reading difficulties and learned a measured technique that, at the time, allowed him to decipher enough words for comprehension. A laborious and painful process which, over ten years, Ash let slide. Too damned difficult to fumble over on his own.

"To hell with it," he muttered.

In the barn's office, he grabbed the ear-tagging pliers and a sack of tags, then headed for the calving barn where his cows, *his* cows, were sheltered from snow, cold wind and frozen nights.

Concentrate on the animals. They're what matters.

Rolling aside the doors, he stepped into the warm cavern. At the Dutch door closing off the hallways, he ordered the dogs to stay before wandering through to the cattle.

Large box pens ran up and down the perimeters while the interior's free space spread like a rectangular field for the animals to take shelter.

This morning, the double rear doors stood open. With the

milder temperatures, most of the herd huddled outside around feed he'd forked onto the snow and into the bins.

A pair of newborn Angus calves lay on fresh straw inside the barn. Twins. The cow's rough pink tongue cleaned their wet coats. Lifting her broad black head, she eyed Ash.

"It's okay, mama," he crooned softly, walking toward the pair. He clipped tags onto the calves' left ears, number one hundred and two and three.

He read the tags five times to make sure, though, oddly, numbers had always been easier than words. He studied the twins. Of the calves born so far, these two tallied forty-eight bulls. Good odds for beef sales.

"Dad?" Dressed in high-topped work boots and her red parka, Daisy came across the barn. "You mad at Grandpa and me?"

"No, honey." *Nothing I can't deal with.*

She dogged him out of the barn, into the herd. "Then why are you hiding out here instead of eating lunch with us?"

Ever the perceptive one, his Daiz. "I'm not hiding. Just checking to see if we have more calves. The pair in the barn were born in the last hour."

"You think Grandpa's wrong letting Ms. Brant interview him, don't you?"

"Not for me to say what your grandfather can or cannot do. He's his own person."

"Okay, then you don't want me helping with the story. I saw it on your face."

"We don't know anything about this Ms. Brant. She blew into town two weeks ago. My question is why? To write an old war story? What for? More to the point, why *now?*"

He pushed through the hulking cattle. Snow breezed into his face along with the scent of hay and hide.

Daisy trudged after him. "You can't judge every journalist because of Mom's death."

"It has nothing to do with her death."

"Yes, it does. You even said so when I wanted to write our high school column last September. The first thing out of your mouth was, 'You want to be like that guy who killed your mother?' Jeez, like I'd run out, get my license and crash a car into some innocent person, all for a story."

He swung to a stop. "Your mouth's getting way too brazen, young lady."

She threw up her hands. "Argh! You're impossible! No wonder no one wants to be your friend." Wheeling around, red hair flying, she stormed through the cattle, back into the barn.

Ash watched her go. His heart hurt. His pixie-girl was on a fast track to independence and there wasn't a damn thing he could do. Oh, yeah, he knew she had a flare for the written word. In first grade, she was already reading the scroll line on CNN.

That same year, Susie bought their daughter the first *Harry Potter* novel. The book had caused a horrible argument between Ash and his wife.

Bottom line: he'd felt the content too advanced for his tiny daughter with her missing front teeth. And Susie, eyes flashing, had retorted, *"How would you know? You can't read."*

Something had died in Ash that day.

Something of Susie and of himself.

She had hoisted his dyslexia as an obstacle flag in the road of their child's education.

He hadn't expected to feel *inadequate* in his marriage. But that day he had. He'd felt unskilled as a man and inept as a father. Later, Susie had apologized, but the words remained. Dangling in his ear for all time.

He stared around at the cows. Dim-witted beasts. Like him. Daisy was right; his friends were few. Caution learned the hard way.

Rachel Brant's soft voice whispered through his mind. *"You're a kind man."* He shook his head. *Hell.*

The last damn thing he needed was another *woman* in his life. Daisy was his life. Tom. The cows.

Damn straight.

They were his life and they were enough.

On Wednesday, Rachel tapped her fingers on her *Rocky Times* desk. Should she call the Flying Bar T about the guesthouse? Yesterday, the greasy-haired manager at the Dream On Motel had sputtered about a month's commitment. The thought of Charlie in that grubby room another night sickened her.

At two-forty-five, she called the ranch.

Tom answered and gave her Ash's cell phone number. "He's the one you need to talk to," the old vet told her.

Of course. It was his wife's guesthouse, after all.

Ash picked up on the second ring.

"Hello, Ash," she said cheerfully. As if she called him every week, as if her pulse hadn't executed a nervous kick. "Rachel Brant here. I was wondering—"

"It's ready."

"Oh." *Were you planning to let me know?* "We can move in, then?"

"Yeah."

She fisted her hand in a yes-gesture. "Would this afternoon be too soon? Say right after school? I'll rent a U-Haul right away to take our stuff to the ranch. It shouldn't take more than a couple hours, tops."

"What time this afternoon?"

"I work till three, then I get Charlie from Lewis-Clark Elementary." And she needed to check out of the motel, buy some groceries for a decent supper. "Say four-thirty-ish?"

"Four-thirty it is. I'll leave the key with Inez."

"Inez?"

"Our housekeeper. I've left instructions with her, in case you have any questions."

"So you won't be there?"

"Probably not." Pause. "Will someone be helping you?"

Was he concerned? "We only have a few boxes and some clothes."

"No furniture?"

"No." What was the point when she moved every other year to yet another town, chasing yet another part of the series?

"I see."

Actually, he didn't, but explaining would incite questions she had no intention of answering. "We'll be out shortly."

"Right."

"Bye—"

Dial tone.

"—Ash."

The McKees were not men of long conversations.

She dropped her camera into her briefcase—a habit she'd established years ago in case an unexpected story presented itself—and pulled her purse from under the desk. Time to get her child from school. *Time to start the ball rolling on why you're in this hole-in-the-wall.*

Shrugging on her long gray coat, she called to the lone reporter left in the newsroom, "See you tomorrow, Marty."

His blond head lifted.

Marty, of the fatal crash that killed Susie McKee. A fool-hardy, energetic kid raring for the next story. *You should be in Iraq or the Congo, not in Podunk, USA.*

"You moving out to the Flying Bar T?"

He'd eavesdropped on her call.

"I am."

His mouth twisted. "Don't let Ash McKee bite you on the ass."

Hooking her scarf behind her neck, she stopped. "Why do you say that?"

"He's a loner."

"He has family, Marty."

He frowned. "Take care, okay? You're only seeing the tip of the iceberg with him."

No, she thought, sitting in the car, waiting for Charlie to exit Lewis-Clark Elementary. Marty was wrong. What you saw with Ash McKee was exactly what you got. No secrets there. Portraits of his wife proved the point. He'd loved her. As he loved his daughter and father.

When she arrived in an hour with the U-Haul, would he be at the house protecting his inside flock rather than outside with his cows? At the thought of seeing him again, her heart hastened. She leaned a little to the right and checked her hair in the rearview mirror. *Good grief.* What was she doing, preening for a taciturn man with a snarky disposition?

You need a life, Rachel. Well, the minute Charlie was finished second grade, she was out of here. Leaving town on a jet plane at the speed of light. His next school year would be in Richmond, Virginia, and they would be living in a little house with a backyard and she would work for *American Pie.* She hoped.

Charlie ran down the steps of the school, parka flapping open to the wind, book pack swaying from an arm. After hopping onto the backseat, he tugged the door closed.

"Hey, baby." Rachel smiled between the front seats. Her little guy, her pride and joy. "How was your day?"

"Okay."

Perpetual kid answer. "Any homework?"

"Have to do some math problems."

Second grade and already homework was arriving two or three times a week. Rachel needed to schedule an appointment with the teacher who continually wrote in her son's agenda: *Charlie read a novel again during lessons today. Class work not completed.*

From the day she brought home Barbara Park's book *Junie B. Jones Has a Peep in Her Pocket* for his fifth birthday, he'd loved reading. But the ability hampered his progress in emotional and social areas. Fantasy offered comfort amidst the angst of new schools and new friends for a lonely little boy.

And she was to blame. *Restless Rachel.*

Disillusioned, she pulled onto the main road.

"Can I play first, Mom?"

He always asked, no matter that her response was the same, that she was a stickler about getting homework out of the way.

"You won't have time for playing tonight, Charlie. We're moving out to the ranch right away."

"We are? Yippee! I get to see the horses now."

Rachel chuckled. "Not so fast, partner. First we buy groceries for supper, then we pick up the trailer, and *then…*" She paused. "You'll do homework while I unload our stuff."

"I want to help."

In the mirror, his bottom lip pouted.

"Homework first, Charlie. And push up your glasses."

He did. "Will Mr. Ash be there all the time?"

"Yes. He runs the ranch."

"But will he show me the horses?"

"Let's not bother him about the horses just yet." Or any part of the ranch. She did not need those dark looks boring into her soul.

"I wanna see the horses," Charlie persisted.

Thrusting horses and Ashford McKee from her mind, Rachel pulled into the grocery lot and centered on what she and Charlie needed to eat.

What's on your supper table tonight, Mr. Rancher?

Most of all, why did she care?

* * *

He saw her the instant he rounded the juice aisle. She stood in the first checkout line with her son, her dark head bent to the kid's wheat-colored one. At twenty feet, Ash studied her face. She had those clean, fine Uma Thurman lines. Sophisticated with a mixture of sweetness.

He debated. Go back up the aisle, or head for the checkout?

His feet chose for him and he walked past the second cash register with its two customers to stand behind Rachel. Like him, she carried a basket and was busy unloading items onto the counter. Potatoes, lettuce, a quart of milk, steaks. A grin tugged his mouth. "Steaks, huh? Good choice."

She snapped around. "Ash."

"Rachel." He reached for the separation bar, set his own filets behind hers on the counter. He couldn't think of another word to say, not with her eyes glued to his face.

Charlie stared up at him behind round-rimmed glasses. Kid had her nose. Small and straight and slightly freckled. Why hadn't he noticed before?

"Hey, Charlie."

"Hey." The boy moved timidly behind his mother; she set a protective arm around his shoulders.

Had Susie given Daisy the same sense of support at that age? He couldn't recall. Susie had been guiding guest riders up ridges and across ranch woodlands when Daisy was seven.

Rachel looked at his purchases. "I thought ranchers ate their own beef."

"Where do you think stores get their beef, if not from ranchers?" he teased, setting his empty basket on the rack.

A smile lifted the corners of her lips. If he bent his head, he figured his mouth would fit there just fine.

Hold on. Where had *that* come from?

"I didn't expect to see you here," she said, suddenly spellbound by the cashier's scanner.

He dug out his wallet. "You don't expect me to eat?"

"That's not what I meant. I thought maybe you'd be—"

She looked so flustered, he couldn't help chide, "Where? Home on the range? Down on the south forty?"

Suddenly, he liked teasing her, liked the sound of her little gust of laughter. Liked a lot of things about her. Things he hadn't thought of in years. Things he hadn't *experienced* in years. She made him feel. He wasn't sure if he liked *that*.

"You should laugh more often," he remarked suddenly. "Does something to your eyes. Makes them bluer."

This time she flushed pink. "Are you flirting, Ash McKee?"

His teasing died. "No," he said curtly, thinking of the last woman he'd joshed around with—Susie, the night before she died.

"Don't worry," Rachel said, but the sparkle in her eyes dimmed. "I'm not interested, anyway." Pulling money from her purse, she guided Charlie forward, then paid the cashier. "Bye." She flung the word over her shoulder and left the store carrying two bags.

Ash watched through the store's wide windows as she walked Charlie through the dark parking lot, then climbed into her car.

He wanted to hurry after them, tell her he *had* been flirting, that he liked the way her laugh lit her eyes and, oh yeah, he was glad she'd be living ninety feet from his house.

Grabbing up his meat package, he strode through the electronic doors. *Hell.* Next he'd be admitting he fancied Rachel Brant, reporter for the *Rocky Times,* as a potential date.

She wasn't interested in flirting, dammit. Not in the least. And certainly not with Ash McKee with his frost-lined attitude.

She understood his abrupt mood change, understood it as if he'd lectured an hour. Flirting meant he thought of her as a woman. He did not want to think of her as a woman. He did not want her living in his dead wife's dollhouse. Well, tough. He'd made his decision and she was moving in.

Snow fell again. Confetti flakes that came out of a nowhere night and zeroed in on the headlights and windshield in long, gossamer needles.

She drove with care and caution on the road out of town. One slip and they could wind up in a ditch, miles from help, impotent against the cold. *With a U-Haul trailer on top of us.*

Tonight, the radio forecasted temperatures dipping to twenty below with the windchill. February, galloping like the great lion, Aslan of Narnia, through winter. On the ranch those mothers with little calves would hunt for protection inside the barns.

Or will you herd them inside, Ash?

Unlikely. His animals no doubt were descendants of the Texas longhorns Nelson Story and his cowboys had driven to Montana in 1866. Cattle that died by the thousands in blizzards twenty years later, but evolved over the past hundred and forty years into sturdy range creatures with hardy hides and thick coats, barriers against freezing winds and drifting snow. Historic details she picked up from the old-timer talk at the coffee shop and in the archives of the *Rocky Times.*

Nonetheless, Rachel shivered for those tiny newborn calves, and looked in the rearview mirror to check her own offspring. "Okay back there, champ?"

"Yeah."

"Want to sing a song?" He loved singing in the car.

"No."

"Something happen today, Charlie?" His mood had been off-and-on from the moment she'd picked him up from school.

"Nuh-uh."

"You'd tell me, right?"

"Maybe."

Uh-oh. Something had happened. Though Rachel understood her son was a quiet student, Mrs. Tabbs may have had a bad-hair day. Or gotten frustrated with the novel reading and daydreaming.

"Have a fight with Tyler?"

"No. Tyler's nice. He's my bestest friend."

"What happened then, baby?"

"I want to live here forever. I don't wanna leave anymore."

"Oh, Charlie, you know that's impossible."

"Why? Why do we have to move all the time?"

"Honey, I've explained it lots of times. The old soldiers live in different states and it takes a while to build up their trust for the story. Besides, we like living in different areas," she added cheerfully. "Right?"

"But I want to stay in one house forever." In the mirror his eyes were hard blue jewels.

One house forever. She had grown up in one house forever and it hadn't been happy. With Charlie, happiness had come naturally—from the moment she knew of his existence, Rachel had loved her child. "Next house," she promised him. "Richmond will be the one forever." If she had to flip burgers for extra money, she'd get him that home, that school, those friends, the dog, a tree house.

"Okay," came his little voice.

"I love you, champ."

"Love you, too, Mom." He drove the Hot Wheels car over the window glass where it left toothpick tracks in its wake.

Through the dark, she saw the ranch house ablaze with light. The collies, black shapes in the night and yellow eyes in head-lights, crept around the car as she cut the engine.

The green truck Ash drove was nowhere in sight.

He said he wouldn't be here.

Had he bought those steaks for someone in town? A lady

friend? One who enjoyed his company, his flirting? Who didn't get the evil eye one minute and a sexy grin the next?

What on earth had her assuming he wouldn't have a woman in his life? Naturally, he'd be seeing someone. *It's been fifty-five months, Rachel.* Hadn't he quoted the exact time frame last week?

She and Charlie climbed from the car. Her nose picked up friendly scents—cows, barns, wood smoke and the perfume of beauty: mountain snow and wind and night.

A sweet-faced Latino woman with a braid that touched the curve of her spine answered Rachel's knock. "Mrs. Brant?" She smiled down at Charlie. "I'm Inez, the housekeeper. Ash let us know you'd be on your way." She offered a set of keys. "For the cottage. There's room to park around the side. Follow the graded area. Ash plowed it out this morning."

So. He'd been expecting her today.

"Thank you." She took the keys and then, following the sheared path rapidly filling with snow, towed the trailer around to the guesthouse.

Someone, probably Inez, had turned on the lights; the windows glowed with warm welcome. Rachel pulled up and shut off the motor. "Home sweet home," she murmured.

Charlie leaned forward. "Do I get to pick my bedroom?"

"Absolutely."

Warmth greeted them the moment she opened the door. Had Ash left the heat on all day in anticipation of her arrival?

Charlie kicked off his boots and ran for the stairs.

"Remember, you have math to do," she called, as he scrambled puplike to the loft. His feet thundered back and forth. She gave him a minute.

"I'm taking this one, Mom," came his shout. "It's got a window bench and everything! You can have the fireplace."

Rachel shook her head. A fireplace in a bedroom? She couldn't wait to see.

A thought rooted. Had Ash and his wife…?

She hurried into the snowy night. If she was to save an extra day's rent on the trailer, they would need to return the U-Haul to the dealership by six-thirty.

The snow had mutated into a storm. A white wall that hit before she reached the county road three miles from the ranch. Three miles of snow and wind battering the car, swaying the empty trailer and swallowing the headlights. *Please. Show me the track, the ditches.*

"Mom?" Charlie's voice, small and frightened from the rear seat. "It's really, *really* snowy."

"We'll go slow, baby. We'll get there."

"Maybe we should go back to Mr. Ash's place."

She would, if she could turn around, if she knew for certain the road would still be in front of her when she pointed the nose of the car in the other direction. Best to keep going.

She drove five miles an hour. The wipers strained against snow buildup and wind blasts.

A shape emerged in the headlights.

"Mom, look out!"

She saw the red eyes a millisecond before the deer leaped—one long, high bound—into snow and night. But already she'd reacted to the animal's sudden appearance. Braking, swinging the steering wheel to the right to miss the animal.

The Sunburst's front tires thumped against a thick drift that spewed snow up and over hood and roof.

"Nooo!"

The rear wheels spun on the icy pavement. She jerked against her seat belt as the car shifted sideways and slid. Slid with the ease of a skater, nose-first down into the ditch.

She heard the scream of metal before she realized the trailer had ripped from the hitch.

"Charlie!"

The U-Haul slammed into the rear of the Sunburst.

Ash left town at 6:55 p.m., earlier than planned. A couple days ago, he'd seen the sun dogs—rainbowlike spots on each side of the sun—and knew a storm brewed before the radio confirmed the weather system hailing from the north this afternoon.

When he'd phoned home, Inez told him Rachel had arrived.

That he inhaled long and loud hearing the news meant he didn't favor the idea of anyone out in this weather. It had nothing to do with her. *Nothing.*

Hell, he'd practically forgotten her when he'd left the grocery store and taken the steaks over to Meggie's house. And when he and his teenage nephew, Beau, stood, bundled up in parkas and wool hats, grilling the meat on her outdoor barbecue, he hadn't thought of Rachel at all.

Liar. Listening to Beau talk cars had Ash remembering Charlie and that palm-size Corvette he carried like a mascot.

Wind whipped snow across the road. Again, a wash of relief went through him that *she* was safe.

Even if it meant she resided in Susie's cottage.

Even if it meant that tomorrow the storm would have blown over and he'd be faced with the possibility of seeing Rachel Brant every day for God knew how long. *Of getting to know her.*

The notion had him losing control of the wheel for a split second. *Careful, Ash, or you'll be in the ditch, freezing your ass off.*

He drove slowly, no more than twenty miles an hour. He could find his way home with his eyes closed, but he wasn't a fool. Top-notch cowhands had found themselves turned around in a storm like this. In another century, some had died.

By the time he reached the four-way stop, the mountain winds had plummeted the temperature to twenty-two below.

Another few miles and he'd be home.

One-handed, he speed dialed the number on his cell phone. Relief washed through him when the satellite connected and Daisy answered. "Dad! Where are you? It's blizzarding like mad here."

"At the crossroads, pix. Be there in twenty minutes or so." At least now they'd know where to look once the storm abated if he didn't arrive in an hour.

"Be careful, Daddy."

"I will." Always, for his daughter. He would not take fate in hand like Susie.

Static fuzzed Daisy's words. "…Brant left…wanted…trailer back…town."

"She *what?*" Why the hell hadn't she waited until morning? Didn't the woman have any sense? The line broke momentarily. "Daisy! Where's the boy?"

"Charl…with her." Words jumping into his ear.

"Daiz, you're breaking up. You and Grandpa stay put. I'll keep an eye out for Rachel." He flipped the cell phone shut.

Goddammit. This storm was no place for a woman and kid.

He hoped, *hoped,* she was in Sweet Creek this minute.

The truck plowed through a foot-high drift, the headlights bouncing down a gap where snow sifted grim as fog over the road—and the specter of a woman staggered along its center.

Chapter Four

Ash braked the truck to within five feet of Rachel and leaped out into the howling wind. Cold and snow slapped him like the back of a work-hardened hand as he strode toward the beam of headlights where she swayed against the storm's fierceness.

"God almighty, woman," he thundered. "What the hell were you thinking to drive in this weather?"

Her familiar gray coat flapped around her legs; her face had the burned look of someone in the sun thirty minutes too long. Under her chin, her black-gloved fingers gripped the sashes of the long woolen scarf wrapped around her head. Ash slung an arm around her shoulders, turning her so he took the brunt of the wind. "Get in the truck."

"Ch-Charlie," she stuttered.

"I'll get him." He guided her to the passenger side, then went for the boy.

Strapped into the front seat, the kid met him with huge

eyes—her eyes. Quickly, Ash shoved the vehicle into Neutral for the morning tow, then unbelted the boy and hauled him into his arms. "Come on, buckaroo."

"Mommy." The wind flung the word into the night.

"Your mom's all right." Ash waded out of the ditch, the kid's arms vicing his neck.

Illuminated by the cab's function lights, Rachel's blue eyes brimmed gratitude as she reached for her child.

Don't thank me, Ash thought.

Thanking meant kindness.

Thanking meant acceptance.

He did not want to accept her.

"The trailer c-crashed into—into the car," she stammered through chattering teeth when he climbed behind the wheel.

He released the brake. "Damage is minimal. We'll get it fixed tomorrow."

The wind rocked the truck. The vents blasted heat onto their legs. Rachel held Charlie close to her side, murmuring reassurances in his ear. Ash concentrated on driving into the snow-blowing night, on the headlights and the road and where the ditches lay right and left.

He could smell her. That faint scent of female. She'd pushed the scarf back from her head. Within the dash lights, her short rumpled hair glinted like a shot of Jack Daniel's in firelight.

His heart had landed in his throat at the thought of her and the kid freezing in swirling snow. Last time he'd had that kind of scare was with Tom's heart attack last summer.

He would not, *would not,* consider the meaning behind the comparison.

Hands gripping the wheel, he drove slowly, carefully, wishing away the minutes, determinedly pushing Rachel from his mind, picturing instead Daisy at home with Tom and Inez.

No one would rest until he drove into the yard. Daisy would be pacing. When Susie died, his daughter had clung to Ash the way kids do, fearing abandonment.

He'd had to drive her to and from school for a month after she refused to ride the bus or leave his side at home. For a year, she'd slept in his bedroom, her twin bed jammed against the opposite wall because, in the dark, nightmares crept over her. He couldn't remember the number of times he rocked her to sleep.

Finally, things had resumed a sense of normality—or as normal as a family could be without wife and mother. Until Tom landed in the hospital with chest pains and Daisy withdrew.

Silent angst, Inez called it.

Gut-wrenching, Ash called it. Watching worry lines cut his daughter's young brow. Watching her pace the hospital corridors. Listening to her walk the floors of the house.

Suddenly the ranch's broad wood and iron sign, swinging back and forth on its hinges, loomed above the road. *Home.*

Through the spiraling snow, he found the lane and drove for the house. From out of nowhere the dogs appeared, small black tumbleweeds with yellow eyes.

The front door flew open. A woman rushed onto the porch and Ash blinked against snow and light. *Susie,* he thought, before recognizing Daisy in his wife's blue sweater.

His daughter leaped down the steps to the passenger door of the crew cab.

"Dad found you," she cried, and just like that she plucked Charlie from Rachel's arms. "Come in where it's warm." Clutching the kid's hand, she dragged him into the house.

Ash followed Rachel up the steps, where the wind fluttered her coat's long panels around the ankles of her tall, slick-soled boots. Useless boots in storms.

Once inside, Rachel removed her son's jacket and mitts.

Around her neck the wine-colored scarf highlighted her cheeks. Ash focused on toeing off his boots.

Inez hovered nearby. "Got some hot chocolate ready." She smiled at the boy. "Like marshmallows, Charlie?"

A shy nod. Sometimes, Ash noted, the boy was scared of his own shadow.

Like you were at his age. At school and in class, especially in class.

Inez looked at Ash. "Tom's in his room."

Interpretation: a private talk. He headed down the hallway to knock on his father's door across from the unlit office.

"Come in," came the gruff reply.

Pops lay on his bed, glasses perched on the end of his bold nose, newspaper on his stomach, a mug of hot cocoa on the nightstand. "Close the door, son."

Ash did, then leaned against the wood, tucking his fingers into his jeans.

"The woman okay?"

"Yeah. Inez took them to the kitchen."

The old man smiled. "Feeding 'em hot chocolate?"

Inez's balm in rough times. Ash felt his mouth twitch. "Yeah."

"How's the boy?"

"Scared." Like a rabbit under the eye of a hawk.

"Probably his first snowstorm. Was she in the ditch?"

"About a mile east of the crossroads. Storm should let up by morning." Ash looked at his stepfather. "Why didn't someone stop her from heading back with that trailer? She and the kid could've frozen out there. Hell, she was stumbling down the middle of the road when I found them."

"She wouldn't listen. Thought there was plenty of time to get that trailer back."

Ash planted his hands on his hips, stared at the window where snow banked the lower part of the glass. "Doesn't she listen to the news?" God, if he let his imagination gallop like a herd of wild mustangs... "If this is a sign of things ahead, we've got a problem on our hands. She's green as they come."

"You'll be able to handle it."

"I don't have time. Greenhorns were Susie's domain."

"Susie's not here, son," Tom said quietly. "So the job falls on you."

Dammit, Ash thought. *I don't want the job.* Why couldn't his family understand that? Didn't they realize Rachel Brant spiked his temper. He glared at his stepfather.

The old man didn't waver. "Let go, boy."

Let go. That was the crux of the matter, wasn't it? Rachel was on their property and he had to let go of the memories, of Susie, of his wife, of the woman he'd grown up with, loved, married and had a child with. Let go of three-quarters of his life. *Piece of cake.*

He turned and strode from the room.

That night, Ash lay under the covers of his king-size, lonely bed, hands linked behind his head, listening to the wind howl around the corner of the house.

"You're a good man." Her words drifted like snow into his mind. Some good man.

Either she was desperate or stupid, and from what he gleaned through their interactions, he'd put his money on desperate.

Desperate to have her story without him blocking the way.

Through the dark he saw her in the blowing snow three hours ago, the relief in her eyes.

"My name is Rachel," she'd reminded him that first day in the cottage. Rachel. A feminine name. Full of mystery.

A faded image of Susie flashed through his mind. Susie. A feminine name, as well, but in a cute, wholesome way, a girl's name. A girl he'd grown up beside and loved from the time he was nine years old. In the end, he'd known everything about her. There had been no secrets between them, no mystery, no surprises.

Until she reminded him he couldn't read.

Still, times like this, in the dark, he missed her so much his body curled into itself with the pain. She would never again put her head next to his and he'd never feel the slight dip of the mattress as she crawled under the covers, seeking the warmth of his skin. He'd never kiss her lips, whisper to her in the night, feel the curve of her hip under his palms.

He hated that she'd died, that they'd argued two hours before she got into her car. Trivial words meaning nothing.

Just the final ones to each other.

He hated the lost minutes.

If only he could see her flashing green eyes once more. Or coax her out of her mood, though there were times in the last years of their marriage when he had tired of the coaxing and simply walked away.

The way he had the day she died.

Now, another woman slept in the rooms Susie had decorated with hope and excitement and fun.

His Suz. He heard her bawdy laughter, her off-color jokes.

Fun. He wasn't a man prone to fun and ribaldry, but Susie had made him laugh and he hadn't laughed—really laughed— in so long his face would fracture like drought earth if he did.

Rachel, he sensed, wasn't inclined to levity. Instead, she was a woman who analyzed life, took it apart detail by detail.

But she was a mystery. Her work, her reason for being in a no-name town. The absence of the kid's father.

Ash wanted no part of the list. Of her.

Right. That's why you can't sleep.

Closing his eyes, he forced himself to focus on the cows he'd be checking in three hours. No mystery there. Just new-born calves.

His heart calmed.

In the 6:30 a.m. dark, Ash plowed out the quarter-mile drive from the house to the main road where the county trucks—lights flashing, motors droning—had pushed drifts before dawn.

With the temperature stable at five below and no wind, the school bus would run today.

He wondered if Rachel would let her son go with Daisy, or if she'd keep him home with the excuse of her ditched car.

He wondered if she was up yet, or still asleep in that cozy little bed, warm and snug under the blankets.

He wondered how she slept.

Knees bent?

Hand under her cheek?

Blanket drawn up around her ears?

Grading back the three-foot drift left by the county plows under the ranch's sign, he cursed. What the hell did he care how she slept? The quicker he got her car out of the snowbank, and her back to her job *in town,* the easier he'd breathe.

Another half hour passed before he could tow the ditched Sunburst back to the ranch, and by the time he stepped into the mudroom where the smell of coffee hit his nose, it was seven-twenty-five.

"'Morning," he said to no one in particular.

Daisy, sleepy-eyed and in her pj's, stared at her toast while Inez set a plate of poached eggs and grits down for Tom.

"G'morning, Ash." The housekeeper poured coffee into his mug, then took a plateful of pancakes and fried eggs from the oven and placed it on his spot at the table, opposite Tom.

His stepfather grunted. "The count today?"

New calves. "Fourteen. Six bulls, seven heifers. One dead."

Daisy picked at her toast. Ash wished his daughter would eat more. Toast had the sticking capability of cotton candy; there one minute, gone the next.

Would Rachel and her son be rising from their beds in the cottage? He glanced through the window. A soft light glowed from the smaller house among the trees. *Not your business.*

Curving a hand over Daisy's unruly red hair, he sat down. "You're up early, sleepyhead." Typical teen that she was, Daisy hated mornings.

"Had to print my essay," she mumbled.

An essay he couldn't read no matter how high her grade.

Face earnest, she looked over at him. "The printer needs a new cartridge, Dad."

Ah, damn. He'd meant to pick one up yesterday before he met Meggie. Daisy had been complaining for two weeks about the faded print. "I'll get one today. I promise."

She spread a dab of peanut butter on the corner of toast between her fingers. "Okay, just don't forget." A glance to the back door. "How's Charlie going to school?"

"Not our responsibility, Daiz." Ash reached for the maple syrup, then dug into his pancakes. Nobody made buttermilk pancakes like Inez.

Daisy nibbled her toast. "Did you get Rachel's car home?"

Home. He supposed the cottage was her home for the moment. "Yup. Towed it in while you were still sawing logs," he teased.

Tom dug into his eggs. "Sweep the walkway?"

Enough already. Ash leaned his wrists on the table, fork and knife spearing the air. "What is this? The Inquisition? I may not like reporters, but I'm not a complete jackass. Windchill brought the temp down to twenty below last night. Just so everybody's clear, I towed the damn car home *with* the trailer. Fixed the hitch and swept the walkway, okay?" He shot Tom a look. "I know what needs done, old man." *I've been doing it for twenty-five years.*

Tom lowered his head, focused on his grits. "No need to get your pants in a knot, son. I know you're on top of things."

Then why ask as if I'm the hired hand, instead of your son who's supposed to be your partner? Ash looked at his daughter. "You'll need to show the boy to the bus this first time."

Before she could respond, a soft knock sounded at the back door.

"I'll get it," Inez said. She walked over and let in a swathe of frigid air along with Rachel and her boy.

"Good morning." Her voice drifted across Ash's nape. She wore a pair of blue snow pants under her coat. Charlie, in a one-piece navy snowsuit, resembled a miniature moon-walker.

Inez gestured them inside. "Come in and join us for pancakes and eggs. There's plenty."

"Actually, we've already eaten. I was just wondering if my car—"

"Mom." Charlie tugged at Rachel's sleeve. "I'm still hungry."

"Great." Inez guided the boy into the kitchen, snowsuit, boots and all. Within seconds, she had him out of the gear and in a chair next to Ash.

With eyes as round as Ash's pancakes, the boy stared at the plate Inez set in front of him. Behind brown-rimmed glasses his blue eyes rose to pierce Ash. *Hell.*

"Want a pancake, boy?" he grumbled.

"Yes, please."

He flicked two small ones off the stacked plate in front of his own. "Syrup?"

"Uh-huh."

"Yes, please," Rachel prodded. Somehow without Ash noticing, she had slipped from her coat and lowered herself to the chair next to Tom. If Ash stretched his feet, he would nudge her toes.

"Yes, please," Charlie recited.

Ash poured on the syrup. Inez set a glass of milk down for the boy and coffee for Rachel. She shook her head at the silent offer from their housekeeper for a full breakfast.

The kid studied his loaded plate. "Will pancakes make me a cowboy?"

"You want to be a cowboy?" Ash asked.

Charlie nodded, small chin bouncing inches from his food.

"You eat those and all your vegetables every day and we'll see what happens." Kid was cute, he'd give him that.

He glanced at the mother. A purple knit thing sculpted her breasts. Great breasts. But they weren't what beguiled him. Her eyes soft on her son caught him square. Gentle, like that first day Tom had talked to the kid about the war.

She met his gaze across the table. A fine pink bloomed in her cheeks. She looked away.

Ash focused on his pancakes. She wasn't anything like Susie, or the few girls he'd dated in high school before Susie. Rachel Brant wasn't what he liked or wanted in women.

Get off it, Ash. You haven't been with a woman other than Susie in over fifteen years. What do you know about likable traits and wants? What the hell have you got to compare?

Susie. He had Susie to compare. *She* was all the criteria he needed. *If* he was interested. Which he was not.

Then stop chalking up reasons.

Damn it to hell. Scraping back his chair, he stood and looked down at the woman he'd thought about half the night. "The roads are clear. Bus will be coming through soon. Daisy can take your boy to school if you want."

Rachel lifted her face. "Thank you. You, too, Daisy. We didn't mean to be such a burden."

"Folks do for each other in these parts," Inez put in, giving Ash one of her Looks as she refilled the reporter's cup.

He glanced at the pantry wall and the sunflower clock Daisy had bought for her mother's last birthday. "Let your car run a few minutes before driving to work."

Rachel's brows bowed. Her Siamese-blue eyes locked on him. "It's here?"

"Out front." He shot a look at Tom. "Hitch is fixed, so you shouldn't have any trouble towing the trailer back to town once the roads are cleared."

"Wow, you fixed the hitch?"

"A bolt popped out. Nothing major." Still, her eyes worried, so he added, "There's only a slight scratch on the bumper." Leaning down, he kissed Daisy's hair. "Have a good day, pint."

"Let me pay for—" Rachel began.

He shoved in his chair. "No need. See you at ten, Pops?"

Tom nodded. "Have Ethan join us."

"He'll be there." Ash headed for the mudroom and his barn gear. Today, they would go over which yearling heifers to keep as breeding stock and which they would list for sale on their Web site. Before Tom showed up in the barn office, however, Inez would help him shower, then do his daily massage. Meantime, Ash planned to check the southeastern section and the eight wintering wild mustangs that had strayed over from the Pryor Mountains.

That should give Rachel enough time to crank up her rusted car and drive to town. Last thing he needed was her wandering into the barn office when Tom and Ethan were reading printouts.

Outside, with the cold, crisp air in his lungs, he breathed easier. The faint scent of her in the heat of the kitchen muddled his head. Was that how it would be every time he walked within fifty feet of her?

He thought of Charlie, asking if pancakes would make him a cowboy. He thought of her smile tipping her lips, the way the sweater lay over her breasts.

He strode for the barns, Jinx and Pedro trotting out front, bushy tails whipping in the icy breeze.

At 8:05, while he was tagging another calf in the home pasture, the school bus stopped in its usual spot at the top of the ranch road. In the wintry distance, Ash saw two figures, one small, one taller.

Slowly, day chased away night as a weak sun broke through the cloud bank in the east. One thing Ash understood was the weather. The temperature would warm to fifteen degrees by midday, giving those first newborns strength before the freeze of nightfall.

He broke thin sheets of ice in the water tanks, then used the Bobcat to clean out the calving barn. His foreman, Ethan Red Wolf, spread fresh straw from a flatbed trailer.

Finished, Ash hauled his saddle into Northwind's stall. Sprigs of hay hung from the stallion's mouth as he turned a heavy-lidded look on Ash.

"Yeah, I know. You'd rather eat than run, but you need the exercise and I need to check your mustang buddies."

He was tightening the cinch when she spoke from the stall's half door. "Ash?"

His hearted banged. He hadn't been expecting her, not here in the barn on his turf. Turning his head as he worked the saddle, he saw she was dressed to leave in her wool coat, her city designer purse clutched under her arm, its short strap slung around her left shoulder. Her eyes were as big and blue as a sky in haying season.

"You shouldn't be in the barn in your good clothes."

"I wanted to thank—"

"Your boy get to school okay?"

"Yes." A smile evolved. "Daisy made the transition fun."

He grunted a response.

"However, I'll pick him up from school. I'm only working a few hours today, before I get off at two-thirty," she explained. "Ash, I want to thank you for getting my car out of the ditch. But most of all, I'd like to thank you for last night. Charlie and I..."

Might have frozen fingers and toes or more, if he hadn't found them.

A shiver which had nothing to do with the frigid air whisked down his spine.

She went on. "I'd also like to pay for your efforts. Is there something you need or would like?"

Kisses flashed across his mind. "Nothing to pay." He brought down the stirrup and jiggled the saddle, checking for stability. "You won't have any trouble on the roads. Plows will have done the bus route and sanded the corners."

She remained at the door, waiting until he bridled Northwind.

"He's beautiful," she said when he led the stallion from the stall into the corridor. "And so tall." Her words were a little breathless.

Aiming for the rear doors, the horse clopping behind, Ash hoped Rachel had the good sense to turn in the opposite direction and leave. He wasn't in a talking mood.

You're a good man. Her words again. Right. A good man *would* chat for a minute, give her the time of day, look into her face and flirt a little. Smile, wave goodbye. A good man wouldn't ignore her when she had desperation in her eyes.

Keeping a distance of ten feet, she followed Northwind out of the horse barn and into the bright, cold day where Ash stopped to adjust the reins. Hands in her coat, Rachel stepped beside him. Her scarf wrapped her neck. He wanted to tell her to snug the wool over her ears.

"This is my first time on a ranch," she said, looking out over the land. Her words puffed out in frosty clouds and the cold pinked the tip of her nose. "It's very daunting."

Daunting? He surveyed the expanse of pasture and field buried under winter, the cattle with crusted snow on their backs working their way through piles of hay. Sights which he comprehended with every beat of his heart.

"And awesome." Her smile was sweet and shy. A first. When had reporters been shy?

She continued, "I'd like to know more about this type of livelihood. My son is crazy about horses and cowboys and—"

"It's a hard life," he said, arresting her thoughts before she made his way of putting bread and butter on the table seem like some Hollywood illusion.

"Yes, I'm sure it is." She studied Northwind, then took off her mitten and edged forward to run her fingers down the stallion's mane. "He has such long hair, like coarse silk. Do you brush it every day?"

"Twice."

Braver now, she worked her hand under the mane to the horse's neck. "He's so warm." She looked at Ash. "And powerful."

He felt the last word course through his gut, as if she spoke of him not the animal.

Her eyes went back to Northwind. "He looks like those Spanish horses you see in movies about old Mexico. Like a horse Zorro would ride." She smiled.

"That's Hollywood," he snapped.

Her smile dimmed.

"Look," he said more kindly. "Northwind's an Andalusian. Most ranches use quarter horses, but this breed is as good around cattle as any quarter horse. They're gentle, intelligent and have a lot of stamina." He liked the way her mahogany hair swept her right cheek as she tugged her mitten back over her fingers.

"Stamina for riding the range all day?" she asked.

"For whatever you want him to do."

Again she searched the distance. "So much land."

"It's a small outfit compared to most. Montana's losing ranches and rangeland to big corporations. Small independents are being bought by mega operations run in boardrooms instead of by ranchers and cowboys. Another thirty years you'll be hard-pressed to see an outfit like the Flying Bar T. They'll be swallowed by conglomerates, or movie stars who don't know what to do with their money, or developers who throw up residential pockets in the middle of nowhere."

Suddenly, he felt stripped, as if his soul exposed a jagged crack. She was a reporter, a newshound, always looking for the next morsel to drag off and sully with printed ink. Next she'd be writing about him bitching about land developers and conglomerates. Great publicity for Flying Bar T cattle sales.

Irate with his foolish mouth, Ash battened down the earflaps on his woolen hat, gathered the reins, swung into the saddle. Northwind frisked under his weight. Leather squeaked, bit rings jingled.

Shading her eyes from the bright sky with a gloved hand, Rachel looked up at Ash looking down from the Andalusian's back. Her face was a pale oval against the ruddy scarf. "Just for the record," he said, "this conversation did not happen. Anything you write will come from Tom."

Wheeling Northwind around, he spurred the stallion into a gallop toward the open range, where the raw wind bit skin and stung the eye. Where Mother Nature was his lover, his foe.

Rachel watched Ash race across the white landscape. Chunks of snow flew from the horse's heels. Ash might not want his story told, but she had heard his words, seen what those intense dark eyes hadn't voiced.

He was one of those ranchers. A small independent against million-dollar might.

And he was scared. Scared of a day in the future when he might be forced to let go of all he had worked to secure, of all he hoped to pass to his children, the love, sweat, blood he forfeited to nurture this soil where she stood.

But more than that, he was afraid she would write up his fears in a negative way.

Once, not long ago, she might have done exactly that. Once, she might have smiled and rushed back to the office and filed away his words, his angst, for an upcoming story.

Whether it was the wariness she detected in his eyes that first day, or the desire she caught last night, or the pain of moments ago, she was tired of getting the story for the "sake of the news" as her daddy had taught her, as he still maintained made a good reporter. What she understood standing amongst the herd, and felt with the very DNA that made her Rachel Brant, was she could not share Ash's words with anyone. Not yet.

Instead, she folded them into her heart to examine in the privacy of her nights.

Tom sat in the den, gazing out the window as Ash, leaning low over the Andalusian's neck, galloped across Flying Bar T fields.

His son was upset. He would not run a horse at such a clip unless he was upset. Not in more than a foot of snow. Good thing the stallion was a strong animal.

Rachel had gone out to the barns to talk to him. To thank him, she'd said. Ash wouldn't take to her thanks, Tom knew. Not because she was a newsperson, but because she was a woman. One who was forcing his son to notice a female beyond Susie. Tom had watched his eyes at breakfast. Like a wary dog he was, but sniffing the wind just the same.

His strong, sad boy. Tom wished he could fix his troubles.

But, hell, if he couldn't fix his own, how could he fix those of his son? Fixing meant turning clocks back, heading in other directions. Heading away from Hells Field.

Away from the VC hiding in tunnels.

It would mean Susie heading down Bluebird Avenue to Meggie's house, instead of around the bend on the county road.

Fixing would mean not giving in to a fifteen-year-old's disappointed eyes to make deals about opening Nam's worm can.

She could do that, this reporter. She could do it with her sharp mind and typing skills, open that can and spew out rot.

Rot that had kept Tom hanging on to the ranch as sole owner for too many years, afraid to let go, afraid to give away another part of himself the way he'd sacrificed his legs and arm.

Ownership of the Flying Bar T afforded reassurance.

Reassurance he was still a man.

But Inez liked her. Said Rachel had a good soul. Of course, Inez was a good soul herself. Only saw decency in others. She trusted in the afterlife and karma and yin and yang. Hereafter mumbo jumbo. She believed Rachel had been sent for a reason.

Tom grunted. He knew different. She'd been sent to shake them up. After thirty-six years, guess that was reason enough.

Chapter Five

After Ash rode off, Rachel walked back to the guesthouse. Inside, she straightened the beds and cleared the few dishes she and Charlie had used that morning. She hadn't expected to sit at Ash's table again, nor had she expected Charlie to eat a second breakfast. But that's exactly what her little boy had done. *Two* pancakes after the Cream of Wheat she stirred on the stove in their own little kitchen.

Pancakes, because Ash ate them and Ash was a cowboy.

Today, she would buy a package of blueberry pancake mix.

By the time she was done unpacking the remaining boxes, it was 9:40. She pulled on her boots and coat and went outside where the sky was a stadium of blue, the air snappy.

A thud to the left brought her head around. Bundled in a heavy green parka, Tom wheeled his chair down the front ramp of the main house.

Catching sight of Rachel, he lifted a hand. "Heading back with the trailer?"

"Yes. The roads should be fine now." She walked toward him. "Do you have a minute, Tom?"

His gnarled brows bunched. "Don't like the cottage?"

"It's fine. Perfect, in fact." She stopped a few feet away. "I was wondering if we could…" She glanced toward the barns. Had Ash returned from his race across the range? "If we could schedule a time to begin the interview. My hours are fairly flexible." As long as she brought in several stories a week and kept the Women's Circuit page filled, the paper's editor and publisher was satisfied.

Tom gazed across the yard. Searching for Ash, too? "How about four this afternoon? Ash has business in Billings today and won't be home till six, but Daisy will be here. Bus drops her at three-forty."

"Thank you." Rachel offered her hand, but Tom shoved off down the walkway his son had shoveled clean while night still hovered over her dreams.

She wouldn't take his brusque behavior as a snub.

He had agreed. That was enough.

She towed the trailer back to Sweet Creek Rentals and paid her bill. The man at the counter checked the hitch when she explained about the storm and nodded his approval when she told him Ash had done the repairs.

"Always was good with his hands," he said, filling out the forms she needed to sign. "Went to school with him, y'know? Both him and Susie. He went a bit nuts after she died, but then who wouldn't? She was a looker with all that red hair. Coulda had any guy she wanted, but she picked Ash. Amazed a lot of people, him not being that smart an' all and her smart as a whip."

Not smart? That wasn't the Ash she'd describe.

Thanking the man for waiving the damage fee, Rachel hurried away. She did not need an exposé on the marriage of Ash and Susie McKee.

But the information tarried in her mind while she drove to the newspaper to finish several articles. She told herself Ash was not her story. Tom was. And on Tom she would focus her attention.

Except, she recalled how Ash talked about his land.

At 2:15 she waited in the school parking lot for Charlie, and by 3:55 was ready to walk to the main house.

Ash's truck was parked down by the barns. Darn, should she reschedule? No, she'd let the old man decide.

Inez answered the back door with a smile for Charlie, said, "Come see what I have," and led him into the kitchen, chatting about his homework as if she did so every day. "Den's the first door to the left down the hall," she said to Rachel.

"Thank you. I owe you, Inez."

"Poosh. Not at all. Been a long time since I had a little fish to make cookies for."

"I'm not a fish," Charlie said, but he grinned.

Briefcase in hand, Rachel found Tom at a computer viewing an expense account. Like the rest of the house, the room was spacious with plenty of access for a wheelchair. Two green sofa chairs and a love seat girdled an entertainment wall dominated by a flat-screen TV. Feet propped on the small, round coffee table, Daisy sat on the love seat engrossed in *Oprah*.

"Hello," Rachel said.

Daisy raised her head. "Hey, Ms. Brant."

Tom shut down the computer before swinging around. "You know I'm not in favor of this," he warned.

"Yes, and I'm grateful that you've agreed." With a forced smile, she chose the chair next to Daisy. The teen clicked off the TV.

Tom harrumphed. "Ash is down at the barn. Heifer's having calving trouble."

She shook off the old man's uncanny insight. The moment she noticed Ash's green pickup the question of his whereabouts had burned in her mind. *Had* he returned early in case she asked too many questions or put the old man in an uncomfortable spot?

Pulling the briefcase onto her lap, she snapped the locks. "We can do this any way you'd like, sir. Daisy and I writing notes—" she handed the girl an extra legal pad and pen "—or using a tape recorder, or both, whichever makes you comfortable."

"None of it makes me comfortable. I'm doing this for my granddaughter. And my kids," he added.

Kids. Yes, Ash had a sister. Meg, police chief of Sweet Creek. Two days ago, Rachel had spoken with the policewoman about a single mother shoplifting at the Rite Aid, after the store's manager phoned Shaw Hanson, who sent Rachel chasing the story. A story she had convinced him to bury on page sixteen at Meg's specific request.

Chief McKee had the heart Shaw Hanson lacked.

Rachel admired this sister of Ash's, who could be his twin.

Same black hair, same intense eyes. But where Ash's cheek and jaw were angular, Meg's offered a loveliness Rachel had wished for the morning she turned thirteen. When Bill Brant said, "If you don't stop growing you'll be tall as a man" and she'd run to the mirror, seeing his image rather than her mother's.

Brown hair, not blond. Blue eyes, instead of gray. Gangly arms and big feet.

"Daisy." Rachel pushed aside her ancient history. "What would you like to ask your grandfather?"

Tom shook his head. "Let's keep it short. Daiz, you take notes while Rachel and I get to know each other."

But when Rachel set the recorder on the coffee table where it would pick up their voices, he waved a hand. "No recorders."

Okay, then. She opened her notebook. "Why don't we start with whatever you'd like to share first."

He pouched his lips. "Why not start at the beginning and end at the end?" She nearly smiled until he said, "I won't give you what you want." His eyes bored into hers. "The good stuff."

"Good stuff?"

"The hell." He looked away, eyes as distant and cold as a snow goose sky. "The gore, the screaming."

Rachel didn't waver. "We'll get there when we get there."

"No."

Moving from the topic, she asked, "How old were you when you were drafted?"

"Eighteen. Had my birthday three weeks before. Uncle Sam didn't waste time."

She nodded. "What did you think when you got that letter?"

"What every guy those days thought. I gotta go to war and I might never come back."

"How did you feel about that?"

"What kind of stupid question is that?"

"Tom, throwing insults won't get this done."

The coolness ebbed; his mouth relaxed. A test. Like Bill, who tested her every time she heard his voice on the phone.

"How do you think I felt? Scared spitless. My mama and daddy cried. Girl I was engaged to cried. Hell, *I* cried. Who wanted to go to some jungle where dying was the highest stake in the game?"

Her father had *wanted* to go—and had come back. Whole.

"Are your parents still alive?"

"Mother died fourteen years ago. Daddy while I was in Nam. Keeled over with a heart attack out there in the corral."

That would have agonized the young soldier, not to see his father one last time, not to be there to put him in the ground, say a prayer, have closure. Maybe his girlfriend had done that for him.

"Did you marry your fiancée when you returned to Sweet Creek?" Had she been Ash's mother?

He barked a laugh. "She took one look at these stubs and hitched a long ride in a short truck. Hightailed it out of Sweet Creek so fast there wasn't even a dust trail to be seen. Ain't been back."

Intent on the floor, his eyes glassed. "Heard she died some ten years later."

Rachel identified with the hollow sound of abandonment; it resembled the voice of her own heart.

Her mother had done the same, dying when Rachel was eight. And then Bill shoving her away from his emotions.

Last but not least, TV cameraman Floyd Stephens, when she told him she was keeping the baby: *"You of all people shouldn't want kids, knowing what you do of the world these days."* Before he'd walked out of their apartment.

Tom lifted his head. His eyes were fierce. "Ash and Meggie aren't my blood, but they're mine here." He tapped his head and his heart with his prosthesis. "They're more than any man could want in his dying age, more than a soldier could want, to chase away the horrors and his memories. They're the reason I've lived for thirty-six years instead of ending it all with my own bullet. And I don't care what you write, miss, but there's one thing you should know. I love my family. More than they'll know. More than you'll be able to describe. Now, we're done and I need to rest."

He wheeled the chair out of the room and left her alone with Daisy. The teenager slowly rose from the sofa, notepad in hand, and silently slipped from the room.

Rachel looked at her legal pad. No one—man, woman or *father*—had given her that kind of love.

She gathered up her materials. *Stop being a pity party, Rachel. Go home, type up your notes. That's what you're good at.*

Thank God for Charlie. Her little boy, saving her life.

The next interview session on Sunday before lunch lasted no more than fifteen minutes. Tom disclosed little about himself and even less about the war. Daisy quietly jotted a few facts.

When Tom ended the sitting, Rachel walked to the guest-house with Charlie dragging his heels the moment Ash came into the kitchen from the mudroom. Four days they had lived on the ranch. Four days in which she and Ash met only at a distance or in their vehicles coming and going down the road. He'd offer a curt nod, she a little wave.

Once, she caught herself peering out the guesthouse window, searching for his tall physique. *Not a good thing, Rachel.*

At 4:50 p.m. the following Wednesday, she finished the third interview. Nothing much gained again, but she would not give up. Sooner or later, Tom would tell her what she needed to know. Already, she had acquired ten pages of notes, a decent start for so few answered questions.

Stepping onto the front porch to call Charlie building a snow fort in a three-foot bank beside the house, she saw Ash and his dogs walk up the pathway from the barns.

As always the sight of him pulled her lungs tight.

With the temperature hovering at twenty degrees for two days, his black vest with a logo of the state and the letters MCA—Montana Cattlemen's Association—hung unzipped. His left hand held leather gloves.

Pushing back the brown cowboy hat from his forehead, he waited for her to pass down the steps. They were side-by-side when he said, "Tom had a heart attack last summer."

Rachel paused. "Yes, Inez mentioned it." The morning after Ash had raced over the range.

"Good. If he doesn't want to talk, don't push it. I don't want him agitated." Bent on the front door, he went past her.

Charlie scrambled up the snowbank, slid on his belly down the other side. She said, "It'll take a lot of interviews if he doesn't open up soon."

In the afternoon dusk, Ash's eyes were black, his jaw above the vest's collar pitiless. "If you're in a hurry for a story, you should find another guinea pig. One who'll run the gamut for you."

"That's not what I meant."

"What did you mean then?"

"I don't want to interrupt your family more than necessary."

His eyes told her she'd done that by coming to the ranch. Still, his look sent a live wire down her body. She may be a disruption to his family, but he wasn't immune to her femaleness.

He said, "If you're worried about Charlie being in the house or getting underfoot, there's a TV in the den."

"I don't let him watch TV unless I'm there to monitor the program."

"Inez can do that."

Rachel shook her head. "That's what I mean. I'm not trying to be difficult, Ash. I just want you to know I have a responsibility to my son. "

"As I have to my dad."

She took a breath. "What do you suggest then? He arranges the interview times. If I had my way I'd do it in two or three sessions and be done."

"Talking about that time in his life bothers him. It makes his heart race. That's why he's only able to do it in short spurts."

Alarmed, she asked, "How do you know his heart races?"

"Inez tells me. He always needs to lie down for a half hour after you leave."

She climbed the porch steps. "My God, why didn't Tom say so?"

Ash snorted.

"Okay." She scraped back her hair. "Stupid question."

"Look. Can't you just go with what he's given you?"

"He's barely given me anything." Frustrated with herself for not seeing this coming, she closed her eyes to think. When she looked again, his gaze was on her mouth. Her tummy spun.

"I have to go." She headed back down the steps.

"When's the next time?"

"I don't know. We didn't set up a time." Blood hot in her veins, she walked to where her son had dug a hole on the other side of the bank. Over her shoulder, she saw Ash watching her from the top step. "But Tom's invited us to lunch on Sunday."

Twenty feet of dusk hid the expression in his eyes. She thought he tilted his head, though it might have been the dying daylight playing shadow tag. *Will I see you there?*

She lifted a hand in farewell.

He did not return the gesture.

Folding her son's mittened hand in hers, she headed down the graded path leading to the little dollhouse among the dark evergreens.

At 12:20 the next day, Rachel was finishing up a story about Sweet Creek's only stoplight short-circuiting that morning to cause a fender bender between Hank Baldry's pickup and Mike Macleod's horse trailer when Ash's daughter appeared at her elbow.

"Hey, Daisy!"

"Hi, Ms. Brant."

"Rachel. Please." She nodded to the envelope in the teenager's hand. "That this week's school column?"

"Yeah, but I was hoping you could look at it before I give it to Mr. Hanson. Maybe show me what to look for."

"Sure. Grab a chair." Shoving papers and binders aside,

Rachel made room in the confined U-shaped space. "Okay, let's see what you've got."

Line by line they went over the two-page article. Rachel explained how to look for ways to tighten or flesh out sentences for a more succinct read.

"You write very well," she said when they were done.

"I want to be a journalist one day."

"You'll make an excellent journalist."

Daisy leaned back in her chair, crossed her arms. "I think Dad wants me to take over the ranch."

"Has he said so?"

"No, but I see it in his eyes every time I help out around the cows."

In other words, the girl was afraid to voice her concerns in case she was right, in case she dashed her daddy's hopes. Oh, but Rachel could relate to that.

Still, she'd watched Ash kiss his child's hair the morning after the snowstorm. *"Have a good day, pint."*

She studied the half-dozen red marks on the pages. The girl had enormous potential. "You need to tell him how you feel, Daisy."

"He won't listen."

"How do you know?"

"I just do." Her eyes veered away.

Okay. Evidently, the topic was not up for discussion. Rachel tapped the edges of the pages together and handed them back. "Don't give up, honey, if this is what you want. Your daddy will come around."

"I don't think so. I think it has to do with his…"

"His what?"

She shook her head. "Nothing." But her salad-green eyes were determined. "I'm not giving up. This is *my* dream." She pressed the pages against her heart, stamping the words there. *"Mine."*

Rachel smiled. "You won't get an argument from me."

Daisy stood. "Thanks, Ms. Brant. I really appreciate your help."

"Not a problem and, please, do call me Rachel." When the girl glanced shyly away, Rachel insisted, "Ms. Brant leaves me thinking of little old librarians."

Daisy giggled. "You're nothing like Miss Ethelwhite. She's, like, older than dirt. Plus, you're way too pretty."

Rachel laughed and it felt good. "Well, thank you." She thought of the tiny, white-haired town librarian she had interviewed last week for a review about a *New York Times* bestseller. "But old can be quite mystical and beautiful."

"Right. Whatever."

"Let me show you." Rachel plucked a binder from the shelf beside her computer. Flipping to the back, she stopped at a black-and-white photograph of an old man. "See this fellow?"

Daisy leaned in. "Wow, he really *does* look old. Who is he?"

"Thomas Many Moons. A Nez Perce shaman who lives in Oregon. He's a hundred-and-two in this photo."

"Yo, that's *ancient*. But he's beautiful, too."

"Yes, he is. Now, look at *him*. What do you see?"

Ten long seconds passed. "Character. And life." Pushing a chunk of red hair behind one ear, the teenager leaned an elbow on the desk. "Thousands of laughs and a lot of sorrow. And wisdom. He looks like one of those old monks that live in the Tibetan mountains. You know, the ones you read about in *National Geographic*? The ones who seem to hold the secrets of the world?"

"Exactly. What else?"

"I think he's, like, at peace with himself." Daisy drew back. "Did you take this picture?"

"Last year."

"Incredible. You got the guy's entire hundred years in this one picture."

"Good observation." Rachel smiled. "That's what a journalist does. Sees things others don't. And if they're good at their job, they'll write so others can understand, too."

The girl traced a finger down the old shaman's waist-long braid flowing over his shoulder. "Can you do that for Grandpa? Take his picture and write about him this way?"

"I can and will." Providing Tom gave her the information she needed—and permission for a photo. She'd had no problem with the other six vets, but Tom was a man who'd suffered deeper and longer than most. He hadn't let go. That much she'd gleaned from their conversations. Yesterday he'd told her as much. *"Won't ever forget the smell."*

No, she didn't think he would. Human death. She could not imagine the odor. Could not.

She closed the book. "We'll write the story together the way your grandpa wants. And I'll teach you to be a fine reporter."

Then she remembered Ash in the middle of the snowy road, glaring down at her from his Crusader steed. *"You're not welcome here."*

Perhaps she wasn't, but come hell or high snow, this office was her turf and in it Daisy would get the chance to grab a great foothold to her dream.

Sunday dawned clear and cold. Ash spent part of the morning with Daisy in the calving barn, pulling breeched calves from two heifers, then moving the bulls from the feed pens to the eastern home pasture. Ethan Red Wolf had Sunday off, as did Inez. The housekeeper visited her sister in Sweet Creek and Ethan spent most of his Sunday in the foreman's house, sketching Native American images or tramping through the woods with his camera.

Ash usually worked the day alone, but today he'd needed Daisy's help. *A good hand with the cattle,* he thought as he tossed a layer of straw into one of the pens.

Daisy hung over the gate, crooning to the nervous new mother as the calf drank his fill.

Ash said, "He's a big one. Fetch a good price come fall."

"I guess."

He eyed his daughter. Selling calves had always been difficult for her. Yet, she understood that not all animals lived to old age. She was a rancher's daughter, after all. And bull calves were never named. Six months or a year down the road they'd be shipped for meat.

Nonetheless, a smile tugged his mouth. One day she'd make an excellent rancher, his little girl—if she so chose. Women ranchers were a tough, intelligent breed and Daisy had a natural instinct required around the animals.

Your mother would be proud, he thought watching his daughter observe the pair in the pen.

Except Susie wasn't here.

Belly full, the calf's legs crumpled, landing it in the deep straw. "Snug as a bug in a rug," he commented, hoping to catch a grin from Daisy. Like the old days.

She swung off the gate. "If we're done here, I'm going up to the house. Rachel and Charlie will be coming for lunch," she reminded him. "What're you making?"

He always made the Sunday lunch on Inez's day off. "Haven't thought about it." On a high hope, he added, "Maybe we could try something together."

"Yeah, maybe."

"Great. See you in a bit, then." He watched her walk away, across the barn's open area, her long red braid swinging against her back. He wanted to call out, "Come back, honey. Talk to your old man." He wanted to sling an arm over her shoulder, tell her he'd protect her no matter what demons plagued her heart. Instead, he waited until she disappeared down the dark corridor and he was alone again among his cows.

He could pinpoint the minute Daisy started slipping into herself the way she had after Tom's heart attack.

The day Rachel Brant had driven up his road looking for his stepfather.

Three-and-a-half weeks ago.

And today she and Daisy would work on the story, put the notes in order, formulate a cohesive story. That much he'd gotten from Pops.

Ash felt something shift inside himself.

Tom, allowing exposure of events he vowed to keep buried. Changing his mind.

Had he altered his opinion of Rachel, too?

Heading for the barn's storage room, Ash breathed in hard. She'd be in the house in fifteen minutes. She'd be at their kitchen table, eyes full of knowledge. And something else. Something that ran between them.

Each time he saw her, thought of her, the rush was there. In his blood. In his heart and head. The soles of his feet. The tips of his fingers. Fireworks crisscrossing his body.

Had he felt like this with Susie?

Yes, of course he had. Hadn't he?

Had it been this intense, this *electric?* He couldn't recall. He *couldn't recall.*

Ah, Susie. I won't lose you, goddammit, I won't.

But he already had, and now another woman made his penis thick.

He hung up the shovel and fork, remembering the notebook Rachel had left in the den after the last session. He had looked inside, stared at the pages. Sixteen as of last Thursday. Each visit dated, that much he identified.

Her slanted scrawl he couldn't decipher. But even if she typed her notes, he'd be hard-pressed to comprehend words of more than three or four letters.

After their Sunday lunch, once Rachel returned to the cottage, he would have Daisy read the pages aloud.

Tamping down the fact he'd be last to know *as usual,* he strode from the barn just as he saw her Sunburst pull onto the ranch road. His feet set him on a course toward her.

Tongues lolling, the dogs loped beside the car while Rachel drove the quarter mile to the main house.

"Lookit, Mom! The horses are racing!" Charlie strained against his seat belt to peer out the window at a small herd galloping in the pasture along the roadside. Snow flew from their hooves, and fog streamed from their nostrils. "I wanna ride a horse, Mom. Do you think Mr. Ash will let me ride a horse?"

"I don't think these horses are tame enough for you to ride, Charlie."

"Daisy said so. I really, really, *really* wanna ride. Can I, Mom?"

"Let's wait and see how things go, buddy. I'm not sure Mr. Ash would appreciate us asking for horse rides. This isn't a trail riding ranch," she said, reiterating Ash's statement the day they'd viewed their present home.

"Doesn't he like us?"

She glanced in the rearview mirror. Her son stared out the side window, the behavior a reproduction of when they drove from her dad's house in D.C., last August.

Forlorn and a little lost.

Because his grandfather often forgot Charlie was seven not twenty-seven and Bill Brant had called his grandson a wuss. *"Doesn't Grandpa like us?"*

She chose her words carefully. "I think Daisy's dad is a very busy man, champ. This is a huge ranch, with hundreds of cows. That's a lot of responsibility and a lot of hours of hard work. When the mama cows are having their babies, Mr. Ash gets up during the night to check on them."

"How do you know?"

"Inez told me."

"Oh." Then in typical little boy fashion, he changed topics. "I wish I rode the bus every day. There's this boy, Cameron? He rides the bus all the time and he likes my cars and stuff."

"That's great, baby."

"Hey, there's Mr. Ash."

Rachel shot a look across the ranch yard. Sure enough, Ash strode toward them, hailing her to stop.

She rolled down the window. Her insides tightened. God, the man was like a tall mug of steamy chocolate. She let her gaze drink him in, top to bottom. A tan ball cap with MCA above its black bill and beneath it, his rich brown eyes. Old navy barn coat draped open. Wrangler jeans of a thousand washes on lean hips. Instead of cowboy boots, he worked in durable Sorel boots. The footwear emphasized the fact he was a rancher through and through. Oh, yes. *Very* steamy chocolate.

"Hey," she managed.

"Coming from church?" he asked.

"No. Did you go?"

His eyes didn't waver. "God and I parted company a long time ago."

When Susie died? "Charlie and I were at the newspaper. I needed to develop some film for tomorrow, and get the camera. Thought I might get some photos of Tom."

"He won't like that."

"I'll be focusing on the face and shoulders, nothing more."

"A mug shot. Huh. Well, good luck with it. Last picture he had taken was before my mother died."

"Oh? Why?"

Ash shrugged, then pointed with his chin to the main house. "Bet you didn't know I'm making lunch."

Warmth waded through her cells, set her nerves aquiver. "Wow," she said on a laugh. "A man who cooks." Then she drove to the ranch house to park beside his green truck rather than at her place.

With wagging tails and welcoming eyes, the dogs greeted Charlie.

Rachel grabbed her briefcase and Ash opened the car door. A chivalrous act that pricked her eyes. Stoic and stubborn he might be, but the childhood lessons he'd learned about gentle- manly manners remained. "Thank you," she said, climbing out.

Taking the briefcase from her hand, he motioned her up the swept cement walkway, wide enough for Tom's chair, to the railed wooden ramp at the mudroom door.

Within seconds, they crowded into the confined space. While she removed her snow boots, Ash waited near her shoulder.

"Should've been wearing those all along," he commented when she set her wool-lined footwear on the mat. "Good thing your boy had them the other night."

The night of the blizzard. "He likes playing in the snow."

"And you get caught in the storms."

She glimpsed bemusement. It took her breath. "I learn fast."

"Huh."

Her heart warmed. Snow boots and woolen socks kept feet toasty in below-zero temperatures. She could almost hear his words.

Daisy opened the kitchen door. "Hey, guys," she greeted.

Charlie grinned. "I brought my play farm set."

"Great, pal. Bring it into the family room and we'll set it up there." Her eyes laughed at Rachel. "Cushions make great hills."

Ash asked, "You take the soup from the freezer, Daiz?"

Her eyes sobered. "Um, there's this new recipe. Can we try that instead?"

"We'll see."

A nod, then, "Come on, Charlie." The door hissed closed; Rachel and Ash stood alone in the mudroom.

"Go on in." He inclined his head.

"I'll wait."

He hung up his coat, stowed his boots beside her smaller set.

"My son likes your daughter," she said to take their minds from the heat arcing between them. "A lot."

"Seems the feeling's mutual." Slowly, he turned, touched her cheek with a callused fingerpad. "But I keep wondering," he said, voice soft, "what the boy's mother feels about the girl's father?"

Light from a small window above the washer tinted his cheeks in sienna. "Depends," she replied, short of breath, "on what the girl's father feels toward the boy's mother."

He wanted to kiss her. She could see it in his Darjeeling eyes. Suddenly, he dropped his hand. "I need to get lunch started."

Swinging open the door, he strode into the kitchen, leaving her to stabilize the air in her lungs.

Chapter Six

W hat the hell was he thinking, touching her like that?

If you need a woman, go into town, see one of those divor-cées hanging around The Cattle Barn Saturday nights.

He shouldn't have touched her. Because now he knew. Knew the feel of her skin, soft as butter, warm as oven bread. Her cat-blue eyes had swallowed him whole and when he felt her breath on his wrist his groin had stiffened.

Too long without, he reasoned. Five years too long.

From the freezer he hauled out the frozen homemade soup, thawed it in the microwave, set the table. He hoped Daisy had forgotten the new recipe. He did not need Rachel seeing him haggle with words he should recognize after years of cooking.

Words, flying from her mind to her fingertips.

Click-clickety-click. Her laptop keyboard. In the dining room, she and Daisy pored over the notebook he'd tried to decipher last night.

From the living room, Tom's soft murmurs to Charlie. The kid had taken to the old man like an orphaned calf to a milk-feeding hand. Ash wondered about the boy's grandfather. The one who'd called the Vietnam war a black hole.

He had seen Tom's eyes at the description, imagined the horror in his father's mind. Horror he spoke to no one.

Maybe to Laura, Ash's mother. His quiet, gentle mother. She'd worked her fingers raw trying to keep that dilapidated roof over their heads while his real father flew choppers over jungles and rice paddies. Before Tom entered the picture with his broken body, and took Ash's mother from near poverty and heartbreak to comfort and hope.

A million times, Ash wondered from whom he'd received his damaged reading gene. Not his real father, reading gadgets and dials and high-tech helicopter panels. Not his mother, understanding the Latin-based language of medicine and therapy. *Just your own twisted gene, Ash. Nothing else.*

He stirred the soup, enjoying the aroma of chicken and basil, sage and parsley.

Daisy came up beside him, magazine clipping in hand. "Dad, this is the recipe."

He slanted a look over his shoulder. Rachel remained in the dining room, clicking away. "Shouldn't you be helping write Grandpa's story?"

"We're done. Rachel's working on something else. Come on, Dad," she whispered. "No one will know."

No one.

Except a reporter.

And a seven-year-old who read *Harry Potter,* the book Ash once rejected for his own daughter, but Rachel embraced for her son at the same age. Daisy had let the bit of information about the kid's ability slip the other night.

Two of a kind, Daisy and Charlie. Two brilliant kids. Ash

grunted. Readers at birth. If he lived to be a hundred-and-ten, he would never gain what they'd secured in kindergarten.

"Please, Dad," she begged. "We can pretend you're teaching me. She won't know."

"Why *now*, Daiz?" he muttered. "Why not *tonight?*" When Rachel was gone.

"'Cause I don't want to cook supper. I want to make lunch." Typical teenager. *I want*.

Guilt sluiced over him. She so seldom asked for anything these days. And hadn't he been mourning down in the barn the fact she barely spoke with him these days?

"'Sides," she went on, "it looks *so* good and it'll be way better than plain old soup and sandwiches. C'mon, Dad. When was the last time we did anything together?"

His anguish winged out the window. She was right. Too long they'd been on a cross-purpose yo-yo. No excuse. She was reaching out.

Her shoulder nudged his biceps; he yearned to draw her in close as he had when she was ten, when she hadn't built her stone wall yet, when he was still her knight in shining armor.

He kept his hand on the wooden spoon, stirring. "What's the recipe?"

"An eight-vegetable ragout." She held up the photo of a mouthwatering concoction in a fancy casserole dish.

"Looks more like supper than lunch."

"Uh-uh. See, it says right there. 'Great for Lunchtime.'" She traced the sentence for him.

"Humph." He scanned the words. *Gretfr lchtme*. "All right." Reconnecting with his daughter was more important than worrying about Rachel Brant and her keyboard skills.

"Love you, Dad," Daisy whispered. "I'll get the ingredients." Humming, she riffled through the refrigerator.

Love you, Dad. His heart did a slow tumble. When had he

heard those words last? A year? Two? He blinked away the burn in his eyes.

"Can I help with something?" Rachel stood in the doorway separating kitchen from dining room. She'd put away her laptop, which meant he couldn't shoo her back to work.

Sweat broke across his brow. *Showtime.*

Spilling carrots, celery and onions onto the counter, Daisy said, "Dad and I are making ragout."

"Really? I love ragout. Is this the recipe?" She wandered to the island and picked up the magazine depiction of a *great lunch.* "Mushrooms, celery, kidney beans, carrots, corn, stewed tomatoes, red peppers. Mmm. Very wholesome."

Thank you. The oral list would allow him to at least know what to rinse in the sink.

"Dad, it says we need a large saucepan."

"In the pantry." Ash dug in the cupboard beside the fridge and brought out cans of stewed tomatoes and kernel corn.

"Stewed tomatoes or whole tomatoes?" Rachel asked.

He paused. "What?"

"You brought out whole tomatoes." She smiled and held up the can. "The recipe calls for stewed."

"Oh." Across his forehead sweat sprang from his pores.

He replaced the can in the cupboard. *Stupid.*

Daisy returned from the pantry.

"We don't have stewed tomatoes," he told her.

"Sure we do. I saw them this morning when I was checking out the recipe."

"Those are whole. I made the same mistake."

A split-second pause before his daughter shot a look at Rachel. "Oh, well. No worries. We can substitute, right? And some extras?" Daisy opened the fridge.

"I think I saw stews in the—" Rachel began.

Dammit, she'd spotted the label he'd misread.

"Voilà." Daisy held up two green peppers. "We can chop in a few of these as well."

Rachel looked from her to him, then smiled. "If you won't tell Charlie, I won't. He hates green peppers."

Relief swallowed Ash. "The chef doesn't tell his secrets. Right, Daiz?"

"Nope." She tossed him a grin that went straight to his heart.

Over Daisy's head Rachel mesmerized him. He remembered the feel of her skin. He wanted to remember other things. Like the feel of her mouth.

He turned his attention to the stove where Daisy filled the pan with sauce and vegetables. He wasn't interested in a woman, and especially not Rachel Brant. Except, she was here, in his kitchen, and her presence pressed on his spine.

"Looks wonderful."

She stood beside him, the way Daisy had five minutes ago. Her breast brushed his elbow. A spark hit his groin.

Dammit, he was *not* that desperate. "Inez made the soup," he said gruffly.

"Actually, I meant what Daisy's making." She smiled at his daughter. "Did your mom teach you how to cook?"

Ash went still. "*I* taught her how to cook."

"Sorry, I thought with all the pictures of—of your wife and Daisy that—"

He turned. Her face was small and pale, her lips full and flush. "You thought wrong."

Daisy stepped between them. "What Dad meant was there hadn't been much time for her to teach me kitchen skills. I was ten when my mom died."

"I'm sorry," Rachel said again. "Truly."

"No worries." Daisy offered a quick smile. "We don't talk about her, is all." She shot Ash a look stockpiled in pain. "Easier that way. Would you like to chop some celery and green onions?"

* * *

Hard for anyone not to notice the pictures, Tom thought, eavesdropping on the conversation in the kitchen. *They're all over the house.*

Susie and Daisy. Susie and Ash. The three of them as a family. Susie and Inez. Susie and Tom. Yet, in all the years, a group picture of the five of them remained nonexistent. Tom regretted that most of all.

Ash, he thought, didn't hear the silence, the absence of Susie's name. But Tom heard it daily, with the clarity of a tolling bell.

Daisy heard it, too.

Inez thought it was unnatural and Tom agreed. A daughter should speak her mother's name freely, frequently. She should remember their times together, times she and Susie and Ash were a family.

All these years and Tom could count on five fingers the times Ash had mentioned his wife's name. Except in his dreams in the months after she died; he would cry in his sleep and mumble her name and Tom would sit at his bedside, watch and mourn with him for those lost moments.

It was not good when strangers like Rachel Brant noticed.

It was not good when her eyes said she wanted to help, but didn't know where to begin, how to start.

And Tom couldn't help her.

He regretted not pushing Ash into therapy. The boy needed to oust the hurt and anger—oh, yes, Tom know about the anger—and find freedom and peace.

Ash needed a woman in his life again.

Laura, Ash's mother, had been that woman for Tom. He'd told Rachel that today, with his granddaughter sitting right there. He'd told them how Laura's healing hands and heart had offered solace. She'd given him peace when he would have rather died. War did that. Damaged body and mind.

Three decades ago, what did he know? Nothing. He had no clue how bad the damage *could* get. He'd heard stories, though nothing had been real until he'd lived the place, the horror, the hell.

Hells Field.

He'd landed in Okinawa the summer of '68. Twenty years old, tall and skinny, a rancher's kid who'd breathed dusty roads and the scent of cow dung most of his life. The only rifle he'd learned to aim was a .22 for pesky groundhogs and coyotes. His daddy did the big game shooting: bear, deer, moose.

In '68, Tom was handed an AK-47 and told to fall in line on a mission to hunt Charlie. *Charlie.* Back home, he'd graduated with a kid named Charlie, who looked nothing like the guys Tom was supposed to hunt.

Thank God for the U.S. postal service. Thank God for the letters from home that kept him sane, that kept alive the memories of softer times.

His mother wrote once a week. His daddy wrote a line or two once a month tacked on the end of one of her letters. His fiancée, Tina, the one whose picture he'd carried in his wallet, wrote nearly every night. He loved getting all their letters, but he'd loved hers most of all.

Tina had been The One.

Growing up together, she and Tom had been pals from first grade when the teacher got ticked at his best friend, Bobby, for sticking gum in Tina's hair and then at Tom for taking the scissors to cut it out. The whole thing had been pretty funny. Tina hated Tom and Bobby for days, until he'd told her how cute that little piece of cut hair looked when she wore a ponytail. And that was that. They were pals for life. Later, when they were fifteen, he and Tina got to be more than pals.

They loved each other.

In Nam, he'd counted the days to get home to her.

* * *

Finally, Rachel had a beginning to the story. Tom had told her about his arrival in Vietnam, about the letters home, about the girl who waited there.

Rachel pieced the notes together, a puzzle slowly evolving from the perimeter inward. But the puzzle nagging her more was the one of Ash sidestepping around his dead wife. Rachel had caught the look sliding between Daisy and her daddy during lunch three days before, and recognized the hurt in the girl's eyes.

Rachel identified the same frustration when Bill Brant refused to share his memories of Grace—except to toss out comparisons that made Rachel feel clumsy and inept.

Susie McKee was off-limits to everyone including, Rachel suspected, Ash himself. Her pictures enshrined her memory. *See the photos, remember, but don't speak of the dead.* Don't talk about the woman who had been part of his life, who had loved him, and left her daughter too early.

Just like Bill, Rachel's father.

She ached for young Daisy.

At six o'clock Tuesday evening, she left the guesthouse with Charlie and walked to the rear door of the main house. Tonight she hoped to move forward, toward the mission of Hells Field. With her sessions lasting no more than ten to fifteen minutes each, she needed to press Tom into revealing the information she sought.

Inez greeted them. "They're in the family room."

Rachel followed the housekeeper to where Ash and Tom were listening to Daisy read the newspaper aloud.

Under the archway, Rachel kept a hand on Charlie's shoulder. "Hi," she said to the trio.

Daisy slapped the paper shut. "Hey. You're early."

Ash shot to his feet. "I'll be in the barns." Barely a glance at Rachel and he was gone.

"I didn't mean to interrupt."

Twenty minutes later she assisted Charlie with his coat. "Thanks for helping, Daisy." Tonight the girl had kept the boy occupied while Rachel talked to Tom.

"Charlie's easy to get along with." The girl winked and handed over his mittens before securing his wool hat over his ears. "And we both like *Harry Potter*."

"Yep," Charlie agreed happily. "An' Daisy's read all the books, Mom."

"She has, huh?"

"Mmm-hmm. She started reading when she was littler than me."

"That so?" Rachel smiled at the teenager.

Daisy shrugged into her jacket. "I began when I was four."

"Wow. Impressive." Charlie had started at five and a half. Rachel remembered the day he'd picked up her *Good Housekeeping* magazine and read two complete sentences without a single error.

Out under the cold stars the girl said, "I have to check on my dad."

"I really didn't mean to chase him out of the house."

"You didn't."

Snow crunched under their boots.

Rachel asked, "Are the cattle still giving birth?"

"They will for another six weeks or so."

"Must be hard on your dad, playing doctor 24-7." And those poor creatures laboring in icy temperatures. Her female instincts empathized.

"It's our life. Without the calves we wouldn't be able to keep his ranch. As it is, there are outfits that would like nothing better than to get rid of small-timers like us."

Small-timers. Tom had said the Flying Bar T ranged more

than nine hundred head. To fathom that number of cloven-hoofed animals in one lump sum boggled her mind. Yet, there were ranches boasting ten times the stock on the McKee place.

Rachel started for the path through the trees. "Have a good night, Daisy."

The teenager glanced toward the outbuildings where light warmed several windows. "Want to see the calving barn?"

"Yes, Mom, come on." Charlie tugged her hand. "Please. I want to see the baby cows and the horses and the dogs."

"You won't be interfering," Daisy assured.

"All right." If Ash glowered at her, so be it. But adrenaline rushed through her limbs just the same.

They headed down the swept walkways, breath steaming from their mouths. Above, the sky was a sugared blueberry bowl, the moon a horn of chilled wine.

Entering the main doors of the largest barn, Rachel's nose picked up the musty scents of cowhide and manure and dry hay and remnants of the clear, vast space that was Montana.

Daisy led them down a short hallway, past a room filled with equipment: ropes, bits of harness, a refrigerator, shelving, cupboards. Ash's coat. They passed a closed room with a metal plaque titled Office tacked to its door.

Rachel felt a smile tug. *A cowboy's office.*

At the hallway's end was a wooden half door. They emerged into a warehouse space lit by softly glowing bulbs. Night-lights for calves. *Oh, Ash, you are a man of surprises.*

She estimated the area took up more than eight thousand square feet. Dozens of Black Angus cows with calves stood or lay in the fresh straw. Some eyed them curiously, others paid no attention, chewing their cud while little calves slept nose to tail in the straw. Charlie took Rachel's hand and she squeezed his fingers for reassurance. Pens lined the two outer walls where bulky shapes moved behind six of the slatted enclosures.

Then she saw Ash. Crouched behind a cow lying on the straw-strewn floor at the far end of the barn. He had his arm deep inside the animal. Another man worked at the cow's head, keeping her eyes hidden with a cloth.

"Calf trouble." Daisy flicked a look at Charlie. "Maybe you should take him home."

"Uh-uh. Can I see?" Charlie's eyes were glued to the birthing.

Rachel stood in front of her son, effectively blocking Ash and the cow. She bent to Charlie's level. "Sugar, this is not the time for a tour. The cow is in pain. I think Daisy is right. We should go back."

"Daisy's not going."

"Honey, you haven't been this close to a cow." Especially one giving birth.

"Maybe it'll be okay," Daisy offered. "First time I helped Dad with a birth, I was six."

"See," Charlie exclaimed. "And I'm seven. If girls can do it, why can't I?"

"Daisy grew up around these animals, son."

"I want to see." His mouth pressed a stubborn line.

Daisy knelt on one knee. "Charlie, I'll take you over." She shot a look at Rachel. "But you have to promise not to say anything, okay? No ewwy noises, no screaming, no talking. This is really, really serious. My dad's trying to save the calf and if you do anything to frighten the cow, she might die. Got it?"

Eyes big as moons, he peeked around her, then nodded. "I won't do nuthin', Daisy," he whispered. "Promise." He hesitated. "Will this make me a cowboy?"

Daisy chuckled. "Depends on how you react to blood." Her eyes met Rachel's. "You going to faint?"

Bemused, Rachel touched her son's shoulder. "I had him."

"Right." The teenager led the way through the quiet cattle to where Ash and the other man worked on the cow. "That's Ethan, our foreman," she murmured to Rachel. "Hey, Dad."

His eyes were closed, his face full of concentration. "Hey, Daiz. Want to push on her belly?"

Rachel observed as Daisy settled her palms on the side of the cow just left of its flank, gently pressing down, massaging toward the tail.

Ash grunted. "Calf's big—and it's—turned."

He worked in green coveralls over a white T-shirt. The MCA cap had been tossed aside on the sweet-scented straw. She recalled the equipment room where his coat and flannel shirt were piled on a bench.

His biceps bunched and stretched under sun-browned skin. Sweat gleamed on brow and cheeks. "Need to find—a hoof."

"Mom," Charlie whispered. "I think the cow is pregnant."

Ash's eyes snapped open and locked on Rachel standing several feet away, then on Charlie. "You're right, sport," he said, his tone humorous. "She is very—" unfocused, his eyes stared across the barn "—ughh—pregnant— Got it. Whew. Okay, here we go. Keep massaging, Daiz."

Rachel couldn't stand by and watch the cow's pain. Stepping beside Ash's daughter, she massaged her palms gently to and fro along the animal's thick black hide.

Admiration flickered in Ash's eyes. "How you doing up there, Eth?" he asked.

"She's wore out," the foreman replied. He stroked the cow's neck, murmuring nonsense.

Ash rotated his shoulder. "Won't be long now. Easy there, little lady." Slowly Ash extracted his latex-gloved arm, bringing a small yellow hoof into the world. Then two tiny legs, the calf's nose.

The cow bawled. "Easy, girl," Ash soothed. "That's it, hang

in there, another push." He held the hoof firmly, lightly, pulling with each contraction, not releasing a gained inch. Moments later, the calf slid onto the straw bed.

Rachel moved to stand protectively beside Charlie.

"It's all slimy," the boy whispered.

"That's because he was in a sack of special water for nine months," Ash explained, removing the pale bluish membrane from the calf's nostrils for that initial breath.

"How come it didn't drown?"

The corner of Ash's mouth shifted. "Because babies inside mommies don't need air. They get oxygen from their mom."

"Oh."

Inserting two fingers into the calf's mouth, Ash cleared mucus from its throat. He tugged off the long latex glove, pitched it aside in the straw near a strange metal contraption.

Free from Ethan's cloth, the cow turned her head to look at her calf. Too exhausted to stand, she offered a low, reassuring moo. The little creature shook its wobbly head, wet ears flopping, navy eyes blinking between two-inch lashes.

Something soft bloomed inside Rachel as she watched Ash's big, scarred hands towel the little animal's wet coat. She remembered his kind tone to the distressed mother and to Charlie and imagined how he must have been once, long ago, with the wife in the photos when Daisy was a baby.

"Can I touch the calf, Mom?" Charlie whispered.

Rachel knelt on the fresh straw, drawing her child beside her. "Let's just watch for a minute, champ. We don't want to scare the cow."

"Good-sized bull." Ethan tagged the ear of the calf, an everyday task in this world of cattle.

Wiping his hands with a clean cloth, Ash rose. "Thought it might be twins. We'll see how she heals. Could be her last year."

"What does that mean?" Rachel asked.

His eyes touched hers. "It means if she doesn't heal she's shipped for meat."

"Should be okay," the foreman reassured. "Didn't need the calf puller." Picking the metal hook from the straw, the man headed for the half door.

Rachel shuddered. *A calf puller? Shipped for meat?*

"This is a working ranch." Ash's definition when she had come looking to rent the guesthouse. He was not a man to waste time on nonsense and things that taxed energy or money needlessly. No wonder he saw her job as frivolous.

A job without purpose.

A job for pleasure.

The way basketball or baseball players provided entertainment.

Unnecessary.

If tomorrow baseball folded, who would suffer? Undoubtedly the players and media employees—but only for the length of time it took to find work elsewhere. And for the exception of preventing emergencies, if newspapers stopped printing and TV news stopped their talking heads the outside world would continue without missing a beat.

Not so with ranchers and farmers. Theirs was a sector which put meals on the tables of the world, shipping produce and meat and dairy products for restaurants and grocery stores everywhere. Ranches like the Flying Bar T.

Ranchers like Ashford McKee.

Without him and his associates, billions would suffer and die. Rachel knew firsthand the state of some of those people. Journalist friends had been in Somalia and Zimbabwe, El Salvador and the Sudan. Places where the lack of food stole people's flesh and children's lives.

And here she was digging up the past of an old war hero,

digging in the past of Ash McKee. For no reason except to appease her father. Suddenly her job seemed silly. Futile.

"Come on, Charlie. We need to go home."

"I want to see the calf some more."

"You've seen the calf."

Planting his feet, her son looked up at Ash. "I wanna stay with Daisy. And Mr. Ash."

"They have work to do." *Not now, Charlie.*

The cow clambered to her feet. Rachel jerked Charlie out of the way, but Ash was already there, between them and the animal, holding out a hand, traffic cop of cows.

"Just step back slowly. She wants to check her calf."

Charlie glued to her side, Rachel did as Ash instructed. On her feet, the cow looked enormous. Her big brown eyes scrutinized the humans before she snuffled her calf and made "mmm-mmm" noises deep in her throat.

"They'll be okay," Ash assured. "Thanks for the help, Daiz." A glance at Rachel. "Really appreciate it."

"Can I help next time?" Charlie asked shyly.

"Charlie," Rachel began. "I don't think—"

"Hey, buddy," Daisy cut in. "Want to see the horses over in the other barn?" She took his hand and led him through the half door and out of sight.

Rachel stood with Ash, alone amidst a throng of cattle. "I'll keep him out of your way from now on. Tonight he begged Daisy to show him the calves." She pushed back her bangs. "We— I didn't expect there to be a birth."

She observed the cow, glad Ash stood a step away. Gentle and docile as it looked, the animal was a new mother. Her protective instincts had undoubtedly climbed skyward.

"As long as he's with an adult or Daisy," Ash said, studying the calf, "Charlie'll be fine." He turned sharp eyes on her. "But he's never to come here alone."

"I understand. Thank you for not yelling at him."

Finished with the calf, he retrieved his cap off the floor. In the dimly lit arena the bill blackened his eyes. "I don't yell at kids."

Heat traveled her neck. "It's not what I meant." She started through the cattle, toward the sanctity of the corridor.

"Rachel."

His voice slid over her skin. Turning, she lifted her chin.

"For what it's worth," he said, "I don't yell at women, either."

He walked toward her. "I might get mad at them, might curse under my breath. But I don't yell." He stopped within arm's reach.

She swallowed. "That's good to know."

Setting a beat-up knuckle under her chin, he tilted up her face. "Who yelled at you?"

Bill Brant's angry mouth and caustic words swam across her mind. She jerked away. "No one."

Ash's eyes narrowed. Rachel stepped back. He couldn't know. She had told no one of her father's rages. "Thanks for letting Charlie see the birth. Good night." Aiming for the Dutch door, she hurried through the cattle.

Softly, so softly it was almost unspoken, came his deep, "'Night, Rach."

Chapter Seven

Daisy and Charlie stood with the chocolate-colored horse the girl had ridden that morning several weeks prior, when Rachel had driven up the snowy county road seeking the Flying Bar T.

"Champ, you did a great job being quiet back there." She tousled her son's hair. "Ready to go home?"

"Mom, this is Areo," Charlie exclaimed, petting the horse's nose over the stall's half door. "Isn't he cool?"

"He's beautiful." Rachel stroked the slender white blaze that centered the animal's fine-boned face. "And sweet-natured," she guessed, studying its gentle eyes.

"Areo's a sweetie," Daisy avowed. "I learned to ride and rope on him, and later he became my first barreler."

"You have more than one horse?" Charlie stared, blue eyes huge behind his glasses.

"Dad's given me two. Areo and a three-year-old I'm training. His name's Ticket."

"Can I see him?"

"Not tonight, Charlie," Rachel said.

"He's in the pasture with the other horses." Daisy patted the pony's sleek neck and started down the corridor.

Charlie skipped at her side. "What's a barely?"

"A barely?"

"You said Areo was your first barely."

She laughed. "Barreler or barrel racer. It's when you ride really, really fast around three barrels set in a big triangle. The quickest time wins."

They stepped into the night again.

"Can boys barrel race?" Charlie wanted to know.

"Boys get to do other things, like ride broncs and bulls and rope calves and steer wrestle."

Their boots scraped against the cold cement walkway. Tom's walkway.

Daisy glanced over Charlie's head. "Maybe your mom'll let you ride in the Little Britches rodeo next summer."

"What's the little bitches rodeo?"

"*Britches,* Charlie," Rachel sputtered. "*Brrr*-itches. It's an old-fashioned word for shorts."

"Oh." His eyebrows drew together. "You gotta wear shorts to ride the horses?"

Rachel and Daisy laughed. The sound rang through the crisp air, a night melody.

"No, honey." Rachel snagged her son's neck in an affectionate hug. "It means kids under twelve compete." Details she'd gleaned from Marty at the *Rocky Times.*

"And," Daisy said, walking backward, "they ride sheep and calves instead of broncs and bulls, and they have a greased pig competition."

Reaching the main house, Rachel stopped at the porch steps. White fog wisped from their mouths. "Thanks for taking us down to the barn, Daisy. It was an enlightening experience."

"Any time."

"Can I ride a calf in the Little Britches?" Charlie persisted.

"I don't think so, son. Most kids are from ranches and farms so they already know how to ride. Come, time for bed."

"But, Mom—"

"Quick, now. Teeth and jammies and then we'll read in front of the fireplace."

"Oh, goodie!" He was off in a flash.

Daisy said, "Mom used to read with me, too." She peered past the muted porch light where Charlie had gone. "I could teach him to ride Areo if he really wants to enter the Britches."

"Thanks, Daisy. You're a sweet girl. But I don't think your dad and grandpa would appreciate us taking riding lessons on top of everything else."

"What if you paid? When Mom was alive she used to give riding lessons to kids from April to October."

Rachel shook her head. "Look. I think we should leave things the way they are. Charlie will forget this by tomorrow."

Daisy slipped her hands under her arms. "I doubt it, but it's your choice." She headed for the mudroom.

"Daisy." Rachel would ask the question for insight to Tom and this ranch, that was all. She wasn't asking because of Ash. "What was your mom like as a riding instructor?"

The girl's face lit, a pearl in the night. "She was great. Especially with kids. It was like she wanted them to love horses the way she did. People came for miles, she was that good."

"Sounds like she was very adept."

"She was the best." For a moment the teen stared toward the barns where lights blazed from all the windows. "Thing is, every year the memories fade a little more."

"Do you talk to your dad about her?"

Daisy's eyes scoffed. "You kidding? My mom's name isn't mentioned in this house. Yeah, we have all her pictures up, but no one so much as breathes her name. Even Inez won't talk. My dad doesn't allow it."

Rachel was stunned. Ash, a shadow of Bill Brant?

Anger beat against her chest. *Dammit.* She'd fought her father over the same problem. And now Ash. Didn't these men realize when mothers died, *everyone* suffered?

Daisy hunched her shoulders. "It hurts him too much, I guess."

And it doesn't hurt you?

Suddenly she wanted to help this young woman with sweetness in her smile and yearning in her words. "Anytime you want to talk about your mom, I'm here."

A wistful smile. "Thanks, but I've forgotten so much about her, like, I don't know, like her favorite foods and the sound of her voice and whether she had freckles."

"Oh, honey. Then you need to write down what you *do* remember. You'll be surprised what will come once you begin. I did that when my mother died."

"How old were you?"

"Eight. By the time I was ten, I'd forgotten a lot, so I started a journal about the things I *could* remember. It really helped. Even now, I'll recall a forgotten tidbit." She smiled encouragement. "So far, I have about two hundred pages' worth. I'll show them to you sometime."

Daisy's eyes were eager. "Would you?"

"Absolutely." Without thinking, Rachel hugged the teenager. "Next time you're by the newspaper, we'll go down to the drugstore and find you a lovely little journal."

"Thanks, Ms. Brant. You're really nice."

"Rachel. And so are you, honey."

"Good night," Daisy whispered before disappearing around the corner of the house.

Ready to start up the path again, Rachel swung her gaze toward the barns one last time. A figure stood backlit in the big open doors. Ash, leaning against the doorjamb, watching her.

How long had he stood there? Had he heard their conversation? A tiny shiver spun over her skin. *Night, Rach.* Words he might whisper under the covers, in the depth of night.

She fled through the darkness to the safety of the guesthouse.

At the elementary school, Rachel waited for Charlie to emerge through the doors. Chased by a wind, flakes scurried through the barren trees along the street.

She turned on the wipers. Five minutes. Ten. Fifteen. Was his teacher keeping him after school?

Rachel shut off the ignition and headed for the school's entry. His classroom was the fourth door down the hall. Empty. Heart bumping her throat, she walked to the office to request Mrs. Tabbs be paged. Half a minute later, the teacher appeared.

Rachel tried to keep panic from her voice. "I'm here for Charlie Brant. Is he with you?"

"Oh," the teacher said. "He left with Daisy McKee. They said it would be all right now that you're living out on the ranch."

"*Rent*ing at the ranch," Rachel clarified, heart easing. "Until we find a more permanent place."

The other woman's eyes were steady. "I apologize. I should have asked Charlie for a note from you."

Yes. You should have. He's only seven. What if it had been a friendly stranger offering him a ride home?

Rachel rushed from the school, ran for her car. Charlie was with Daisy on the bus. She'd go to the ranch and wait. And reprimand her son when they were alone.

By the time she arrived at the Flying Bar T, the wind blustered in gusts down the mountain foothills and across the timberline.

She stood on the porch of the main house, waiting, studying

the white arrow of road to the wrought iron sign, her hands gloved against the burst of February's meanness.

Finally, the bus came into view. Two figures started up the quarter-mile driveway, scarves blowing in the wind.

"Mom!" Charlie, bundled in his blue snowsuit, called excitedly as they neared the house. "I rode the bus home. Can I ride the bus forever?"

She came down Tom's ramp. "Did you not think I'd be waiting at the school like always, Charlie?" From the corner of her eye she saw Ash stride across the yard. Snow swirled between them.

Gala apples rosed Charlie's cheeks. "But I thought you knew."

"How would I know? Did you ask or tell me? Did I give you permission? I had to find out from your teacher, son. Do you have any idea how worried I was?"

Of course he wouldn't. He was seven. Worry was an adult contract.

Daisy said, "It's my fault, Rachel. I should've called and let you know."

Rachel took in the teenager's sober eyes, her wind-pinked nose. "Yes," she said. "You should have, but—" she turned to Charlie "—my son is also at fault. He knows the rules."

"Does this mean I'm grounded?" he asked in a small voice.

Ash stopped beside Rachel.

"It means," she said, aware of him watching the kids, watching her, "no more bus rides until I say so."

Charlie's face drooped, but she held firm when all she wanted was to gather him into her arms and kiss his child's skin. *I love you, Charlie, but this is a lifesaving lesson.*

"Okay," he mumbled.

"Hi, Daddy," Daisy whispered as she trudged past them and up the porch steps.

"Daiz."

"You may go," Rachel dismissed Charlie. The boy ran down the snowy path in the trees. When both children left, Rachel sighed. "Thank you for letting me handle this."

Amusement crinkled his eyes. "Seems you were doing fine on your own." Serious again, he said, "It won't happen again, Rachel. Daisy's impulsive, but she's a quick study."

"It's not her, it's Charlie. I taught him about Stranger-Danger the second he was old enough to talk. And," she hurried on, "I know Daisy's not a stranger but—"

"It's the principle of the thing."

"Yes," she said, relieved.

The front door opened. Daisy, coat and knapsack gone, peeked out. Her eyes zeroed on Rachel. "I'm truly sorry for making you worry, Rachel."

"It's forgotten."

The teen nodded. Her gaze moved to Ash.

He said, "You'll clean up the supper dishes for a week."

Her punishment for impulsiveness.

Again, she nodded. About to turn back inside, she hesitated. "Dad? Will you chaperone our school's St. Patrick's dance on March 17th? It's a Friday."

"Daiz, this is not a good time." His eyes said, *I'm upset with your behavior right now.*

"Well, um, I wanted to ask if Rachel would take photographs for the paper."

"Daisy—"

"It's okay," Rachel cut in. "I'll check with Mr. Hanson to see if some can be printed."

Like a candle the girl's face brightened. "Cool. Maybe you guys—" she darted a look one to the other "—could go together."

Together? As in a couple? "I think—" Rachel began.

"Rachel has to take care of Charlie." Ash started up the ramp. "And you're letting good warm air out of the house."

"But, Dad, I need to know."

"Later." Ushering his daughter inside, he shut the door.

Rachel stood in the wild, cold wind. One moment Ash was on her side, the next he literally slammed the door in her face.

Disillusioned by the day's events, she headed for the cottage where Charlie undoubtedly waited for a life's worth of grounding.

Ash headed upstairs to Daisy's room. Her door stood half open. Propped by pillows, knees holding a book, she lay on her bed, reading. Or pretending to read.

He knocked and she lifted her eyes above the page. "I don't think I'll be able to chaperone the dance, Daiz."

"Why? Because I asked Rachel to come?"

He entered the room. "Because it's calving season."

"Can't Ethan handle it for one night? Besides, it's not like you'll be gone the whole night. The dance ends at ten." Her mouth flattened. "You'll be home in time for your precious cows."

"Don't be snide. And you're making a mountain out of a molehill."

"Am I? Dad, how many times have I asked you to volunteer for anything at school?" Her eyes glimmered. "Or even to come to the parent-teacher meetings."

Susie had been the school liaison in their home. No justification for his negligence. *Oh, hell, admit it. You're afraid some teacher will say, Read this great essay she wrote.* Truth be known, he ached to read her words.

She continued, "I'm on student council and we can't get chaperones. Aunt Meggie's coming, but we need at least two more parents."

"What about teachers?"

"We've got four confirmed. If we don't get at least eight chaperones, they'll cancel the dance."

He sighed, rubbed his neck. She was fifteen, a good kid; he had a lot to be grateful for. She could be involved with the wrong crowd. The dope smokers. The street racers. She could be one of those boy-crazed girls he heard Meggie worry about with her son, Beau. "All right," he said. "Put me on the list."

"Thanks, Dad."

He turned to leave.

"If Rachel comes to take pictures, you two should go together."

Halting midstride, he swung around. "It isn't going to work, Daisy."

"What?" Eyes too innocent.

"Your matchmaking."

"I'm not matchmaking. I'm thinking it would be company for you and, well, think of the gas you'll save carpooling." She frowned at his you're-not-fooling-me look. "Come on, Dad, she's hardly a toad. And everyone can see you like her. Jeez."

"Stay out of it, Daiz." He slapped the doorjamb and headed for the stairs.

"Fine," she called after him. "Pretend you don't like her. What do I care? You're the one who'll be left behind. Especially when Pete Richards or Ethan asks her out."

Ash stopped on the landing. Pete Richards worked at the *Rocky Times.* Another reporter he could understand, but…*Ethan?*

He strode back to the bedroom. His daughter resembled the cat who'd swallowed the two-ton canary.

"Ethan?" he grumped.

"Uh-huh. He asked me if she was dating anybody. I said no. Then he asked where someone like her would enjoy dinner. I told him to take her to The Cattle Barn because she likes country music."

She does? "How do you know?"

Daisy rolled her eyes. "God, Dad. Get with the program.

It's called girl talk. Do you really think all we discuss is Grandpa's story?"

Yes, that's exactly what he thought. Okay, he figured they'd done a little "girl" talking, but not about who Rachel should or shouldn't date. Dating was personal.

God almighty. Did Daisy ask Rachel about *boys?*

Searching his daughter's face, he realized she'd grown up when he wasn't looking.

She wasn't fifteen. She was twenty-four. Hell, make that thirty-four. And she knew things he'd keep secret for a million years. The embarrassed heat climbing her neck told him so.

Things like sex. And condoms. And what guys her age wanted from girls. Hell, what guys *his* age wanted with a woman.

What you want with Rachel Brant.

Daisy slapped the book closed. "Don't look at me like that. Rachel's a nice person. She's sweet and smart and isn't afraid to talk about things."

And, Ash envisioned her thinking, *she's doing what Mom would've done.*

But *would* Susie have talked with Daisy about the birds and bees? Maybe. Then again, maybe not. Susie was about Susie. Yes, she had loved her daughter. Fiercely. And she'd loved him just as fiercely. But she hadn't always been there for either when it counted. She hadn't been there when eight-year-old Daisy wanted to take ballet lessons.

"Ballerinas are tall and slim," Susie had told their daughter. *"You're going to be like me—short and shapely."*

He'd found his little girl in Areo's stall, crying so hard her shoulders shook with hiccups and mucus streamed from her nose. She hadn't wanted to be short and shapely, she had wanted to grow up tall like him. And slim.

And she had wanted to be a ballerina.

Hard as it was to acknowledge, Susie was right. Daisy had

grown into a petite and *feminine* five-two. Over the next couple years she might gain an inch or two in height, but she wouldn't be tall like Rachel, or have that willowy, dancer physique.

Still, he'd bet the ranch Rachel would've told her to go for the ballet lessons.

And that difference bothered him. "I don't care who you gossip with, Daisy. As long as you leave family out of the conversation. Is that clear?"

"Whatever. You're the last guy I'd want to discuss anyway."

That stung. "Good." He turned for the door.

"She's going to help me make a journal about Mom."

Slowly, he spun on his heel. "She's going to what?"

Daisy lifted her chin. "I want to write things about Mom so I don't forget them. Rachel's going to help me. She did one for her mom and—"

"You're discussing your *mother* with a newspaper woman?"

A dramatic sigh. "Dad, she's not doing it for a story. Sheesh. Chill, okay?"

"When it comes to writing," he snapped, "everything she does is for a story."

"Well, not this." She put aside the book. "Don't you get it? I want to remember Mom and this is the only way I can." Her voice rose. "We've got her pictures *everywhere,* but it's like she's a stranger. *I need to talk* about her, even if you don't. I want to know the good times along with the bad. I want to *know* the woman in all those pictures!"

Tears clouded her eyes. Her arms wrapped her knees. "I don't want to wake up one day, Daddy, and wonder if she ever sang me a lullaby or brushed my hair or kissed me hello. Is it going to take thirty-six years for you to figure out that her death can't be shoved into some box with the lid locked?"

Like Tom and Nam. "Daiz." *Dammit to hell.* He wanted to tell her everything would be all right. But it clearly wasn't.

Disgust darkened her eyes. "I can understand Grandpa," she went on. "His problem was his own. But Mom was part of us. You *and* me. We made memories and you're ignoring them like she didn't exist or matter."

"She mattered," he said, helpless to stop her anguish. How could he explain that it was his fault she ran into Sweet Creek that day, his fault she sat drinking at The Cattle Barn? That they'd argued—a down and dirty fight—fifteen minutes before she drove off the ranch?

Daisy turned to the wall. "Please leave."

"Honey, I—"

Over her shoulder she held up a hand.

Right. Talk to the hand.

With a heavy heart, he left her alone.

Journal on her lap, Rachel sat beside Daisy on the guesthouse sofa. Outside, another cold night pressed against the windows. After putting Charlie to bed at eight, she'd invited the girl to work through Tom's story—which they had done for an hour, sorting through notes, adjusting sentences. More and more, Rachel allowed Daisy leeway to write her grandfather's story.

At nine-thirty they'd finished for the night.

Rachel opened the journal. Smoothing back the first page, she said, "These are my memories, Daisy. This is what I meant the other day when I suggested you start a journal about your mom." She lifted the book onto the girl's knees. "Go ahead, read it."

"I shouldn't," the girl said, tracing Rachel's inscription: Mom and Me, Our Times Together. "This is too personal."

"Yes, it is personal, but it's also cathartic for me to share it with you because I know how much you miss your mom."

Reverently, the teenager turned the page, scanned the words. "Can I read it out loud?" she whispered.

"If you'd like."
Daisy began.

"I was eight when my mom died of cervical cancer. She was the light, the sun, the moon of my life. I loved her with my heart and soul. I still love her. I will always love her. These pages will honor and remember her, and one day, I hope, her grandchildren will understand the woman whose genes they carry."

"Wow, powerful." Daisy studied the picture of thirty-year-old Grace Brant beneath the introduction. "She was beautiful. Just like you."
Rachel shifted uncomfortably. "I look like my dad."
The girl shook her head. "No," she said. "You have her exotic eyes and her smile. With the corners tilted up."
Something warm ran through Rachel. "Well, thank you, honey."
"I wish I was more like my dad," the girl said. "I wish I was taller and had his straight black hair. I hate being short and having this—this carrot mess."
Rachel set a hand over Daisy's on the book. "Don't put yourself down. We need to love ourselves for who we are. Besides—" she winked "—if you looked like your dad, you wouldn't have this cute nose and those green eyes or glorious curls. Those are things your mother gave you." *Pay attention to your own words, Rachel.*
Daisy's face was a beacon. "Yeah?"
"Yeah."
The girl stared ahead. "You're right. I mean, I love my dad. He's the absolute best, but I loved Mom, too."
"Of course you did."
"I'm not going to forget her. Not the way Dad wants to."

"Your dad will never forget your mom, Daisy. All he has to do is look at you."

A slow smile. "No, he really won't, will he?" Daisy sat straighter. "I'm really glad we had this talk."

"So am I, sweetie."

Chapter Eight

Two days later, a siren had Ash slamming his brakes as he pulled onto Cardinal Street from Bartell's Feed & Seed. Lights flashing, horn blaring, a Sweet Creek fire truck raced past. Easing his Dodge Ram onto the street, he followed the commotion at a slow pace.

On his way out of town, he had planned to stop at the *Times* and talk to Rachel about Daisy and that damned journal.

All night and all morning, he'd thought about it. Oh, he understood Daisy's plea. Hell, if he could, he'd write a journal about his life with Susie, too. He'd write about the day he met her at a Little Britches Rodeo, their parents urging them to enter the sheep-riding contest and her beating him with a one-second better time. And about the years they'd ridden over the range, talking and laughing, sharing goals and dreams. How in school she had tried to help his handicap.

He'd describe the day he had won her heart from Shaw

Hanson Junior, jock and high school football star whom she'd been dating, when the three of them had met at a Cattle Barn dance and Hanson scoffed at Ash's tenth-grade education, saying nothing counted more than getting a college scholarship.

Joke was Hanson might have achieved the scholarship, but he'd flunked out his first year; come home with his tail between his legs. By then Ash and Susie were engaged. Hanson still grumbled about it to anyone who would listen, though he was married and had two kids.

The fire truck jerked to a halt at the intersection of Cardinal Street and Bluebird Avenue.

A cold sweat rushed across Ash's skin. Was the fire at the *Rocky Times?* Hanson had restored the building with a stone-and-brick face several years ago but, like more than a dozen stores lining Cardinal, the newspaper rested on its wooden structure of 1873. Wood harvested from Montana's mountain forests.

And dry as drought grass.

Firemen jumped from the truck and rushed toward the intersection.

Not a fire, a traffic accident. Had a pedestrian been hit?

"Not Rachel, *please,*" he muttered.

He found a spot two doors down from the police department.

His sister stood on the sidewalk in her tan uniform shirt and dark brown slacks, shivering against the cold February wind. She was taking notes as she talked to Jesse Hasker.

"Hey," Ash said, coming up beside her and shrugging from his vest. Trying not to think of Rachel. "You shouldn't be in this weather without a coat."

She glanced up. "Hey, Ash. Did you see it happen?"

"The accident? No, I was heading out of town when I heard the sirens." He looped the vest around her shoulders and dared a look toward the intersection where Jesse's half-ton had smashed the driver's side of a beat-up blue Honda hatchback.

Not Rachel. Old Joe Gamble.

"Will the old-timer be okay?"

Meggie surveyed the Honda. "Hope so. The medics will likely take him to the clinic in a few minutes."

Admiring Meggie's discipline, Ash nodded and thought of the six years she'd been police chief of Sweet Creek. At first her career change had bothered him until, reluctantly, he realized that in some way the job had saved his sister after her divorce and return from California.

A medic and two firemen huddled around Joe with his bruised and bloody face, the wind snatching his words: "Can't go…my business…lose too much."

Abruptly, Rachel, holding paper cups of coffee, elbowed through the crowd, coat winging open like a dark bird ready to swoop down on its prey. A camera swung from her neck.

Ash scowled. Concern veered off and irritation parked itself. *Jeez.* Couldn't she leave the old guy alone? Did she need to take photographs now? Grab the story *this* minute?

She walked straight to Meggie. "Can I give this to Joe?" she asked without a look at Ash.

Meggie eyed the coffee. "If the medics say it's okay."

Rachel strode to the nearest medic, spoke briefly, then bent and set the steaming brew into Old Joe's hands. The sight stirred memories of two nights ago in Ash, when she had helped a calf enter the world.

Dammit to hell. Could the woman confuse him further? Who would've expected her to aid a battered old man amidst chaos, instead of capturing Kodak moments for the press?

Ash set off through the crowd. He caught Rachel's arm as she came around the trunk of the car. "Can I help?"

"Joe needs a doctor."

"They'll get him to the clinic."

She cast a look to where medical personnel were easing the

baker into the passenger side of the police cruiser. "He's worried about having to close his business if the doctor puts him in the hospital or insists he take a week to recuperate. Look, I have to go. Shaw wants pictures."

Ash frowned. "Now? Can't you wait until they've taken Joe away?"

"He knows what I do for a living, Ash."

His jaw dropped. How could she be concerned for the old man one minute and so calculating while a man's livelihood went up in proverbial smoke the next?

"Who gives a rat's ass if it's your job. That old man—" he jabbed a thumb toward the cruiser with its flashing lights "—needs some understanding."

"I know that. I also told him Shaw wants photos." Distress sharpened her words. "And who knows? The police might be able to use them."

She had a point. Relenting, he stepped aside. "Fine."

"Ash." Her eyes begged him to understand.

"Go."

She strode away, hauling the camera up to her eye as she went. He headed for the cruiser. "You okay, Old Joe?"

"Tell 'em I don't need to go to no hospital," the old man muttered, but he lay unmoving in the seat. "Can't afford to close my business."

"They're doing their best." Ash glanced over his shoulder; Rachel's shutter clicked away.

Meggie peered around Ash. "Joe?"

He turned sad, watery eyes to her. "I don't feel so good."

"We're taking you to the hospital."

Frustrated he couldn't do more, Ash contemplated hustling his sister—and Old Joe—back to the ranch, back to safety, to security.

The muttering crowd stirred. Ash raised his head, seeking the woman who kept him awake long into every night.

She stood with Shaw Hanson. From the fixed line of her mouth, Ash sensed she wasn't pleased with her boss. A moment later, she tossed the camera into the man's hands. His face reddened, but the tow truck's arrival drowned his words.

Rachel plowed through the people, bent on distancing herself, Ash figured, from the accident, gawking bystanders and Shaw Junior. *Leave well enough alone.* Problem was, Rachel Brant had set up camp in his mind the morning he stared down at her from Northwind's saddle and she hadn't left.

Every bit of common sense flying off with the bitter winter wind, Ash strode after her. What the hell did he think he'd do when he caught up with her? Hold her? Kiss away her owie? *Get a reality check, Ash.*

But that's exactly what he wanted, and damned if his feet weren't agreeing.

He broke into a jog.

Hugging her coat against her chilled skin, Rachel hurried down the street. Shaw would fire her now. Arguing with him in front of half the town had not been smart. But then when had she been smart, according to her father?

"If you were smart, you'd apply to the Washington Post. *I can get you a damned good job there."*

"If you were smart, you'd marry Floyd. He's going places, that young pup."

"If you were smart, you would have taken him to court for child support."

"If you were smart, you'd know freelancing won't pay the bills."

If you were smart.

Well, she wasn't smart.

Telling Shaw Hanson, publisher and editor of the only newspaper in Sweet Creek, that she could handle her own stories, thank you very much, had been downright stupid. She might as well have told him to mind his own business. A paradox, really. The paper *was* his business.

"Rachel!"

Ash. Her stomach twisted. She'd seen the disgust in his eyes. God, sometimes she hated her job.

Pushing through the front door of the newspaper, she nodded to the receptionist and walked to her desk. The newsroom, a tiny, cramped area consisting of three desks—hers, Pete's and Marty's—was empty.

Pete was out of town, running down a coyote slaying story on Able Jax's land. A story she'd received, but Shaw had ordered Pete to write. *"Pete knows the rancher."* Even though she'd taken Able's call. Told him she'd be out to see him within the hour.

Then, she'd heard the sirens and ran to investigate while Shaw had been upstairs in the layout room. Camera in hand, she'd been first on the scene.

Two stories, back to back, snatched away by a man living in a fifties time warp when women were useful for sewing, cooking and keeping both the kiddies and the house clean, not necessarily in that order.

Slumping in her chair, she closed her eyes. Shaw Hanson had hired her for one reason only: pressure from the Sweet Creek Ladies Aid. Scuttlebutt had been the biweekly was dying. Who needed a newspaper when you could watch real-time news 24-7 on CNN? The saving graces were those women wanting their spotlight moments. They wanted a "feminine" side to the paper, someone they could call to advertise bake sales and bazaars, write "society" blurbs like weddings and births and christenings, someone to feature recipes, craft days, pie and African violet contests at the August fair.

So the Women's Circuit page was born with Rachel as its token female artifact.

"What happened back there?"

Her head snapped up.

Brows jammed together, Ash stood staring down at her.

"Nothing." She scraped both hands down her cheeks, then booted up her computer. "Shaw's covering the accident." Her throat constricted. Old Joe's shop and her job were in the process of annihilation and here she was, calm as a turtle on a sunny rock, preparing to work.

"That your choice?"

She shrugged.

"Rachel?" Worry wove through her name, worry that something was amiss.

And, he was right. God only knew what she and Charlie would do if she lost this job. The Hells Field freelance series wasn't done and, if she had no way of keeping a roof over her child's head, she'd be forced to move on to another town, another paper, or, God forbid, home to her father. But worse, the contract with *American Pie* magazine for her Nam series would be severed if she didn't get Tom's story.

"Rachel?" Knees cracking, Ash crouched beside her.

"I'm okay," she said, staring at her computer's request to type in her password. "I may lose my job, but I'm okay."

He reached across and punched the machine's Off button.

"Come with me." Taking her hand, he pulled her out of the chair. "Grab your purse."

"Ash, I have to work."

"And as you said you may lose your job. If that's the case, it can damn well wait."

He preceded her through the newsroom, out the back door and into the alley. His big, callused hand sent currents up her

arm. Next to him, she felt petite, feminine. He didn't let go o
her fingers, but kept them curled in his palm.

Silent, he led the way through the snow-encrusted alleyway
to Bluebird Avenue. There he let go of her hand.

Because of public view.

She ignored the pinch. He wasn't ready to acknowledge a
reporter as a friend—or possible *girl*friend—to himself or the
world. They walked down the street, away from the police
cruisers and fire trucks, the commotion around Old Joe.

Please, let him be okay. And let Charlie and I be okay, too

Not a prayer. A plea of hope.

She had no idea if she would have a job tomorrow. She had
said some nasty things to Shaw.

Depressed at the thought, she swung her arms for warmth
and lengthened her stride with Ash.

At the street corner, he stepped up to the door of a tiny tri
angular shop called Coffee, Anyone? The place had been he:
first Women's Circuit story: Have Your Wicked Chocolate
Cupcake and Eat it, Too.

Ash paused. "They make the best coffee in the state."

"Then you're in luck. I could do with a cup right now."

Gallantly, he held open the door and waited for her to step
inside. With everyone at the accident, the coffee shop wa:
empty except for the proprietor.

"Hey, Ash." A woman in her midthirties flung him a grin
"Long time no see."

"Darby." He removed the Stetson, chose a window booth
"We need a couple mugs of your brew."

"Coming right up." Her eyes flicked between them, settled
on Rachel. "Didn't the sirens go off a few minutes ago?"

"A truck hit Old Joe's car," Rachel said, sliding into the
bench opposite Ash.

"He okay?"

Rachel nodded. "They're taking him to the hospital."

"Poor man." The words sounded blasé, but Rachel understood their sincerity. Darby was Tyler's mother and Tyler was Charlie's new friend. With publication of her story on the coffee shop, the two women had shared a steaming mug or two. Like most in town, Darby cared a great deal for Old Joe.

"So, why aren't you getting the story?" she asked.

"Shaw's covering it."

Darby would hear about their disagreement soon enough; half the town had heard his guttural "Let *me* handle things."

Darby's eyes slitted. "He wouldn't let you do the story."

Rachel shrugged. "If the photos help the investigation—"

"You take way better pictures than Hanson," the woman huffed, clearly on Rachel's side. "The Women's Circuit page gave the paper the oomph it lacked from the time of its founding seventy years ago. That article you did on Mrs. Harkens was priceless. Did you see it, Ash? A hundred and four and the old gal looked liked a princess in Rachel's photo." She winked at Rachel. "You captured her *essence* in that pic. Shaw Hanson should *be* so lucky to have you on his team."

"Well, thanks."

"Give credit where credit's due as they say." She walked back to the coffee bar.

Darby's right, Rachel thought. *I should be taking those pictures and doing the story.* Aware of the man sitting across from her, she studied the empty street.

Suddenly their eyes caught, held. *He's a loner.* The picture painted by her colleague, Marty, fell out of sync with the man sitting across from her. "How long have you known Shaw?"

"Went to school with him. We're not friends."

Darby set two mugs of dark roast on their table. When she'd left again, Ash smiled. "This should hit the spot."

The drink landed in her stomach, a fireball that spread heady heat through her veins. Like the tall, silent rancher looking at her with his dark eyes.

"I'm sorry Shaw upset you," he said.

"I can deal with it." Just as she'd done with a dozen previous incidents. An old hand she was at wrangling male machismo. Bill Brant had taught her well for over twenty years.

When Ash remained silent, she offered, "He's not used to having a woman on staff. It was the same when Daisy—"

Damn, she'd said too much. His eyes narrowed.

"What about Daisy?"

She shook her head, set down her mug. "Look. I have to go. Thanks for the coffee."

His hand caught hers. "What about Daisy?"

"Talk to your daughter, Ash. It's not for me to say."

His lips thinned. "If he's said something to hurt my kid—"

"He hasn't said a word to her." Not directly. His words were to Rachel *after* Daisy had relayed her intentions about the high school column. *"This is a newspaper. We're not in the business of catering to teenage drama."*

In the end, she'd won and Daisy had gained her five inches of space at the bottom of the Women's Circuit.

Ash pulled back his hand, folded his arms across his chest. Putting up walls. "What did he do to Daisy?" he insisted.

She had promised the girl confidentiality, yet lying to Ash felt wrong. Carefully, she said, "He didn't want the Students' Union events in the *Times.* Said it was too juvenile."

"Some of those kids are tens times smarter than Hanson," Ash muttered.

"You don't need to convince me." Rachel stirred a dash of cream into her cup.

"Was Darby right?" he asked softly. "Did Hanson take your story?"

"Something like that." More precisely: *"I'll take the pictures and talk to the police. You go back to the office and do some research on the last accident at this intersection. We'll need to include it."*

She'd begged him to let her at least take the pictures while he got the story.

He hadn't budged. Her boss, she was learning fast, was a Bill Brant clone. *Do as I say, it's the only way.*

That was when she'd tossed the camera. Hanson hadn't been pleased. *"I'll talk to you later."*

Suddenly Ash covered her hand again. "Slow and easy," he said. "Slow and easy." As if he were gentling one of his cows. "Let him have his glory. There's nothing you can do. *Nothing."* He gazed out the window to the street, where a pickup passed, flinging dirty snow.

She watched him turn deep into himself. *Don't think of her, look at me.*

What hadn't *he* been able to do for Susie? To change, to fix?

Her heart tumbled. He was a tough man. A rancher and single dad, facing hardship and heartache every day.

His face was ruddy from nature's elements, his black hair flat against his forehead from the broad-brimmed hat. His shave this morning had missed a tiny patch beneath his chin. For an insane second, she wanted to reach across the table, touch the spot, soothe the grief she'd glimpsed in his eyes.

"Ash," she said quietly, calling him back from the distance that was his wife.

He raised his head, blinked. He *had* been thinking of her.

"Tell me," Rachel encouraged softly. "Tell me about her."

He snorted softly. "Ever the reporter, aren't you?"

"No," she said, offended. "I'm asking as a friend."

"*Are* we friends, Rach?"

Rach again. "No one calls me Rach."

A corner of his mouth lifted. "I'm the first?"

Her own lips curved. "Don't let it go to your head, cowboy. I'm not partial to the name."

"As a friend, you won't mind." A lightning grin shot a crease into his right cheek.

Air struggled in her lungs. "As a friend, you'll respect my wishes." Her brows lifted.

He sobered. "And you mine."

Touché.

"I will say this," he added, eyes piercing hers. "I loved my wife."

They finished their coffee in silence and when they were done, he tossed down a few bills before they pushed through the door into the cold afternoon. A weak sun shuffled toward the mountains, lengthening shadows. Ash reached over and pulled her coat collar up around her ears. "Want me to talk to Hanson?"

"You'd do that? For a hard-nosed, go-get-'em-no-matter-what-it-takes reporter?"

He grinned, ran his finger down her nose. "Not so hard-nosed, I've discovered."

She let out a half laugh. "You haven't seen me in action."

"I can only imagine." He clamped on the Stetson. "I'm surprised you're not in some warring country."

"I could've gone." If she'd listened to Floyd and had an abortion. Which had been absolutely, one hundred percent out of the question. The second she knew of Charlie's existence, *he'd* become her life.

Ash looked down at her for several heartbeats. *Handsome lashes,* she thought. Long and thick as the prairie grasses, black and curvy as a raven's wing.

"I'm glad you didn't cover those wars." His fingers brushed against her left temple, toyed with her earring.

She wanted his warm palms pressed against her neck, her

face. She wanted that half-zipped fleece-lined jacket—preferably with him inside—cuddled around her body.

"Thanks, Ash." A glance at the shop they'd just left. "For sanity."

His eyes clutched their secrets. But over coffee his heart had opened a fraction, though his final words smarted a little. He had loved his wife.

Loved, Rachel. Not love. Past tense.

He said, "You're the sanest woman I've ever met, Rach."

She had no comeback. In one brief sentence he'd emptied her mind and mouth of words. The sidewalk with its gritty snow suddenly looked intriguing while she blinked hard once, twice.

And then she was jaywalking across the street, leaving him. Hurrying toward an uncertain future.

On foot, he plowed through the snow toward the Douglas fir where he'd strewn her ashes. She'd wanted cremation. No hole, no headstone she'd told him when they were kids riding fences. He'd kissed her under this tree, and she'd said, *"When I die I don't want to be put in a black hole."*

He'd shivered then and he shivered now.

A black hole. Had Susie known her life would be cut short? Had she seen some innate karmic vision, prodding her to spew out instructions about death and black holes at the age of sixteen?

He cursed aloud. He'd known Susie all his life. A quick-minded, funny, energetic girl who had grown into a hummingbird flitting here and there with the zest of a Thoroughbred colt at the starting gate. She would have hated resting for eternity in the ground. *In a black hole.*

Like Tom's war. According to Rachel's son.

Rachel.

To empty her from his mind, he had ridden Northwind a mile and a half to this tiny meadow, an appendage to one of the four creeks winding through McKee land. In summer, the acre danced in flowers of every shade and color. The old fir spread its branches like the protective wings of a giant nesting bird, snuggling whatever sought shelter under its long green needles. Planted by Tom's great-grandmother, the tree was the last remnant of the homestead place on which she and her husband had lived nearly a century ago.

Ash had brought Susie here for the last time, scattering her cinders to the soft breeze.

Today there was no sign of her. Just crisscrossing tracks of rabbit and coyote on a half foot of snow under Christmas tree branches. He stared down at the prints and thought of Susie. Of Rachel. One he had loved and married, the other he was beginning to feel things for that, dammit, he couldn't seem to control.

Things that should still remain with Susie.

He tried hard as hell to recall her face. And could not.

Frustrated, he looked across the creek's banks, to the horizon where the Rockies hemmed the late-afternoon skyline. Rachel had taken Susie's place in his mind. Rachel, clenching that mug of coffee, worrying about Old Joe and Daisy.

He recalled the tears she'd blinked back at the newspaper, how her lips had trembled around Shaw Hanson's disdain.

He mulled over the reasons he couldn't get her out of his mind, couldn't stop touching her after those seconds in the mudroom when he'd felt the softness of her skin.

And now he had taken her to that coffee shop, let Darby Lowe see them together. Darby, once Susie's best friend.

Ash knew what Darby thought of reporters. Yet, he couldn't deny her concern for Rachel had been genuine.

Doesn't matter. Rachel Brant was, simply put, a moment's

diversion. A month down the road and her name would be a forgotten memory.

Cold silence laughed across the meadow. He rolled his shoulders against the chill.

He would leave here and not return for a long time. Years, maybe. When he was an old man.

'Bye, Suz.

Whirling around, he strode to the Andalusian.

"You going to be okay drawing for a while?" Rachel asked Charlie as they stood on the stoop to the McKee house Thursday after school.

"Yeah."

"Good boy." She ushered him into the kitchen just as Daisy entered from the hallway.

"Grandpa's ready. Hey, Charlie. Whatcha got there?"

"My drawing book."

"Can I see?"

"You like drawing, too?"

"Yeah," Daisy said, taking the boy's hand. "But I bet you're way better."

"No way."

"Yeah, way." They disappeared into the living room. "I'll be right there," the girl said over her shoulder.

Guilt. A raw-bitten sore that festered each time Rachel came for Tom's story. Charlie stood in second place. Not that he complained, but Rachel was finding it harder to set her job before her child.

Soon, son, she thought. *Soon it'll be over and we can go home. To Virginia and* American Pie.

She almost stumbled when another thought pierced: *What's so great about Virginia? You have no family there, no friends. Your daddy's in D.C.*

But Virginia was close to DC. Closer than Montana. Charlie could visit his grandpa more often and she could work on her relationship with her father.

Somehow, the thought left her chilled.

"Smells wonderful," she said to Inez standing at the stove.

"Teriyaki chicken. Would you like to stay for supper?"

"Thank you, but I already made a tuna casserole."

"Next time then." The older woman's smile offered sustenance. The guilt dug deeper. A hardworking lot, these McKees, who opened their doors to strangers like her.

In the mudroom Ash's coat was not on its hook. Just as well he toiled in the barns. Their encounters were blooming into a friendship Rachel was not certain how to manage. She almost laughed aloud. As if Ash McKee was a man to let himself be *managed* by anyone.

She found Tom in the den browsing the Internet. A copy of Saturday's *Rocky Times* lay on his lap.

"Come in, girl." The old soldier motioned to one of the sofa chairs. "Sit down." He slapped the newspaper with the back of his hand. "How's Old Joe?"

Depressed. "Hanging in there."

"Damn shame. He and his wife built that business from scratch. Been in that building going on forty years."

That surprised Rachel. "I didn't know he had a wife."

Tom set the paper aside. "Not anymore. She died thirty years ago in childbirth. Damn near killed him, too."

Evidently the baby died or lived elsewhere. Rachel set her briefcase on the floor. "I wish I knew him better."

"Most who've lived here all their lives don't know Joe. He's a loner."

Like Ash, according to Marty in the newsroom.

She pressed back a clean page in her notebook. "Old Joe's talking about retiring."

Tom grunted. "Can't blame him. Meggie used to work part-time for him when she was in high school."

"Yes, Joe said she made the best lemon muffins and garlic bread he'd ever tasted."

Tom smiled. "Nobody bakes like our Meggie."

Our Meggie. A family term. Rachel had no doubt family meant everything to Tom McKee. As it did to his stepson. How would it feel to have a father say *our Rachel?* Or a man—*a lover*—refer to her as *my* Rachel?

Tom pointed a finger at her poised pen. "No sense putting off what you're here for."

She bent over the notebook.

She was a woman of independence.

She needed no one to get her through life's bumps.

The story was all that mattered. A story which would give her prestige and security. And, hopefully, her father's praise.

Chapter Nine

"Rachel." Over the phone Ash's voice slipped into her heart. "There's been a fire in the cottage."

"What?" She shot out of her chair, knocking a stack of line edits off the desk. "When?"

"Ethan noticed the smoke about an hour ago—"

"An hour? Omigod." Their possessions, their meager possessions. "I'll be right there." Purse in hand, she searched frantically for her keys. "Oh, God. What am I going to tell Charlie?" Her little boy. Sweet, dear Charlie, who at this moment was at school and didn't have a clue what was happening to his home, to his bed, his posters, the toy puppy he hugged every night in his sleep. *Oh, Charlie!*

"Rachel, take it easy. No one's hurt—"

"I'll be right there," she repeated and hung up.

"What's going on?" Shaw Hanson yelled as she raced past his office, toward the back door.

"I'm going home."

She slammed into the alley and ran to where the Sunburst was parked.

Home.

For the first time the word held warmth and welcome. And now it was burning along with the few things she and Charlie had collected over seven years.

She hadn't driven a block when worry set in fast and deep.

Had she shut off the range?

Had she left the furnace on too high?

Had she shut off the iron she used this morning, or the dryer or unplugged the toaster? She'd taught herself to do all those things instinctively, but this morning…

Had she missed something because she'd been running late and Charlie turned his nose up at his oatmeal and whined about wanting Sugar Pops instead?

She drove as fast as the winter roads allowed, her mind spinning with what Ash and Tom would do if the fire was her fault. How would she repay the damage? Did they have insurance? Had the fire department been called? She hadn't heard the sirens. Yes, the Flying Bar T lay twenty miles out, but a truck could make it in twenty minutes. *Fire destroys in five, Rachel.*

Susie's dollhouse would be ashes by the time they arrived.

Calm down. He said no one was hurt. That's all that matters. The rest can be rebuilt.

Except for those irreplaceable treasures.

She wouldn't think of them. Instead, she focused on her savings, enough to provide some of the renovations. Extra funds she would beg from her father.

Gray smoke crept from the open front door of the guesthouse and seeped through the top bedroom window—Charlie's bedroom—as she drove into the ranch yard and parked.

Ash and Ethan and a group of men and women she didn't

recognize gathered around Tom and Inez on the walkway between the houses.

Someone had backed a water truck to the door of her home; a long canvas hose, its mouth emitting frozen crystals, lay on the churned snow.

Grateful the fire had been doused, Rachel could only stare. How much had burned? The roof was still intact, as were the walls, but inside? What hadn't been destroyed by the fire would have succumbed to the water and smoke.

Her home, damaged. *Her home.* This house, this one place in her life she'd felt at ease, at peace, and Charlie had been happy and eager to go to school.

She must have released a small sound because the group turned and in one swoop she felt their censure.

Ash broke away, striding toward her, his Sorel-clad feet consuming the distance. Soot drew a quarter moon across the left side of his jaw and sweat plastered his hair across his brow. His hat and coat were missing.

"Ash…" Defeat squeezed her throat.

"You okay?" His voice was gruff.

She nodded. "You?"

"Fine."

She could see he wanted to touch her, but the men watched, caution in their eyes. Because she was *the reporter.* A news-hound. "I'm so sorry," she said.

"We figure it might be faulty wiring in the stove fan. That's where most of the damage was sustained."

"Oh." She looked at the group surrounding Tom and Inez. Ranchers and neighbors rushing to help, men and women doing for each other, looking out for each other. A community drawing together. She would give anything to be part of them, but she'd missed the boat when she forgot to turn off the stove fan—after she'd burned this morning's toast.

Now, because of her, Ash would need to reconstruct his wife's dollhouse. Oh, yes, these people would remember Rachel Brant for a long while.

"The kitchen took the brunt of it," Ash said. "Part of the ceiling was destroyed. Good deal of smoke and water damage." He ran a hand through his hair. "Rachel, your bedroom is a mess."

Her effects. Oh, God, her effects. Smoke meant soot and stink, fire meant cinders, water meant rot.

"You won't be able to do anything about your stuff," he told her as she stared at the guesthouse. "Not until Burt says it's safe to go inside." Burt, he explained, was a foreman on a neighboring ranch who patched as a volunteer fireman. "Look, why don't you go on in the house? You're getting chilled out here."

She was cold. In her haste she'd forgotten her coat at the paper, and now stood in ten degree weather in a light sweater, denim skirt and her useless tall boots.

"Come on," he said when she bit her lip.

Taking her arm, he guided her to the main house. Once inside, chills railed her body. From a hook by the door, Ash snatched a coat, slung the warm corduroy around her shoulders, then led her to the kitchen table.

"I'll get Inez," he said.

"Ash."

His eyes were a shelter from the storm. The garment held his scent. *Oh, God. Ash.*

Once, she had believed she interfered in his life. Today they connected. She hugged his jacket, his home, his family to her chest.

"I have some savings—"

"It was insured."

Of course. Buildings on a ranch would have financial security against such a risk as fire, which could spread within a matter of heartbeats and destroy everything.

"I'll make it up to you," she vowed. "I promise."

A crooked smile. "I'll hold you to it." And then he was gone, back to the ruins of his wife's innovation.

Through the kitchen window, she watched him jump into the water truck and drive the vehicle out of sight. Several men walked to the open door of the guesthouse and peered inside. Another began rolling up the water hose. When Tom wheeled up to the group with Inez at his side, Rachel turned away and called Hanson from her cell phone.

"I won't be coming back today," she said when he picked up. "The place I was renting had a fire and Charlie and I need to find somewhere else to stay tonight."

"Got your camera?" he asked without preamble.

Rachel scowled. Trust Hanson to peck like a vulture for his precious paper. "I was a little distracted at the time."

A pause. "Make sure you get a shot tomorrow." He hung up.

Jerk. She had no intention of getting a photo of her burned home to satisfy Hanson's curiosity. God knew what she and Charlie had lost. Pictures of Charlie as a baby? At one, two, three.

The photo of Floyd in the baby album?

Her mother's picture? Her dad's?

Charlie's first baby outfit, a little blue two-piece with matching booties?

Please, not his first lost tooth.

His precious Hot Wheels.

Oh, her little boy's tears, pearls of sadness. Her throat ached. So much of their lives.

Not five hours ago, the scrapbook with her first published story, the photos of people Rachel had interviewed, of the places she and Charlie had lived lay open on the kitchen counter along with the journal containing memories of her mother. The journal of memories that had excited Daisy to start her own.

Both books in the confinement of the kitchen. *So stupid.*

A sob broke from her heart.

Unable to stay in the big, quiet house, Rachel headed out the front door. She had no idea where she and Charlie would sleep tonight. They hadn't lived in Sweet Creek long enough to knit friendships.

Ash was storing the hose onto the water truck when she stepped onto the front porch. The driver's door stood open, as if at any second he'd jump in and rumble off.

"I'm going back to town," she told him. She would keep her one o'clock appointment with Ellie Dinworth celebrating her beauty salon's twentieth anniversary two doors down from the *Times.* The story would appease Shaw; Ellie was his cousin.

Ash lifted his head. "Inez is planning lunch for everyone. Why don't you stay?" The Stetson was back in place, low over his brow, but his eyes gifted her with a *please.*

She pushed at her bangs, turned from that searching, all-knowing gaze. "I need to arrange things."

"For tonight?"

"Yes." She and Charlie were homeless now. Had they ever had a home? "For tonight."

He shoved the hose into a drawer under the barrel of the tank. Breath exhaled his mouth like smoke. "We have extra rooms in the main house."

"Thanks, but we'll be okay." She would not impose further. She'd done that with the guesthouse and now it contained a fire-eaten kitchen, ceiling and bedroom. "The Dream On isn't so bad." If you ignored the dust balls under the bed, the grime along the molding in the bathroom, the musty blankets. "Charlie won't be impressed but it's better than the car."

Now why had she said that? Sleeping in the car was a piece of history she'd rather forget. What mother made her child, her sweet-faced, innocent five-year-old, sleep in a car for a week?

Ash stared at her. "You slept in a car?"

"A long time ago. Years, in fact." Tugging on her gloves, she came down the steps. "I was young and foolish." And desperate to find a place to rent.

He grabbed his coat from the front seat of the truck. "I can't see you being foolish."

For the first time in over two hours, she smiled. "There has been an occasion or two."

She wasn't petite or sweet and feminine. She wasn't his kind of woman. She was a hard-nosed reporter. But suddenly she wanted more than anything to go to him and hug his big body, set her hand against his sooty, sweat-dried cheeks, kiss his stern, masculine lips.

Something must have shown in her eyes. He blinked once, slowly, then a second time. "Reconsider our rooms," he said. Then climbing behind the wheel, he slammed the door.

She waited until Charlie, dragging his knapsack, got in the Sunburst, slowly buckled the seat belt, then picked up the tiny Corvette from the seat where he left it each morning.

In the rearview mirror, she saw he'd forgotten everything but the toy.

"How was your day, champ?"

"Fine."

Unsnapping her belt, she turned to face him. "Charlie, look at me."

Leaf-long lashes lifted.

"Something bad happened this morning."

Wariness.

"There was a fire in the guesthouse. It destroyed most of the kitchen. Honey, some of our stuff is—is gone."

His face was all eyes. "What stuff?"

"The firemen won't let me look, because it's not safe."

"HD?"

Hound Dog. The brown-and-white toy puppy that kept the bogeyman out of his dreams. "I don't know, Charlie. HD was in your bedroom, right?"

"I think so," he whispered. Suddenly, his eyes widened and she realized his concern. "My cars!"

"Safe." She smiled to lighten his heart. "The firemen said the fire hadn't reached the living room. And I remember you leaving your shoe box by the front window this morning." Twenty feet away from the kitchen. "Your cars should be okay."

"We can still sleep there, right?"

She shook her head. "I've booked us into the motel for a few days. There was a lot of smoke damage and Mr. Ash wants to begin restoration, which won't happen overnight. Meantime, I'm going to look around for a new apartment."

"Can we go back to Grandpa Bill's?"

"No, champ, we can't. I have a job here and you still have to go to school."

"I don't want to go to school anymore. Every time I go to school something bad happens."

Rachel bit her lip. He was right. Four midyear moves because of some unforeseen factor—Floyd showing up and wanting back in her life, but ignoring Charlie; her causing hard feelings amongst residents over a ghost story; two relocations when her veteran interviews were completed—had branded her little boy with a sizable inferiority complex.

Well, the moment she delivered the completed series to *American Pie,* they would go to Virginia. Hopefully to a permanent job on staff. In a permanent house.

She ignored her heart suffering over Ash.

Beyond the windshield, children ran across the school yard to climb into buses and cars or head down the sidewalk for home.

Despite Shaw-Machiavelli-Hanson, she liked this town. She

liked the camaraderie, the wholesomeness of its residents. The gentle pace. She loved the sturdy Rockies, the quiet vastness stretching from their foothills; the hardworking, sun-browned farmers and ranchers.

She liked Daisy and Tom and Inez. And Darby Lowe. In Darby she'd found a woman friend. A new venture for Rachel, who nurtured few friendships. But here, *here* she'd allowed Darby and her son Tyler into their lives.

Most of all, Rachel liked Ash. Oh, yes. *A lot.*

Trouble was, Ash still loved his wife. And Rachel knew better than to give her heart to a man in love with memories or ambition. Firsthand experience—her father and Floyd Stephens.

"Don't worry, sugar," she said. "We're not moving away from Sweet Creek, just to a new place *in* Sweet Creek."

"I want to live with Daisy."

She sighed. "Charlie."

"Okay." His bottom lip poked out. "Then can I get HD now?"

She pulled into the traffic creeping along the school zone. "Probably not, Charlie. I need to speak with the fire department before we can retrieve any of our belongings."

He slumped in the seat, head bent, bangs hanging in his eyes. "I hate motels."

Ditto. They'd stayed in enough over the years to know the Dream On was of the Least Desirable venue. Two hundred and eighty bucks for seven nights in a fifteen-by-twenty-foot room with a closet-sized bathroom and kitchenette, cigarette-burned carpet, fingerprinted walls. And God knew the nature of the stains on the sheets.

Charlie's round blue eyes hit the rearview mirror. "How come there was a fire?"

"We're not sure." *Yet.* "They're investigating it."

"Miss Inez lets me lick the bowl when she's making sugar cookies."

Such a small thing. "Yes, she does."

They rode in silence the rest of the way to the motel. Rachel parked in front of room number eleven.

"I want to play with Tyler," Charlie whined.

"Not tonight, son." Tonight she had a dozen things to do, foremost find a more permanent place to live.

Opening the motel room door, she ushered Charlie inside. In her tote were the new rental listings she had gleaned from Sally, the paper's ad designer. Shaw would throw a hissy fit if he knew Rachel had scooped the ads before they hit tomorrow's edition. She didn't care. Her son needed a place to live.

"We have extra rooms."

Don't think about the house on the Flying Bar T.

Charlie hopped onto the bed with his mini muscle car. "I'm hungry."

She checked the refrigerator where earlier she'd stored a few groceries, including blueberry yogurt cups. As Charlie tore into one, Rachel took the ad list, sat on the bed and reached for the phone on the nightstand.

The minute Ash entered the mudroom after his evening calf check, Daisy slipped in from the kitchen and closed the door.

"Dad," she whispered urgently. "Let's get Rachel and Charlie. She can't argue if we're in her face."

He hadn't taken off his hat. Now he did. Slowly. After driving the water truck down to the barns this morning, he'd sat and watched Rachel take that old Sunburst down the road. She hadn't returned, nor phoned, nor sent Charlie home with Daisy on the bus. *Damn the woman.* No clue about the rules of the land. Rules that said a man offered a helping hand to those in trouble.

He shrugged out of his coat. "She's made her choice, Daiz."

Methodically, he removed his boots. One thing he understood clear as a damn bell was when a female made up her mind about something, hell or high water were just words.

Like Daisy and her mule-headedness.

She said, "I can't believe you won't fight for her."

Fight for her? What the hell was that supposed to mean? Rachel wasn't his girlfriend, he wasn't losing her to some other guy. The only woman he'd ever fought for was Susie, seventeen years ago. And he'd won. He had no interest, *no desire* to do that battle again.

Daisy went on. "You know what the Dream On is like. Hooker haven on Friday and Saturday nights, for Pete's sake."

He frowned. "How would you know?"

"Oh, Dad. I wasn't born yesterday. *Everyone* knows about that sleazy hole. Rachel and Charlie are there because she doesn't want to inconvenience us—and because you don't want to ask her to stay here."

"I asked and she refused," he replied wearily, running a hand through his sweat-stiff hair. He needed a shower.

"Well, maybe you need to be more convincing." His daughter slanted him a look. "Or are you worried she'll find out about your reading if she's living in the house?"

His heart kicked. "What are you getting at?"

"Come on, Dad. You know what I'm talking about."

He did. With Rachel living in the house, he'd be on edge every minute because of his damned dyslexia, because reading was an arduous and painful chore. Oh, he could see the print, but the words were always jumbled with letters missing.

What had they called it? "Difficulty processing sequential and linguistic data in the brain." As a kid he'd called it as he felt. *Dumb.* As an adult he had understood the difference, but that understanding hadn't relieved the situation.

Not everyone sees learning disabilities as a curse or weapon of torture, Ash.

Except he had trusted Susie. And Susie had used his disability against him over their daughter.

Now Daisy wanted to bring Rachel into the house. Rachel, who had his common sense galloping like his wintering mustangs.

He did not want her where he could *touch* her. Touching led to other things. Like kissing. And he wanted to kiss her more than he'd wanted to do anything in a long, long while.

Except take her to bed. That he wanted most of all.

Rachel of the long legs and cat eyes, the cherrywood hair that flowed around her slim neck like a small, shadowed waterfall.

Who would eventually see him as Susie had years ago.

"Dad?" Anticipation in Daisy's eyes. "You know I'm right. Besides, you always taught me that it's a person's responsibility to help the underdog. Rachel needs our help. Little Charlie needs our help."

"Daisy."

Her expression grew jaded. "I can't believe it. You won't help her *because* she's a reporter?" His daughter waved a hand at the door that, thank God, was closed to the kitchen. "That could be me one day, you know. I could be a reporter someone dislikes and treats—"

"I don't dislike her." *I like her too damned much. And, hell, you might change your dreams.* These days kids changed directions with the prairie wind.

She crossed her arms, eyes keen as a red-tailed hawk's. "Then what's the problem?"

Rubbing his forehead, he exhaled a long breath.

"Look," Daisy went on before he could gather two words together. "We have to think of Charlie. The little guy needs a decent place to stay. Rachel won't ask. I *know* her."

Better than he did. From the beginning, those two had girl talked. About Tom's story. About Shaw Hanson scoffing at the Students' Union. About dating.

"Ah, Daiz."

"It's okay, then?" Her eyes pierced him.

"Fine. Let's see what she has to say." And may God help him.

She grabbed his shoulders, kissed him square on the mouth. "You're the best, Daddy."

Dashing into the kitchen, she called, "Inez, Gramps. Dad and I are bringing Rachel and Charlie home."

Home. A blanket of comfort stole over his heart.

By nine o'clock Rachel knew she was in trouble. Sweet Creek, Montana, was no booming hub. The ads sent her on a merry-go-round, bad to worse. From cobwebby, sunless basements, to mice-infested trailers to houses out of her price range.

At 9:10, she and Charlie traipsed into the motel.

"I'm hungry," he whined, climbing on the bed to watch TV.

Four hours ago, they had dined on fish and chips at a small fifties diner at the edge of town that specialized in burgers, deli sandwiches and quick fish feasts.

Rachel opened the yellowed refrigerator, reached inside. "How about an Oreo with some milk?"

He nodded, his eyewear slipping to the end of his little nose. She set the cookies on a plate, filled a glass, kissed his hair. *Love you, little man.* "I'm sorry for keeping you up so late, baby."

"'S'okay." He flopped back on the pillows. Another minute and he'd be asleep.

She was shrugging out of her coat when a knock sounded. Charlie sat up. "Who's that, Mom?"

"Maybe Mr. Gosley." Expecting the landlord with the extra towels she'd ordered, she went to the door, peeked past the ancient beige curtain. Daisy stood under the murky glow of the stoop light. Rachel threw the bolt and chain lock.

"It's Daisy!" Charlie charged across the room.

"Hey, guy." Ash's daughter ruffled his hair. "Dad and I came to get you guys. You're staying with us at the house."

Rachel's eyes fastened on the man standing beside his truck. The night breeze sifted through his hair. He said, "I'll have the cottage fixed in a week." The line of his mouth said he wasn't here to argue.

"Mom." Charlie nudged her hip. "I want to live with Daisy."

Before she could refuse, the teenager intervened. "Dad's hired some carpenters. And anyway, I promised Charlie a lesson in currying Areo tomorrow."

"Yeah, Mom, and you always say a promise is a promise."

Rachel laughed. "Yes, I do. Guess I'm outnumbered." Again, she and Ash exchanged a long look. "We'll follow you back to the ranch after I settle up with the motel."

He came forward with a palm full of bills. "Taken care of," he said. "All you're paying for is to have the room tidied."

Stunned, she stared at the two hundred and sixty dollars she'd doled out this afternoon. "Well. Nothing like taking the bull by the horns." Again she laughed and it felt good.

He had come for her.

"Can I ride in Ash's truck?" Charlie asked, breaking the hot look linking Rachel to the man in question. "It's got cow stink and if I'm gonna be a real cowboy, I need to smell like cows and horses."

Ash cracked a grin. "Sorry to disappoint you, buddy. Cowboys only smell like the barns when they're *in* them. Other times, they wear clean clothes *and* they keep their trucks spick-and-span in case a lady might need a lift." His eyes held Rachel's.

Lord, she was doomed. Half a day and, believing their crossed paths were concluded, she had missed him. Missed his night-deep voice, those dark fathomless looks, that stern mouth.

"All right," she said.

Charlie cheered. Daisy grinned. Ash stepped into the room. "Let's get your stuff."

Five minutes later, with a sack of groceries from the refrigerator and a pack of uneaten Oreo cookies on the front seat of her Sunburst, Rachel followed his taillights through the night, back to the Flying Bar T.

Chapter Ten

Ash carried Charlie into the house. The boy had fallen asleep halfway to the ranch, chattering like a squirrel one minute, slumped in a netherworld on Daisy's shoulder the next.

"Hey, britches." Ash set the sleepy child gently on his feet on the front mat. "We're home. Ready for your cookies and milk?"

The boy knuckled an eye. "Tired," he mumbled. Ash's heart did a slow revolution. With Daisy at that age, he'd snuggled her into his arms, kissed her cheek and carried her off to bed. The dad in him wanted to do the same for Charlie.

Behind them, Rachel said, "Son, you should eat something or your tummy will be growling in the middle of the night."

"Peanut butter and jelly."

Ash looked to his daughter. "Daiz?"

"On it." Taking Rachel's groceries, she herded Charlie toward the kitchen.

Alone with Rachel in the entranceway, Ash thought she looked beat. "Come," he said. "I'll show you the rooms."

They went down the hall past the den where she had dug into Tom's war memories, past the old man's bedroom door that remained closed, up the stairway to the second floor.

He strode past Daisy's turret room with its unmade bed, shoes scattered across the floor and posters of Leonardo DiCaprio and Orlando Bloom. "Don't mind my kid. She's in teen mess mode."

Rachel chuckled. "Which I'll experience in six years."

Stopping at a smaller bedroom, he caught the light. "Figured Charlie could sleep in here."

With some pride, he watched as she took in the twin bed with its blue-and-white comforter, the prints of horses on the walls. Last summer, Daisy hung the posters when her town friends, staying for slumber parties, had gone a little horse crazy.

"It's perfect, Ash," Rachel said. "Thank you."

He stood slightly behind her in the doorway. The faint scent of her hair, like the jasmine that Inez grew in a Mexican pot on the kitchen windowsill, lured his nose.

Tapping the doorjamb with a palm, he stepped back before he did something foolish. Like turn her in his arms and kiss her.

"Your bedroom is—" he moved across the hall to open the door beside the bathroom, flicked the light "—this one."

"Lovely." Tiredness washed from her face.

Slowly she studied the knotty pine bedstead, the matching furniture, the yellow quilt and creamy curtains on the corner windows, the prints of gardens and country cottages hanging in wooden frames.

The room replicated a photo Susie had once cut from a magazine. Ash had always thought the decor too prissy for a ranch house. For a man like him to stand in the center of its floor.

Until this moment. Until Rachel, with her tall, graceful body, short, chic hair, those ballerina arms. Once, on TV, he'd heard the words *quiet elegance,* and understood the description tonight. Her presence erased the room's cool facade and, instead, brought in life and warmth and…peace.

She turned, caught his look. "Ash—"

He didn't give her time to finish. One step and he was cupping her face in his hands and lifting her mouth to his.

A soft, startled breath escaped her lips and then she was dancing the courtship ballad with him. Lips, tongues. Fingers, skin. Heat.

She was everything he'd imagined—and more. *So much more.*

He'd kissed women before Susie.

He'd kissed Susie thousands of times.

But this…this was *different.* Maybe because it had been so long. Maybe because she was a danger he couldn't afford to risk. And maybe, just maybe he was tired of the grief and anger and loneliness and the ragged hole in his heart.

His fingers found the thick satin of her hair, stirring the scent of jasmine, making his senses crazy. With her. *Only her.*

Someone groaned. Was it him? Her? He wanted to pull her into his skin, have her swim in his veins.

They were in a bedroom. Two paces and he could have her under him. *Rachel.* His hand skimmed spine and buttocks, ready to lift her into his arms—

"Mommy? Where are you?"

Charlie's voice sent Ash stumbling back. For three long seconds, he and Rachel stared at each other, breathing as if they'd finished a grueling wilderness run. His kisses had dampened her lips, his fingers muddled her hair.

Swiftly, he brushed a thumb over her mouth, eradicating telltale signs. The power of her warm flesh pooled in his groin and he stepped toward the bed and sat down, elbows to knees, hiding *his* telltale sign.

"In here, Charlie." Her eyes were dark as a snow-loaded sky in the moments she repaired her hair with two quick swipes.

Footsteps hurried down the hall. Charlie stood in the doorway, Daisy eyeing them from behind the boy.

"Hey, love." Rachel went to her child. "Ready for bed?"

"Yeah," he said. "But I don't have a toothbrush."

"Don't worry about it for tonight. I'll get us a new one tomorrow."

"We have new ones under the sink," Daisy offered. "Come on, Charlie." She frowned at Ash before tugging the child into the bathroom next door.

Ash pushed off the bed. "Get some rest." Sleeping in the room next door, *he* sure as hell wouldn't.

"You should've left me at the motel."

Whatever he'd expected her to say—I'm sorry, or this shouldn't have happened, or I don't do cowboys—that she would say he should have left her at the Dream On Dive grated a little. Did she think he brought her back so he could tiptoe into her room in the middle of the night?

"I won't touch you again, Rachel," he assured and walked from the room.

Several days later, Tom rolled out to the front porch after lunch to soak up the warming late-February sun. Ash worked in the corrals again, training Daisy's young colt, Ticket, to the rope.

He's edgy, my son. Too much on his mind.

Tom knew some of it had to do with the ranch, with the fact he had not brought the boy to partnership in the Flying Bar T. Something Tom needed to arrange soon, before calving season was done, before it was too late. Heart attacks might allow one chance, but seldom two.

Ash clucked to the young gelding at the end of the lunge, and the horse tossed its head. Good stock, that one. Like Ash. Strong, dependable, trustworthy.

But lately a little wary. Tom saw it in his careful words around Rachel, in the way he looked at the woman.

Tom was edgy, too. He wasn't sure if he liked Rachel's constant presence. He couldn't hide from her the way he had when she'd lived in the cottage. Now, he saw her every day, and each time her eyes hit his they queried: *Is this a good time?*

She wanted the story done.

Tom wanted it done.

He *needed* it done.

Daisy was a wonder. She worked with Rachel tirelessly, and had read long portions to him of what they'd put together. Some parts were okay, others Tom didn't like.

Still, he worried. He might be old and crippled, but he wasn't dense.

He worried that Ash couldn't see what Tom had come to know: that Rachel was a decent woman, one with strength as well as kindness.

She wasn't without flaws, nor was she a saint. But Ash didn't want a saint. He wanted a woman. He wanted her.

She was a continent apart from Susie, God rest her soul. Where Susie was a chickadee flitting from this to that, Rachel was a robin, observant and systematic. A loner.

That, most of all, attracted Ash. Once, when he was young, Susie's spontaneity held his heart, but he was a grown man now, past the flush of youth. He needed a soft place to fall.

Like Laura had been for Tom after the War.

Like Inez kneading breads with her capable fingers, kneading his sore shoulders, his glutes.

His two women. They had given more than Tom thought he deserved in one lifetime. Besides their love, they had offered him calm hands and soothing hearts.

In the beginning, Laura had helped him through the ignorant questions from folks in town. Like how many villages had he burned, how many kids had he killed. Stupid questions that made him feel like pond slime and had him wanting to hole up in the brush for twenty years.

And Inez. Dear woman. He loved her as he had loved Laura. Damned lucky he'd been to find them both.

And then there was Tina. Tom snorted. Whirlwind Tina. Meeting him at the front door of this house after his discharge from the veterans' hospital in Boston.

He'd been home two days when she drove up the road in her daddy's big '66 Ford convertible, blond hair whipping in the wind, scarf flying from her hair like the Stars and Stripes.

His mother had opened the door. Called Tom. While he'd been laid up in therapy, she'd hired a carpenter to convert the front steps into a ramp for his chair.

He'd heard Tina ask, "What'd you do to the steps?"

And then he rolled out of the kitchen. A gimp in a chair.

He hadn't told Tina about his legs or his arm. Hindsight was a great thing they say. Withholding those kind of details from your fiancée was not great.

But then after Nam there wasn't a whole helluva lot that was great. He could attest to that.

Tina's mouth gaped. She took one look at his stumps, and said, "You didn't tell me you were a cripple" and broke into tears.

His mother had damn near slugged Tina.

Tom had tried to console her, tried to explain, tried to justify that telling about the missing limbs made his deformity real and he wasn't ready for any of it to be real. Not then.

Hell. Was anyone ever ready for this kind of life alteration?

He and his platoon sure as hell hadn't been prepared for Charlie crouching in underground tunnels, waiting for them to come walking along like dumb deer.

The next day Tina phoned, said they should "take a breather."

Not as if they hadn't been on a two-*year* breather with him in Nam and her here.

A week later she left town.

With his best bud.

Life's a bitch and then you die.

Trouble was, for some, dying was a thirty-six-year-long haul.

The temperature changed overnight and for the next two days warm Pacific air rolled over the Rockies and across the undulating range. Snow melted, ice withered in creeks and ponds, grass patched hillsides. Everywhere tiny crocuses poked their purple heads from the raw earth. And, according to Ash, calves were dropping by the dozen every minute.

Amazingly, Hanson had given Rachel three days off—after she told him the damage to the ranch guesthouse hit eight grand.

Thank God for the insurance Ash renewed last fall, she thought, carrying a box of clothes smelling of smoke to the back door of the main house. This morning the Fire Chief had allowed her to transfer some of their belongings.

She went through the quiet house. Ash was in the barns with Ethan; Inez and Tom had gone to Sweet Creek to visit her sister.

Upstairs in her bedroom, Rachel sat at her laptop and worked on Tom's story, manicuring words and ideas to find the rhythm and flow she had gathered over the past years from the other Hells Field survivors.

Daisy's input helped enormously. The girl had talent. Rachel wished Ash would rethink his opinion about writers—and reporters.

He was an enigma, a conundrum. She'd been wrong when she'd thought him a what-you-see-is-what-you-get kind of man.

Those hard masculine lips, she knew now, were shockingly soft and warm and mobile. He was a man full of passion and response, kissing her and kissing her again, here in this

bedroom during those three minutes, his hands molding he
flesh, his mouth urgent and tender in the space of a breath.

Yes, Ashford McKee was a man of a million facets. And i
would take a lifetime to unveil them. The thought had he
pinching her knees together. *Oh, Rachel, you are so pitiful.*

Nonetheless, she was helpless to her emotion. Whether he
intelligence balked or not, her *heart* wanted to unveil thos
facets, craved to know the Ash hidden beneath that somber
brusque surface.

She heard the quick, brisk thud of boots on the stairs. He
breathing slowed as the sound continued down the hall, a de
termined tattoo against the hardwood.

Were those spurs jingling on his heels?

He stopped at her closed door.

"Rachel?" Deep voice through wood.

"Come in."

She rose and stood by the desk.

Slowly he filled the door frame with his big, range-toughene
body. Worn navy parka, Stetson and—leather chaps.

Oh, Lord.

Not just a man, but a true blue, heart and soul *cowboy*.

Her eyes latched onto his.

"Hey," he said softly. "Thought you might like to go riding
this morning."

"I'd love to." She stood anchored to the desk, anchored to him

His smile faltered. "What is it?" Spurs ringing like wind
chimes, he moved forward.

A sigh tumbled through her lips. In deep water, deep, silen
water, was where she stood.

Halting in front of her, he lifted her chin with a thick
knuckle. "Rachel?"

"Let me get my coat," she managed.

His gaze swept the desk, the laptop. "If you're working, we can take a rain check."

"No, I want to go. You just…" *Floor me.*

Humor in his dark eyes. "I just what?"

"Nothing. Let's go." She stepped past him, but he caught her waist, brought the scent of sun and snow and animals. Intoxicating her. "If it's something I did, tell me."

He was not a stupid man. She stepped back. "All right. I'm confused. One minute we kiss, the next you avoid me like the Avian flu for three days. Now you ask me to go riding."

She looked square into his tea eyes, that full-bodied breakfast tea. A morning-after tea.

"I won't be some kind of diversion when it suits you, Ash."

"Did I say you were?" He sighed. "Look. The other night was a mistake."

She laughed. "Well. A girl definitely knows where she stands with you."

Under the Stetson those eyes turned midnight. "You'll always know where you stand with me. And for what it's worth, the mistake was mine, not yours."

"Thank you for clearing that up." She wanted him gone. Out of her room where he dominated her space, her senses. Her heart.

"Rachel." A corner of his mouth hitched. "I didn't come to argue. I came because I thought you were interested in knowing about a working ranch."

Of course. The other story. The one she'd been considering since the morning after the snowstorm when he had talked about conglomerates and struggling independents.

Forget he's a man or that you can't stay calm when he's around. All that matters is what you write.

"Show me," she said and, dignity intact, preceded him out of the room.

Down the hall and stairs, the song of his spurs wrote itself on her soul.

Ash cinched the McCall saddle onto Areo for Rachel.

He wanted her experience to be a good one. A well-worn saddle, an old gelding that would give her a gentle, easy ride while they checked fence lines.

Next month, he'd let the cattle back onto the range. Already, due to the thaw, some had wandered to the corners of the home pasture. Ash figured a few would drop calves in stands of trees and along creeks.

Leading Areo to the corrals, he skimmed a look over the old army jacket he had dug from the pile in the mudroom. The material hung several inches below the curve of Rachel's shapely rear. For that he was sorry.

She shot him a grin. As if he held up a placard relaying his musings. He nodded toward the saddle. "Need some help?"

"Nope. I can do it."

Fine. He waited while she grabbed the saddle horn, stepped into the stirrup and pulled herself up. When she'd settled, he moved her long, slim calf aside to get at the stirrup strap.

"What are you doing?"

"Adjusting the length for your legs. Yours are longer than Daisy's."

"Oh."

His palms brushed soft denim and felt the tension beneath. Her skin would be pale and smooth, the shape of feminine muscle.

He peered up, caught her gazing down. Her cherrywood hair rimmed her woolen, wine-colored hat; the scarf fell on her breasts. *Dammit, Ash. Get ahold of yourself.*

Giving the leather a final tug, he commanded, "Stand up in the stirrups."

She did.

Mechanically, he scanned the space between the saddle and her trim butt. A fist's width. "Good. Wait here."

Hard as stone, he spun on his heel, and headed into the barn. He shouldn't have asked for her company this morning. Or any morning.

For the past month he'd been waking with a woody. And that kiss the other night…hell, he'd been hard 24-7. And now he'd be with her out on the range. Alone. What the hell had he been thinking, asking her to come along?

She'd be pumping him with questions about his life and God knew what else.

Guilt steamed his cheeks. *She'd only asked once, knucklehead.* In the coffee shop. *Your fault for feeling sorry about her job with Hanson.*

He saddled Northwind, led the stallion down the barn's corridor. *You can't have it all your way, Ash. Either you accept her for who she is, or you ignore her.*

Which he'd done for three days.

"I'm confused," she had said.

He wondered what she'd say if he admitted the same?

Like a brand, the heat of Ash's fingers marked Rachel's leg. Her eyes strayed constantly to the man. He rode tall and straight, in complete harmony with the Andalusian's quick-paced walk. A Cheyenne warrior of old, riding across the plains.

"Saddle sore yet?" he asked, his mouth lifting.

They'd been out for a half hour. "Not at all."

Areo obeyed each motion of her hand. In contrast, Northwind worried his bit, though Ash maintained an easy rule.

"Areo has a nice, broad back. It's like rocking on a beanbag chair."

Ash laughed, the sound slip-sliding across her skin. "You won't be saying that by the end of the day."

"Is that how long we'll be?" She'd planned to be home for Charlie.

"Daisy will look after him."

Other women would have found his perception annoying, the way he could interpret her emotions, her thoughts. Rachel found it intriguing. No man had understood her before. The sense of empathy was new indeed.

Suddenly, he reined Northwind to a stop and studied the ground. "Let's head that way." Pointing north, toward the Crazy Mountains, the limitless stand of trees and evergreens blanketing craggy foothills, he said, "I want to see where this cow is."

"What cow?"

"The one we're following." He gestured toward the soft earth. "See the tracks."

A lone set of cloven hoofprints headed northwest. Rachel appraised the hills, more dark now than white with the temperate winds from the mountains melting the snow.

"Why would she go off by herself?"

"To calve."

Like creatures of the wild. "You think she went today?"

"Probably yesterday, from the looks of the tracks. They aren't fresh."

"We should've brought the dogs," she pointed out.

"They're herding dogs, not trackers."

They rode in silence, Ash studying the trail out front. Reaching the trees fifteen minutes later, he dismounted to analyze the direction of the cow, then examined the range. Across hillsides, cattle foraged in clusters on the dun-colored grass bared by a fortified sun.

"What is it?" Rachel asked. Had he lost the track?

"Storm brewing."

She scanned the sky.

He lifted a thumb toward the southwest where in the graying sky a pair of rainbowlike spots bracketed the sun. "Sun dogs."

"What are they?" she asked, intrigued. The man complemented the land the way a lyric complemented a melody.

"They're caused by ice crystals in the atmosphere. Means bad weather's coming." Catching Northwind's reins, Ash mounted again, but kept the stallion in place, spot-dancing, eager for a run. "Listen."

Tilting her head to catch the whereabouts of sound, Rachel held Areo still. Faintly, above the jingle and squeak of gear and leather, came a short, hoarse lowing.

"Let's check it out." Wheeling Northwind about, Ash headed into a thicket of pine and cottonwoods.

Rachel urged Areo after Northwind's charcoal tail. The terrain was rough with underbrush and rocks and crusted snow. Ash zigzagged down the hill, easing back branches for Rachel, calling out a warning as he let go.

Ahead, she heard the gurgle of water freeing itself from ice and frozen mud. The air tingled with the scent of crisp snow and thawing earth.

The lowing grew more audible.

"There." Ash pointed, but Rachel saw nothing past his broad shoulders. "In the creek."

He coaxed Northwind down the last leg of the slope, then was out of the saddle before she saw what had caused his urgency.

A cow stood stuck to her flanks. Mud caked her front quarters from her struggle to pull free. Sighting riders, the animal lowed to her hunchbacked, shivering calf at the edge of the creek's bank.

Rachel climbed from Areo, looped the bridle reins around the trunk of a cottonwood. "How long do you think they've been here?"

Ash untied the rope looped at his saddle's pommel. "Couple days. Mud's dried in the grooves she's cut. Means she's quit thrashing for a while. Likely dead tired."

He backed the Andalusian to within a few feet of the Angus. "I need you to hold Northwind in place." He handed Rachel the reins, then with quick fingers, removed jacket and chaps, tossing the latter onto the mud beside the cow.

One end of the rope in hand, he crawled across the covered surface. When he'd fed a loop around the animal's hips, he called, "When I say, lead him forward one step at a time."

"Where will you be?"

"Pushing her out of the mud."

Dark goo surrounded the beast. A rivulet of water flowed under broken icy patches twenty feet beyond. Had thirst driven her into the mire? What if Ash…?

At Rachel's hesitation, his eyes squinted. "You gonna be okay with this?"

No, she was not okay with this. She was terrified. Of the horse. For the cow and calf. For Ash. Most of all, for Ash.

"We should get help," she said.

"If we called on every little scrape, nothing would get done."

We. He and other ranchers. Cowboys, foremen. Their womenfolk. Stalwart women like Susie.

This is a working ranch.

Rachel did not fit this arena, Ash's arena. The fear running in her veins spoke the truth.

Ash scooped mud from around the cow's hindquarters. Seconds later, he hurled his filthy gloves aside and worked with bare hands. The cow struggled, her muddy tail slapping Ash across the head and shoulders.

"Tighten the rope," he called.

Rachel urged Northwind forward, the rope jerking taut against the cow's hindquarters.

Come on, Bessy. Climb out of there.

Northwind took another step, then another.

The animal floundered and Ash scrambled to level the rope harnessing her body. Suddenly, in a valiant effort, she bawled and, fighting the mud, snapped the rope against her hide. Lunging awkwardly, her cumbersome body snaked to the left and collapsed into the mud—on Ash.

Rachel's stomach hit her toes. "Ash! Omigod!"

The cow had pinned his right leg at a skewed angle.

"Lead him forward, Rach." The cow struggled to stand, whirling clumps of mud through the air. "Don't let him—stop."

Heart ramming, Rachel urged Northwind up the bank. *Please.*

The cow hurtled upright once more and Ash dragged free.

Thank you. Rachel rushed to the creekside. Face storm-gray, Ash lay spread-eagle beside the cow.

Heedless of the mud sucking at her knees and elbows, Rachel crawled to Ash. She couldn't breathe. Was he unconscious? "Ash." Or dead? *"Ash."* His name clutched her throat.

His eyes fluttered open and she bowed her head in relief. "You're alive." His face swam through her tears.

"Heeey." His mouth, that sexy mouth, twitched. "Don't cry. I'm just having a little rest."

She hid her face in his muddy throat. Her tears pooled in the creases of his skin. She, who had learned years ago not to cry. "You scared fifty years off my life."

"Only fifty?" he teased.

She lifted her head. He'd lost the Stetson. Mud caked his hair, streaked his cheeks, coated one ear.

He was a man of few words, a man holding honor and decency and kindness as rules of thumb. He labored in barns, on the range and most days smelled of the outdoors and animals. But in that moment, Rachel knew. Knew as sure as the sun pouring through the naked trees above that she loved him.

She *loved* Ashford McKee as she had no man.

Her chest billowed with the knowledge.

Her veins danced with it.

Heedless of the muck, she leaned over, kissed his mouth.

"Hold that thought," he whispered when she was done.

Oh, she'd hold, all right. Forever and just for him.

"Gotta get up," he said and winced when he tried.

"Your leg?"

"I think the old girl busted it." Pain stammered his voice. "Should've listened to you. Cell phone in my jacket. Call Eth."

She glanced at the cow. If the animal rolled onto its side again, Ash would be in worse danger. "I'm getting you out first. Wait here."

"I got someplace to go?" he chided.

A stern look and she set to work. Mud coated her jacket, jeans, boots, webbed her fingers. Nothing mattered but Ash.

Several minutes later she had him on the dirty, crystallized snow, out of harm's way.

Rachel touched his cheek with a muddy finger. "You're safe."

"I'm safe." Suffering glazed his eyes.

She retrieved his jacket, found the cell phone.

"Speed dial two," Ash mumbled. "Eth's cell."

The foreman answered on the third ring. Without preamble she said, "It's Rachel. Ash may have broken his leg. We need you to come to— Where are we?" Tempering her worry, she looked at the man on the ground.

"Southwest pasture, down by the creek from the twin pines. Tell him about the cow."

Rachel relayed the information. After flipping the phone shut, she removed the horses' saddles and gathered the warmed saddle pads around Ash.

A crisp wind swayed the trees; the sun had disappeared. He'd been right. A storm brewed. She cradled his head in her lap.

"Rachel," he whispered hoarsely.

"Shh." Gently, she plucked at the mud drying in his hair, watched as his lips pushed words through his chattering teeth.

"If I'd known y-you'd hold my h-head like this, I'd'a b-busted a leg long ago."

"You talk too much, cowboy," she admonished.

Several long moments passed. The calf nuzzled noses with its mother, and let out a hungry bawl. Once more the cow struggled feebly against the creek's muck.

"Poor things," she crooned.

"You surprise me, Rach."

"I do?"

"You're braver than I figured."

She shrugged. "We reporters are a tough bunch, what with war zones, diseased areas, natural disasters. Cows in mud."

"I'm not talking reporters," he said.

Her pulse booted. "No?"

"No."

A chickadee chittered in the trees. Close by, the horses nibbled at the frozen, brown grass.

"I'm talking heart," he said, dark eyes on hers. "Yours is out there."

Tears stung a second time and she looked away. "It wasn't always." Heart didn't get the story.

"It's good people can change, then."

She stroked his hair, adored its glossy thickness. "Don't we all at one time or the other?"

"No," he said on a sigh. "Not always."

The forest offered its silence, until Ethan and three ranch hands arrived with the truck and ropes.

Chapter Eleven

Ash had torn the quadriceps tendon in his right thigh and bruised a kidney. No broken bones, thank God, so no cast or crutches. Just a damn sore muscle and abdomen. The doc had taken a number of X-rays, bandaged him up and sent him home with orders to stay off his feet for seven days.

Right. As if he was about to play couch potato for a week. In the middle of calving season. Doc needed his head examined.

Limping through the cow barn Saturday morning, Ash thought back to Thursday. Rachel, reporter, news hack, media person, *woman,* had shown him a side that surprised him still when he let the details of that morning wind through his head.

In a crisis when he had needed her, she hadn't cringed, whined or protested.

She probably saved your life.

Tracking his cows alone, he would have been in that creek,

under that animal, for God knows how long. Maybe until one or the other or both died.

Fool. You never *discard your cell phone in the bush.*

He'd done just that. Taken off his jacket and walked into a soup hole.

"Are all these cows gonna have babies?" a small voice beside him asked.

Charlie, trailing Ash's heels into the barns.

The kid wore a green corduroy jacket and wool hat and mitts. His little Sorel boots were on the wrong feet. After the fire, he had tagged Ash at every turn, a puppy lost then found.

I'm not your hero, boy. Save that for athletes and movie stars. She cried for you.

"Are they?" Charlie asked again.

"Most will calve, yeah."

"Is it bad if they don't have a baby?"

"Not bad, just not good. And it's calves they have, Charlie, not babies. People have babies."

"Oh."

In the dim interior, the child's face was a small, pale moon with freckles peppering his skinny nose. Rachel's nose, Rachel's mouth, her clear blue eyes.

Ash wondered whether the kid's dad had blond hair—or whether the man even lived. *Ask her. She'll tell you.*

No, asking meant exchanging pasts. *Show me yours and I'll show you mine.* Wasn't that how it went? Well, dammit. Not with personal history and for damn sure not with Ash McKee's.

"What happens if a cow doesn't have a calf?"

"She's shipped for meat."

"But why? She didn't do nothing wrong."

"Because she'll cost us money for a year and we can't take the chance that she won't calve the following spring. That's how a ranch works. Cattle are our livelihood. If we don't sell them, we don't eat." He looked down at the boy. "And people like your mom can't buy meat at the store."

Ash could see the gears grinding behind the kid's eyes. "Do cowboys *have* to eat meat?"

"They can eat whatever they want. But I've yet to meet a cowboy who doesn't eat meat."

"Will I be a cowboy?"

"Depends on where you live."

"I'm living here."

"But not forever." *Jeez, Ash, do you have to be so blunt?* Maybe not, but how else would he get through to the boy that the ranch wasn't his permanent home? That his mother had other plans?

He limped toward the birth pens. The first heifer-calf pair could be released back to the herd tomorrow. The next pair, new this morning, would stay penned forty-eight hours. A sturdy, healthy calf would bring a better price come fall.

A shriek wheeled Ash around. *What the hell?*

Charlie beelined toward him. Forty feet away, a big-bellied cow stood guard over her newborn. The animal shook her head in warning.

"Ash!" Charlie skidded to a halt in the straw. "That c-cow— She tried to ch-chase me."

"What were you doing over there, Charlie?" Ash swallowed hard. Next to that eight-hundred-pound mother, the kid was the size of a peanut. "Didn't I tell you to stay with an adult when you come into the barns?"

"Yes, but—"

"No buts." Taking the boy's hand, Ash limped to the half door where the collies waited. Opening the gate, he said, "I want you to go back to the house and think about what could have happened because you didn't listen."

Charlie's eyes blurred. "I didn't mean to," he whispered. "I just wanted to pet the—the c-calf, 'cause it's s-so cute."

"Charlie." Ash lifted the boy's chin. His bottom lip quivered. "They are cute. But not as cute as you and if anything happened—" *Stop right there.* "Go," he said gruffly. "You're not allowed in here again until I say."

The boy ran for the main door.

At Ash's feet, Pedro and Jinx watched the kid disappear. Both dogs turned mournful eyes up at Ash.

Goddammit. He felt as if he'd clipped a butterfly's wings.

Over the past six weeks, Rachel had come to understand the basic operations of a ranch.

She'd been with Ash in the barns and on the range, listened to him speak with Tom and Ethan and Daisy. In town, she overheard men and women in the coffee shop, bakery and diner. She read the archives of Shaw Hanson's *Rocky Times* and talked to ranch wives during this year's calving season. And before spring was done with the Flying Bar T, she would witness the branding and castrating of those same calves.

Moreover, she had experienced the rude side of ranching. How, in the blink of an eye, a cow could crush a man's leg.

She did not understand how that same man could terrify her little boy to the point of hiding in a bedroom closet.

As she walked through the muddy yard to the calving barn, Rachel contemplated what she would say. Likely, when it was over, Ash would request she pack her bags.

Then so it would go. She and Charlie had been booted out before. Ash McKee would simply join the ranks of men who found her and Charlie deficient for one reason or another.

Accustomed to the sweetness of hay and cowhide, she stepped inside the barn, her vision adjusting in the dusky light as she cataloged shapes in the corridor: a bucket, a stack of bales, a bridle hanging from a nail.

Ash, in the doorway of his unlit office.

"Rachel. I was expecting you."

Her breath quickened. She strode to where he waited, big, tall, motionless in his domain. "You've hurt Charlie," she said when she stood several feet out of reach.

He pushed back the Stetson.

Determined, she wrapped her arms around her middle. "He admires you, Ash. He's never had a man in his life to admire. And you made him cry." A gnarl in her throat, her child's agony. Still Ash said nothing.

"He's just a little boy," she went on. "He doesn't understand the dangers on a ranch. Heck, for that matter, I haven't grasped the half of it myself." *Please, say something.* "But I'll keep him out of the barns, don't worry." She backed away. She would not beg.

"Did he tell you why I sent him home?"

"Because he wanted to pet a calf."

"Because he left my side."

"To pet the calf," she repeated.

"No. I sent him home because he went among cows who don't know him. Because he walked up to a new mother and she became distrustful." Ash stepped into the hallway. "Do you know what mothers do when they fear for their calves? They lower their heads and charge. What do you think would have happened to Charlie then, Rachel?" He limped toward her, eyes boring into hers. "You saw what can happen to a man. Just like that." He snapped his fingers. "I was thirty feet away from Charlie. I wouldn't have gotten to him in time."

Not with his injured quadriceps, his bruised kidney. Hadn't she witnessed that slow-motion clip down by the creek? How a man in perfect health fell under danger?

For a long moment, their eyes held.

There was no other choice.

"We'll move back to the motel today."

His brows jacked. "Why? All the boy needs to remember are the rules and he'll be fine. Daisy had to learn them, too. It's part of life here."

"Rules have nothing to do with it. Your attitude does."

His head reared back as if she'd slapped him. "My attitude?"

"How you say things to people, Ash. There's a kind way and there's a harsh way. Charlie—" she took a sustaining breath "—is a sensitive child."

"Then teach him how to protect him*self*."

Instead of hanging on to his mother's skirts.

The words hung like a grain bag between them.

Okay, she had reasons to be overprotective of her son—thanks to Bill Brant with his snide comments in Charlie's presence. *Can't the kid tie his own shoes yet? Boy his age should be roughhousing, not playing in his room by himself.* And the winner of them all, *Kid shouldn't be stupid around guns.*

Words withering Charlie's spirit.

Rachel blamed herself. Somehow, someday she needed to repair the relationship between herself and Bill. Encourage him to attend counseling with her, get to the root of her father's cold demeanor, his constant requirement for her to be as good as Grace Brant. Her problems, not Ash's problem.

Looking into his dark eyes, she felt like an island in turbulent water.

Teach him to protect himself. "I'll consider your advice," she said stiffly. "But you might take your own advice, Ash."

"What's that?"

"With Daisy. By teaching her to protect her heart."

"Her heart."

Rachel took a step. "Every time she sees her mother's photos, she hurts. Talk to her. She needs your help."

His eyes burned.

Rachel continued. "She comes to me. For the same reason Charlie comes to you. But I will never turn her away."

His body was deathly still. "My lesson to Charlie could save his life one day. It doesn't compare."

"Depends on how you look at it." She walked out of the barn.

Damn her. Where did she get off, telling him how to behave around his daughter?

Staring at the evening sitcom on TV, Ash scrubbed a hand across his whiskered jaw and peeked over at Daisy snuggled on the couch, at Tom reading the paper, Inez crocheting.

He was doing his best—wasn't he? Burying himself in the ranch, trying to keep them all afloat, trying to make a life of well-being for his family.

Okay, so he didn't have time for humor and good times. Didn't have time for—

Daisy.

Talk to her. Teach her to protect her heart.

He'd let it go too long, this seesawing between him and Daisy. He no longer knew how or where to find the even keel.

You've gotta take the risk, man.

Fine, he'd start with the boy. Favoring his stiff knee, he got up. "I'm going to lie down awhile."

"Need a compress?" Concern in Tom's eyes.

Ash shook his head. "I'll be fine. Stay where you are, Inez," he told the woman, who was setting aside her needle and thread. "Just gonna stretch out the leg. Be back in thirty."

Slowly, he climbed the stairs to the second-floor bedroom. If Rachel slammed the door in his face…

The boy sat cross-legged on his bed, playing with his red Corvette. Ash offered a smile. The boy looked away.

Well, hell. Did he expect the kid to make it easy after he and his mother sat silent as fence posts at the supper table?

"Hey, Charlie." Ash moved carefully into the room.

"Hi."

"Like that car, do you?"

"Yeah."

"Me, too. Wish I had one."

"When I grow up, I'm buying a real one."

Ash held out his hand. "Can I see it?"

Brief hesitation, then the car lay in Ash's hand. "Fine-looking vehicle," he said. "Drove one once."

"You did?" The boy's eyes were big as pancakes.

"Yep. My mom's cousin had one. Drove it up from Texas the summer of my sixteenth birthday."

"Wow."

Ash lowered himself on the bed, restored the car to the boy's palm. "Charlie, have you thought about what I said in the barn this morning?"

The boy spun a tiny mag wheel under his thumb. "Yes."

"Think you'll remember it?"

"Yessir."

Ash breathed easier. "All right. Here's the deal. You come down to the corral in the morning and I'll give you some riding lessons on Areo. But only if you can tell me what the number one rule is."

The boy grinned. "I know it. I'm supposed to—"

Ash held up a hand. Kid was a cute one with those blue eyes round as lamp shades behind his glasses. "Not now. Tomorrow. If you remember it down at the corral, you ride Areo. Deal?"

Charlie's head bobbed.

Ash held out his hand and they shook. Small, sweaty palm against callused skin.

"Am I a cowboy now?" Charlie asked.

Ash ruffled the kid's hair, pushed off the bed. "You're a novice cowboy. How's that?"

"That means beginner."

"Right. Smart boy."

"Sometimes I'm not." He ducked his head.

"Well, that's why you're seven. You still have a lot of growing to do."

"Mom says so, too."

"I'd listen to your mom."

"And you." The boy's smile healed a spot in Ash's heart.

"On this ranch, that's a given. Your mom in her room?"

"Uh-uh. She's right behind you."

Ash struggled around. She leaned in the doorway, hands hidden under her arms, defensive and a little wary, the gesture pure Rachel. He'd done that. Subtly, silently. Over the weeks here at Flying Bar T.

Kissing her had not been clever.

He couldn't stay away.

An itch in his skin, she zinged to the tips of his body's extremities. One look from those blue cat eyes, one word from that expressive mouth and he was as lost as her son with his boots on the wrong feet.

He moved across the room, nostrils flaring at her scent. *For crissakes, Ash. You're like Northwind when the mares are in heat.*

"Um…" He massaged his nape. Would she think he was playing the kid against her? "I told Charlie I'd teach him to ride Areo tomorrow."

"I heard." Her eyes went to her son. "Time for bed, champ."

"Aw, Mom. Can't I stay up till eight-fifteen?"

"Eight-ten, but only if you've got something to read."

"Daisy's reading me *Watership Down*." His blue eyes widened. "Hey, maybe Ash can read with me."

"Can't tonight, Charlie." Ash backed toward the door. His heart thumped in his throat. "I still need to check the barns."

"Aw, pleeease. Just a page. It won't take long."

"I'll call Daisy," Ash offered. He shot Rachel a helpless look.

"No, I want—"

"Son," Rachel interrupted. "Ash can read on another night. When all the calves have been born," she said pointedly. "Now, go brush your teeth and get ready so Daisy doesn't have to wait."

The boy scooted from the bed, bounded past them to the bathroom across the hall. "See you tomorrow, Ash!"

"'Night, Charlie."

When the door clicked closed, her eyes softened. "The riding lessons were a nice offer, Ash. You've become his hero."

God help him. "People should be their own heroes."

"Another Ash rule?" Humor jeweled her eyes. Together they stood in the doorway, inches apart. The humor dissipated and tenderness pulled at his bruised and lonely heart. Brave-of-heart Rachel. Saving him from mud-swamped creeks and injured cows. Riding Areo to inspect fences…

Losing treasures in fires.

Soothing old men in smashed cars.

Massaging prolapsed heifers.

Battling snowstorms for her son.

Helping Pops purge Nam.

Helping Daisy find Susie.

He was headed for a truckload of trouble.

Charlie, brushing his teeth six feet away behind a bathroom door, was a sanity Ash could deal with. Rachel made him wild and tender and crazy.

For the first time in his life, fear marked his soul. He did not want Rachel seeing him the way Susie had.

The afternoon was warmer than usual for March.

Tom sat out on the porch with Inez. She'd gathered a blue afghan around his stumps to ward off the chill while he watched Ash teach Rachel's child how to ride. Areo, Tom knew, was a good pony, gentle, kind and fat as a drum. The tyke's legs were doing the splits—like the grin on his face.

Rachel, vigilant for her son, had her arms hooked over the top of the fence. Tom should've told her not to worry. Ash was nuts about kids and would die before he'd let anything hurt them physically. Emotionally, well, he had some work to do there. One look at Daisy and Tom knew how much it bothered her that Ash avoided speaking Susie's name.

Maybe Inez was right, believing Rachel was bringing Ash around. Maybe there was hope. Hell, maybe there was hope for *him.*

Take this morning. He and Rachel had had another chat. Tom called them chats because "interview" alluded to her profession and considering what their family had endured at the whim of journalists, he'd rather think of their get-togethers as chats.

Besides, he discovered Rachel was easy to talk with. 'Course, that might be because Daisy was their buffer through this writing-researching project.

Good for her, he thought, and recalled his granddaughter's avidity to work with Rachel. Whether Ash liked it or not, Daisy deserved her dreams.

The breeze drifted Rachel's words toward the house. "Way to go, Charlie. You're riding high now." Encouraging words.

From the little she revealed during their conversations, Tom sensed she wanted to emulate her mother in order to please her daddy. Not a good thing.

Children needed to be their own people. They shouldn't have to bribe their parents—or *anyone*—for love.

He'd told her that today. Told her about bribing Tina to stay with him, after Nam. How he'd offered to build her a house here on the ranch, would've given her anything she wanted, if she'd just stayed.

He'd been that desperate.

Having three mangled limbs did that to a man.

Tears fogged Rachel's eyes when he'd told her. "You won the Purple Heart," she'd said. "Twice. I can't imagine that kind of courage."

Thing was, courage hadn't made him loveable. It had made him angry. Furious. Enraged.

And, here was another truth. He would exchange those goddamn metal trinkets any day if it gave him back just one leg.

Recon missions weren't heroic. Deep in the jungle he'd been exhausted to the bone, sweat in his eyes, mosquitoes big as birds, dirt between his teeth. And the enemy so close he had heard their lungs exhale air and their hearts tattoo their ribs.

Recon was seeing the whites of the enemy's eyes as his platoon lunged forward, AK-47s and M16s blasting. Rushing down trails hollowed out beneath their feet.

Recon had been tunnels filled with VC stabbing good American soldiers trapped to their armpits, unable to move. Blowing flesh and bone God-knew-where.

Not heroic. Just doing a duty. Doing what they thought right, what they believed helped the folks back home.

He told her that, too, today.

"Don't think so much." Inez set her hand over his, warming his old flesh.

"I'm not."

She smiled. She knew him well. As well as Laura had once.

"Got an appointment with Jarvis Torquil tomorrow," he said. "Changing the ranch deed over to Ash."

Inez squeezed his hand. "Good for you. Ash will be pleased."

"Won't be telling him for a little while yet."

"Take your time. It'll be on paper."

That it would. Finally, Tom could go to his grave at ease. Letting go felt like the warm spring winds on his cool flesh.

He'd hung on too long to this ranch, trying to assuage his war wounds with the land, trying to fill holes in his soul. Wasn't land that filled holes. It was love.

Down by the corral, March whipped Rachel's hair around her face as she continued to encourage her boy, a good mother, intriguing Ash.

Tom watched his son glance over at the woman, again and again. Yes, she *was* different.

Not at all what anyone expected.

He wondered if Ash understood the meaning of that.

"Mom, I'm gonna be a rancher like Ash when I grow up." Cheeks rosy, Charlie rushed into the kitchen from the mudroom.

Rachel caught sight of the man in question as he closed the door behind her son and wandered over to where she stirred a rich beef and vegetable stew in a big slow-cooker on the stove. A little ping hit her belly. Such intense eyes.

"What happened to being a fireman?" she asked Charlie. After the fire, her boy had been on a mission to become one of America's heroes.

"Can't ride horses if I'm a fireman. Ash says you need to know how to ride horses to be a rancher and I'm getting real good. Right, Ash?"

"Right, buddy."

Charlie hopped onto the stool beside the desk phone and spun in quarter circles. "See? I told you."

His enthusiasm gladdened her heart. "Are you listening carefully to Ash's instructions?"

"Yep. Have to 'cause the rules are very important."

Her gaze took in Ash. Arms folded, he'd stopped to park his fanny against the counter. "That's good, Charlie," she said. "Just remember to do the same when you're at school."

Sullenness. "That's different."

"How so?" In her peripheral vision, Ash unfolded his arms and straightened.

Charlie spun faster. "School doesn't teach about ranching."

"There are still instructions you need to listen to, son."

"But not like here. These rules are easy and fun."

"No, champ," she said. "They're not. They're hard and you better know them with your eyes closed if you want to be as good a rancher as Ash. But," she added, "it also means you need an education. So listen carefully in class when the teacher is talking."

Charlie looked at the man he adored. "What do you say, Ash?"

"Your mother's right."

"But—"

"Get an education, Charlie. Go to college. Then you won't be shoveling— Do as your mom says. Listen in class." He pooched his lips at the stew pot. "Where's Inez?"

"Giving your father a massage. His hip is bothering him."

"That why you're cooking?"

"I offered because I thought she could use a little help." To Charlie, she said, "Go wash up, puppy." When her son scrambled off, she offered Ash a smile. "Cooking is the least I could do after what you've done for my son."

"Haven't done anything he wouldn't learn in time." He stepped closer, sniffed the steam trailing from the slow-cooker.

"Smells like heaven." His voice softened. "Trying to win my heart by way of my stomach, Rach?"

He stood close enough to lean against. To kiss.

If cooking is what it takes.

The thought sprang out of nowhere. He was a one-woman man and she was not that woman. The photos around the house, the unspoken decree about a certain name chained his heart.

"You're blushing." His voice rumbled softly near her ear.

"It's the heat." *Wrong description, Rachel.* "From the stove," she clarified.

A slow, slanted smile. "If you say so."

I'm more than sex, Ash. But she let him kiss her anyway. A soft lingering of lips, a hint of tongue. Fingers tracing breasts. And she knew right then standing there in the kitchen, that she would welcome his desire always.

Whether or not his wife watched from her multiple frames.

Ash knew he'd sidetracked Rachel with that kiss at the stove. Hell, *he* had been sidetracked.

Looking at her across the table, he could taste her flavor again. Tangier than the stew she brewed, sweeter than the apple crumble she'd pulled from the oven ten minutes ago.

Oh, yeah. She understood cooking. And how to please a man with her mouth—if her kisses were cues.

He wondered about her relationship with Charlie's father. Had she pleased *him* with her mouth? Evidently. The kid wouldn't be here otherwise.

What's gotten into you, Ash, for Pete's sake? Rachel's exes are not your business.

Reaching for his coffee, he cursed himself for the envy rolling in his gut. And it was envy. The thought of her touching another man, kissing another man? *Making love* to another man?

Yet, she would. One day she'd go down that road with her boy, find another town, another paper, meet another man.

And Ash would let her go—because Charlie believed school wasn't as important as running a ranch. Ash could not be that kind of hero. The uneducated kind.

He kept his fingers from curling, clinching.

If you want to be as good a rancher as Ash...you need an education. If she only knew. She, who would see him as Susie had when they fought over Daisy's reading material years ago. *You can't read.*

God almighty. Had he known she harbored those thoughts

over the years... He would *not* take that risk with a woman again. Nor would he sleep with one he didn't love.

He nearly shot out of his chair. *Jeez-Louise.*

Where the hell had *that* come from? He didn't love Rachel. No, he did not.

He liked her, thought she was pretty, enjoyed her company, liked her eyes, her kisses, her scent.

The fact she had him endlessly aroused had nothing to do with love. Nothing. Just normal male reaction to an alluring woman. That was all. *All.*

"Dad."

He dug into his wedge of apple crumble.

"Da-ad."

"Huh?" Ash brought up his head. Damn, he'd been so lost in Rachel he hadn't heard Daisy though she sat on his right, beside Inez. "Sorry. What did you say?"

A giggle. "Sheesh. Talk about being totally out of it. I said if your leg still hurts, I have someone to take your place at the dance Friday."

"Dance?"

A gusty sigh. "The St. Patrick's dance you promised to chaperone, remember?"

"Oh, right." He set down his fork, cleared his throat. With his injured leg and trying to find another hand to help in the barns, the dance had been all but forgotten. "I'll be fine. What time does it start?"

"Doors open at six. You and Rachel need to be there by seven."

At the other end of the table, Tom spoke. "Might as well go together." When Ash glared across the food, the old man added quickly, "Save some gas."

"Um..." Daisy hesitated. "Can I go with Beau?"

Beau, Meggie's son, had obtained his driver's license last summer. From what Ash had seen, the kid was a careful driver.

"Anyone else going along?" he asked. Teen passengers made a difference in the way drivers behaved.

Daisy studied her plate. "Jay Danner. He's on the student committee for the dance."

"Good kid." Tom again.

Ash stared down the length of the table. *I can handle my daughter, old man.* "All right. You can go with Beau and Jay."

"Can I go, too, Mom?" Charlie whispered to Rachel.

"What about your sleepover at Tyler's?" She caught Ash's gaze briefly. "He'll be disappointed if you don't go."

"Oh, yeah, I forgot." Charlie nodded happily and Rachel pushed his glasses up his nose.

Ash focused on his dessert.

Rachel, alone Friday night.

Alone in the cottage she planned to move back into once Ethan and the carpenters Ash hired last week completed the reconstruction of the kitchen this week.

He didn't know whether to sing or curse his luck.

Chapter Twelve

At her desk in the newsroom, Rachel's stomach fluttered. For the past four days with Ash instructing Charlie on riding, nerves ate into her sleep and appetite.

Her son trotted after the man at every chance. In and out of the barns, around the corrals, a small, relentless shadow on the heels of his hero.

She released a sigh. *Don't put all your hopes in one basket, little one.* Truth be known, she was still learning that lesson.

She thought of the bundle of pages sitting on her night table. Nearly two hundred and forty. Enough for a book, if she chose, if *American Pie* reneged, if Tom reneged.

The more she talked with the old man, the more the thought of a book niggled. Writing books could mean living in one location, any location. A place that offered community, friends, a sense of belonging. A place with a house, a yard for Charlie and his buddies, a garden. She would like to learn how to grow flowers and vegetables, to can and pickle. She would like to live in a place where people asked "how are you?" in the post office and meant it. Where you walked home from work or school without fear.

A place like Sweet Creek.

She would not think of Ash, of what making her home in *his* town could mean for her and Charlie.

Don't be that big a fool, Rachel.

She concentrated on the computer's screen, on the article she'd written about Montana's independent ranchers. Families struggling to maintain their heritage, their land, their bread and butter. The story Ash had inadvertently given her in January.

She had mailed the piece to *The Rancher,* a small weekly magazine in Billings devoted to the state's rural communities. "Riding Into The Sunset" would see print next week.

What would Ash say when he read her article? And he would. The magazine arrived each Monday in the Flying Bar T's roadside mailbox.

Oh, yes. She was learning about options.

The question was, could she teach her son that lesson in lieu of Ash McKee?

Friday at six-thirty, Ash drove into Sweet Creek with Rachel sitting two feet away on the truck's bench—smelling of summer and looking like a river lily.

He knew about river lilies; his mother had planted a cluster on the east side of the house, next to the mudroom stoop, and each haying season the plant produced a host of red blooms. Tall, slim, exotic.

Like Rachel.

He looked across the cab. Over the past six weeks, her hair had grown and now swung an inch below her slender jaw. He thought about sliding his fingers up that line of bone, into her hair—tonight. He thought about a lot of things concerning Rachel tonight. When Charlie slept at Darby's house.

The boy sat between them, straining to see out the window.

Rachel looked over her son's head at Ash and he wanted to pull the truck over and kiss her. And kiss her.

Had they been alone...

He concentrated on the path of his headlights, on getting to town, to the school gym where he could escape the truck and her.

Right. As if he could forget how she looked ten minutes ago, coming down the stairs in those tailored black slacks, that silky green blouse under a classy suede jacket.

He felt gauche in his new jeans and pearl-buttoned tan-and-black shirt. And his boots. Hell, he'd spent two hours last night buffing and polishing and still age marked the leather.

Doesn't matter what you do, fool. She's out of your league.

Question was, did he want to be *in* her league? Oh, yeah, he wanted, all right. He wanted *her.* In his bed.

His belly jumped just looking at her.

His skin tightened with her scent.

Means nothing if you're not willing to take the whole package. Including the fact she could read and write rings around him.

Mind on a seesaw, Ash pulled in front of Darby's house. He waited in the truck while Rachel walked Charlie to the front door. He told himself he needed to save his knee before it suffered through five hours of walking halls, the school yard and boys' washrooms. Waiting in the truck had nothing to do with being seen with Rachel. Like a boyfriend.

Beneath the porch light, he watched her hug her boy, kiss his hair, fix his knapsack. Then Tyler yanked him inside and Rachel said goodbye to Darby.

A minute later, she was back in the cab, intent on the house fading into the night as Ash drove down the street. "I've never left him overnight before," she said.

"He'll be okay."

"He probably won't even miss me." Her voice wavered.

Adult growing pains. He recognized them from his bouts with Daisy. Reaching across the seat, he took her hand.

"You're a good mother. But the boy needs a little independence."

Her cold fingers flexed around his. "I suppose so."

Suddenly, waiting seemed endless. He pulled into a dark, deserted alley, cut the engine.

"C'mere." He tugged her across the seat.

Her lips were warm, soft, giving. He'd missed her, missed this with her. He lifted his head, stared into those blue cat eyes that drove him crazy. He wanted to lie in the depths of her soul.

"Ash," she whispered.

"Rachel," he whispered in return. And in spite of all his logic about types and leagues, he smiled.

She said, "This has to stop." Yet, she remained in his arms.

"I agree." He pretended to misunderstand. "We won't get to the dance if we don't." He kissed her again, stroking his tongue along hers, wanting to stroke her elsewhere. Deeper.

When he was done, she pushed back to her side of the truck. "I mean us. Charlie's getting too attached to you. It'll break his heart when we relocate to Virginia come summer."

Such sober eyes, voicing a truth he knew. *Knew.* She was a woman on the move wherever a story took her. An educated woman, accustomed to city ways. She was not of the land that cultivated him, a land with snowstorms and below-zero temperatures, blackflies and mosquitoes, dust and mud and bawling cows.

He could not offer her fine sweaters and fancy boots and chic hair salons.

He could not give her stories.

So, what the hell was he doing falling for her?

It's not like that.

Right. He cranked the ignition. "Let's not disappoint Daisy." Without another look or word to the woman beside him, he drove to the high school.

Kids were arriving by the carload as Rachel hopped from the truck the moment Ash parked in the Sweet Creek High School lot.

Spotting Daisy among a group near the gym, she waved. The girl waved back and trotted over in her black miniskirt and pink knit top.

"Hey, Dad, Rachel. This is so cool you guys could come." Her green eyes sparked. "Did you bring the camera?"

"Have it right here." Rachel patted the rose-colored denim bag looped over her shoulder.

"Great. I told everyone you'd be taking pictures for the paper, so we need, like, a ton."

"I'll take as many as I can, Daisy, but it all depends how much space Mr. Hanson gives the event in the paper."

The girl's smile dimmed. "I know. But the last dance barely paid for the music. This one needs to at least break even on everything or the teachers won't let us have another."

Ash rounded the truck's hood and stopped beside Rachel. "Want me to have a chat with Shaw?"

Daisy's mouth dropped. "No, please do not, Dad." Her gaze flicked between them. "That would *so* not be cool." The girl shot a look toward the gym where someone called her name. "Look, I have to run. See y'all later." She began jogging backward. "And, Dad? Don't forget to dance with Rachel." Before rushing away, she winked. "He does a great two-step."

When the teenager disappeared among her friends, Rachel and Ash started toward the school doors. "Is that right?" she teased. "You can dance?"

"I've been known to cut the rug a time or two."

She was intrigued. Big, serious Ash, light on his feet on the dance floor. Who had taught him? His mother? Inez?

"I didn't learn," she murmured, glad for the darkness hiding her abashed cheeks.

"Why not?"

She studied the ground. "I was the school wallflower."

"Huh. Somehow I can't picture it."

That brought up her head. "Why? Because you know me as brash Ms. Brant, out to get her story no matter the cost?"

"Not at all. I was thinking more along the lines of damn, but she's a looker. A guy would have to be stupid not to ask her to the floor."

Her breath caught. Before she could utter a response, they entered the school. Kids, teachers and parents—most wearing a splash of green in honor of St. Pat's—crowded the foyer and wove in and out of the gym doors. Excitement bounced from the walls. Teenagers took personal note of each other and teachers took note of those entering the main doors.

All eyed Rachel.

Ash leaned in close. "Look around. They're entranced by you. Your wallflower days are over."

"Pure curiosity," she shot back. "I'm the newcomer on the block."

"Maybe, but check out the men. There isn't one who won't want a dance."

His tone of jealousy played a refrain in her head and she let the corners of her mouth lift.

They entered the gym. Shamrocks, pots of gold coins and green top hats decorated the walls. Leprechauns and charm bags dangled from the ceiling and basketball hoops. On the stage, a deejay was at his station sorting through his music.

When Ash stopped to talk with a couple Rachel didn't know,

she walked toward a cluster of kids near the stage and readied her Canon. The teens waved and goofed around for the shots and, suddenly, she was caught in the exhilaration of the night.

For two hours she and Ash lost sight of each other. It wasn't until she stood in the open rear doors taking in the cooling air that she saw him again, walking out of the crowd of jiggling adolescents.

He looked fatigued, his limp more pronounced than when they arrived. Unsure of what to say, he stood for a moment glancing around before their eyes clung.

How are you?

Great. You?

He said, "Caught two boys smoking in the washroom. How's it going with you?"

"Nothing except a few groping couples outside. And, no," she added when his gaze flashed to the door and his Adam's apple shifted, "Daisy wasn't among them."

"Of course she wasn't."

Rachel smiled. "Ash, you wear your heart on your sleeve around her."

"Huh." A nod at her camera. "Get lots of pictures?"

"Dozens."

"Kids will be pleased."

"How's your knee?"

"It'll hold." He reviewed the packed floor. "Want to dance?"

"Ash, I told you. I don't know how."

"You know how to sway, don't you?"

Swaying she could handle. Swaying with him… That was another account.

"Come on," he said, taking her hand and leading her to the edge of the crowd. "It's a slow one. Just listen to the beat."

The beat. All she heard was her heart careening in her ears.

Their bodies aligned, a perfect fit. Under her suede jacket, his hand jetted heat into her spine. Tucking her left hand against his chest, he bent his head beside hers, his breath whispering like dandelion down along her neck.

If she turned her head two inches their mouths would tangle. His body was as rugged and strong as his land and she loved him, but in three months she would be leaving Sweet Creek for what she hoped would be permanency in Virginia. The series would be done. In three months Ash would be another part of her history and she—

"When do I pay you to play on the job, Ms. Brant?"

She stumbled back. "Shaw—hi!" She swiped at her bangs, nervous female that she was. "You're attending the dance."

Her newsman boss smirked. "When my reporters volunteer for a job, I want to see what the attraction is."

Disregarding the way his beady eyes darted between her and Ash, she said, "I've taken about eighty photos—"

Ash cut in. "I asked the lady to dance, Hanson. If that's a problem, take it up with me."

"No, no." The man held up a benevolent hand. "If she's done her job, she's free to dance."

Beside Rachel, Ash's body tensed. "I'd say she's free to dance *any* time."

"Your opinion." Dismissing Ash, Hanson spoke to Rachel, "By the way, heard you're writing another story." This time, a glance at Ash. "Interviewing Tom McKee, are you?"

"It's freelance. For an out-of-state magazine," she added, and kept her tone even. "It won't interfere with my job on the *Rocky Times*."

"Good to know. People around here might take offense, you making heroes out of vets from a war everyone protested."

Rachel stared at the man. *Did you not pay attention in history class?* "If you recall, Shaw, in the sixties they had no choice. Conscription was still in effect."

"Humph. Coulda gone underground."

Was the jerk serious? Breathing slowly, carefully, she said, "Thousands of those men gave their lives for our nation. Some gave up their soul. You might take care with a statement like that." Thinking of Tom, she momentarily observed the crowd—teenagers, teachers, parents—moving to the music. Several quick-stepped swing-country. "There's a soldier in nearly every family's history."

Hanson's smile was not amiable. "Maybe. But I suggest *you* don't write yourself out of a job. Have a nice night."

When Hanson vanished into the crowd, she muttered, "I'd leave his paper in a heartbeat and go elsewhere if I could."

Ash's gaze cut to her. "But you still have Tom's story to finish."

"Yes."

He studied her. "Has Tom read any of it?"

"Not yet. Daisy has. She's writing part of it herself. She's a good writer, Ash. I'm recommending that *American Pie* allow her words to stand."

She saw the shift before he spoke. "Daisy's not a journalist. Don't try to make her into one."

"I wouldn't dream of it. She'll be who she is all on her own. Care to dance?"

The song's tempo shifted to wriggling bodies spaced a foot or more apart. "Thought you were afraid of dancing." But a corner of his mouth worked.

She reached for his hand. "Not afraid, just unsure. There's a difference."

When Ash pulled the truck up to the main house at ten-thirty that night, Rachel made a decision.

"Do you have a minute?" she asked. Then, before he could respond, she slipped from the cab and shut the door.

Guided by the porch light, she walked around to her house.

With the completion of the restored kitchen and ceiling, she and Charlie had moved back in yesterday.

Ash's footfalls sounded quietly behind her. Her imagination took flight. He'd come in for a nightcap, a chat, maybe more—if she asked, which she wouldn't.

She sighed. She was leaving Sweet Creek the moment Charlie finished second grade. Tom's story would be complete and she'd have no reason to stay. After Ash's comments tonight about Daisy, Rachel realized he would never understand her work.

From her purse, she withdrew the key. Likely to Ash a key seemed absurd in a community where people trusted one another, but she'd been raised in a city, a latchkey kid. Another difference, another abyss they needed to close before understanding came full circle.

Leaving the door open with him standing on the stoop, she hurried to the stack of pages on the coffee table.

"Here," she said, returning to him, offering the manuscript that one day would run as a series in *American Pie*.

He stared down at the bundle she cradled. "What's this?"

"Stories of the Vietnam vets I've interviewed. The yellow tab marks Tom's part. Even though his portion isn't finished I want you to read it along with the rest."

His eyes narrowed. "Why?"

"Because it's the only way I can show you I'm not a bad person, Ash." In the soft glow of the porch light, she saw his head jerk. A sucker punch. *I'm sorry.* She shoved the manuscript forward. "Take it."

He stepped back and almost lost his balance off the stoop. "No, that's okay. I trust Daisy."

Something in Rachel shrank. Right. Trust. Good for one, but not the other. Why had she expected more from him?

She bit back the sting in her eyes. "I had a lovely time tonight, Ash. The best in a long, long while. Daisy spoke the truth—you are a great dancer. Please, if you won't read this, give it to Tom or Inez. Please."

His throat bobbed twice as he gazed at the pages. When he still refused to take them, she laid the bundle gently on the stoop, next to his buffed left boot. Then she smiled.

"Good night."

And she closed the door.

When he'd entered the house with Rachel's pages fifteen minutes ago, only the stove light burned. He didn't expect Daisy for another half hour. Heading the student recreational committee, she also directed the cleanup crew.

Across from where he sat at the table, the package taunted. Rachel's words—and Daisy's.

God, how he wanted to read them, *wished* for some miracle to erase his handicap, give him a glimpse into their world. Into the world Daisy cherished, but never offered to share because of his self-imposed restrictions, his shame.

His hand crept forward. His fingers touched the smooth surface of the top sheet. Rotating the manuscript around, he contemplated the big, bold print midpage. The title.

What did it say?

His body chilled, sweated.

The first word...

Lgcyofte.

No... *Remember what the instructor in Billings said. One letter at a time.*

He set his index finger over the first letter, moved slowly to the right. *L.*

The next letter produced an *E.* Then a *G. LEG.*

Leg? Why had she begun with a limb Pops lost? Couldn't be right.

He moved his finger again. *R.*

Not *R*. He stared hard. Sweat beaded his lip. *Come on, Ash. You can do this. It's just a flippin' title. Can't be that difficult.*

Covering the *G* with his other index finger and enclosing the letter, he finally saw it: *A*. Not an *R* but an *A*. *LEGA.*

Lega... Now a *C*... Yes. The *k* sound or the *s*? *Y*... Leg-a-ky? No. Leg-a-sy. *Legacy.* He got it.

Groaning relief, he looked at the next letter. *O*... *F*... *T*... *H*.... *Too fast. Back up.* O. F. *Of.*

Legacy of. THE. Good old THE. Easy as pie THE. *Legacy of the. Don't lose your spot.* H. E. A. R. T. *Legacy of the hurt?*

Goddammit. He'd read it wrong. Again. *Again.*

Stupid brainless dummy. Can't read, can't read, can't read.

In and out of his mind, childhood voices fluttered, moths around a pole lamp. A kettle drum pounded in his chest.

One more time—

The front door opened.

Daisy.

A wash of guilt swept through Ash. Caught up in deciphering Rachel's title, he'd forgotten his daughter. He turned to the sound of her tiptoeing into the kitchen.

"Hey, Dad," she whispered.

"Hey, pint," he whispered back. "Have a good time tonight?"

From the fridge, she grabbed a bottle of water. "Yeah. I think we made some money this time. Most everybody showed up. Thank God. Now our dances won't be canceled." She gave him a sideways look. "You and Rachel seemed to have a nice time."

"We did." A noncommittal response.

"Run into any problems?"

"Just one. Mike McLeod's boy brought some beer. I asked him to leave. He did."

She grinned. "I'll just bet."

Ash shrugged. "Guess he figured tangling with an old cowboy like me wasn't worth the trouble."

"An old cowboy. Dad, you're, like, six-foot-four of range muscle. Mike may be a linebacker for our school team, but he's not that tough."

"I'm not looking to strong-arm anyone, Daiz."

"Humph." She walked to the table. "Whacha got there?"

"Rachel's Vietnam series."

She read, "'Legacy of the Heart: a Tale of Nam.'"

Heart, not hurt. A second's worth of reading that had taken him ten minutes of fumbling and bumbling. And Daisy had read it upside down.

Her eyes were puzzled. "Why'd she give it to you?"

"I'm supposed to go over it."

"Oh."

He pushed the manuscript across the table. "Read it. Make sure it's what she claims."

"And what's that?"

Her tone brought up his head. "Stories about the war. I want you to look for any discrepancies, things that don't make sense. Things that sound sensational." He didn't like the mulish expression crossing his daughter's face. Rubbing a hand around his neck, he said, "You know what I'm talking about, Daiz."

"No, actually, I don't. Rachel's been living on the ranch six weeks, and in our house for a week. She helped you from that creek. I can't believe you still think she's out to get our family."

"Hush your voice, girl. Grandpa and Inez are sleeping."

Standing in the soft glow of the stove light, her jaw clenching, his daughter resembled a small bantam hen defending her chicks. "Dad, do you trust me?"

He didn't hesitate. "With my life."

"So if I was a reporter one day, you'd trust my words."

Where was she going with this? "You're my daughter."

"Aside from that. *Would* you trust my words?"

"Of course. You don't tell lies."

She sat opposite him. "Not intentionally."

He frowned. "What are you getting at, Daiz?"

"You just said you trusted me, trusted what I'd write. Well, I do write, Daddy. I wrote half of Grandpa's story." She paused. "And I'm writing a weekly column about our school for the *Rocky Times*. The first one was published six weeks ago. I'll be writing another about the dance tonight to match Rachel's photos. I'm going to be a journalist."

His breath rasped from his lungs. "She knew this?"

"Yes. And so do Grandpa and Inez."

He sat flummoxed. Hurt dug like a thorn in his gut. Everyone had known but him. Ash McKee, ever the last to know, dammit.

"I wanted to tell you," she hurried on. "But you were so—so *stubborn*. And distrustful. Maybe it's your dyslexia that makes you that way. I can't imagine how I'd feel if I couldn't read."

Tears stood in her eyes. "Daddy, please. Try to understand. I love the ranch. I love everything you do, but this won't be my home forever. I want a career in media." She pushed back her bangs. "Who knows? I may hate it, but at least give me the chance to find out."

He stared at the pages. *My daughter's words.*

She went on. "Rachel's taught me a million things. How to see things in my head, how to feel them with my heart. How to not just regurgitate facts."

He wanted to get up and pace. He couldn't move. "Does Rachel know about my…"

"Your reading? No. I never told her. She thinks you don't know it's me writing the column because I don't have a byline."

The writer's name. "She should've told me about this," he grumbled.

"I made her swear not to. She didn't like it, said it wasn't honest. She wanted me to go to you and explain. But I couldn't. I know what you think of reporters. They hurt Grandpa years ago. They sent you to jail for three days after Mom died. They *killed* Mom." A shaky breath. "But I'm not those journalists. Rachel isn't those journalists. We're good people, Daddy. Good people who happen to like writing. It has nothing to do with you and it isn't a reflection on your dyslexia. It's time you realized that."

On a long sigh, she snatched up the pages, rose. "I'll see you in the morning."

Five seconds later, silence surrounded him with its brick walls.

Chapter Thirteen

He remained seated for a long time envisioning Daisy's eyes, full of hurt and regret and sorrow. Maiming his heart.

He'd seen the same expression on Rachel's face. *"I trust Daisy."*

What he'd really meant was, *I trust Daisy's writing.*

Rachel had comprehended *his* words well.

He checked his wristwatch: 11:09. *Not too late to apologize, Ash.* If she'd gone to bed, he would phone over. He could not crawl under his own covers knowing he'd hurt her, knowing she might be sleepless with his cruelty.

Slowly, he rose from the chair. His knee stung worse than a grease burn.

At the back door, he tugged on the boots he had danced in. Old, beat-up boots with a polished facade. The way he felt.

Outside, a wind plucked at his hair, nipped through his shirt. Shoving his fingers into his jeans' pockets, he headed for the cottage. The main floor windows were dark. A faint cast—a night-light?—beckoned through the upstairs window where the shades stayed open. The boy's room.

Charlie, sleeping at Darby's tonight.

Ash almost turned around—except he stood on her stoop. And then, behind the curtains, the bottom windows reflected light. She had come down to the main level.

Had she heard him?

He knocked softly, waited.

The door opened. She stood in a blue ankle-length robe, her feet bare, toes pink tipped. She had long, slim feet. Dancer's feet. Except she couldn't dance. Or so she thought.

"May I come in?" he asked.

"It's after eleven, Ash."

"I know, but I need to say something."

"Can't it wait?"

"No."

She let him inside. On the kitchen counter, the kettle steamed, then clicked off.

"I'm making some tea. Would you like a cup?" She appeared tired, drained. Looking at her bloodshot eyes, he wondered if she'd been crying. She closed the door, went into the kitchen.

He followed. "Rachel. I'm sorry."

She stood half-turned in profile. "For what?"

"For not trusting you."

With my life, he'd told Daisy. Six days ago, he'd put that life in Rachel's hands. Her *trusting* hands.

"Don't worry about it," she said now, measuring leaves into a mesh tea holder before dropping it into a two-mug teapot.

Reaching, he took her hands away from their task, cupped them with his own. Cold hands, warm heart. Chafing her fingers between his palms, he said, "You're a good writer. An honest writer."

"You read the work?"

"Part of it." Okay, not even half a title, but reading wasn't what he'd come about. "Daisy's got it at the moment." A truth. "She told me about her column and—and her dreams of being a journalist. How you've helped her. We haven't talked much, Daiz and I, these past years."

She attempted to tug from his hold. "Ash…"

He hung on. "It's okay. We're okay."

"Are we? I know about Marty," she whispered. "That he crashed into your wife's car." Her eyes searched his.

"It wasn't just Marty." And finally his heart spilled.

About Tom and the ASPCA.

About how they had suspected Shaw Hanson Senior. And how Shaw Junior had wanted Susie for years, though she chose Ash.

He talked about the grief he felt when Susie died, about punching Marty in the mouth and finding himself in the town jail for seventy-plus hours.

He talked for twenty minutes. And when he was done, his throat hurt and tears rode her eyelashes.

"Don't cry," he whispered as one rolled down her cheek. "It all happened a long time ago."

Unable to stand her pain, he cupped her face and kissed her mouth. "Rachel." *Rachel. Rachel. Rachel.*

His palms found her under the robe.

Warm, silken skin.

Curves that surprised him.

She was merlot dizzying his head, a country song strumming on his heart.

"Stay, Ash. Stay the night."

Her whispered request cut off his air and he looked down at her, dying in her blue, blue eyes. The last time had been with…

A long, long time ago.

He kissed her. Kissed her again. And again.

Openmouthed hunger, touches in soft places.

The robe dropped and she stood in a pink T-shirt and tiny white panties. Another surprise, considering the season. Through the winter months Susie had slept in head-to-toe flannel.

His hands slipped around her bottom, lifting, slowly fitting, denim to silk, until her legs wrapped his waist and her arms wrapped his head. She bent over him, tugged his bottom lip into her mouth. A spear of heat flared between his legs.

"Easy, honey," he muttered. "Or we're not gonna make it."

Giggles. Drifting in his ear, bubbles against his tongue.

He headed for the stairs, drunk on summer scent, satin hair, butter-soft flesh.

One hand on the wall, she guided him. When they finally found her bed, he lowered them onto the mussed-up covers where she'd been nesting before he arrived on her stoop.

"Ash." Clinging to his neck. "Don't be cautious. I won't break."

"No?"

"No." Her eyes were summer pools, the type he had skinny-dipped in as a randy teen. "I don't want slow this first time."

This first time. Other times would follow. Possibly three tonight, if he counted the condoms in his wallet. Condoms he bought yesterday. In hope.

Her hand slid to his crotch and hope was a thing of the past. Within seconds, they stripped him of boots and clothes. Her T-shirt landed on the chair by the fireplace, the panties somewhere near the door.

"Rachel." He was heavy, ready. He took her face between his palms, looked into her cat eyes. He ached to tell her he had never wanted like this. "Rach."

"Come here, cowboy," she whispered. "This is for us."

She opened her arms, her body, and his lonely heart went gladly into the haven she offered.

* * *

Rachel woke by degrees, aware first of warmth, a real warmth she'd never experienced. She snuggled deeper into its cocoon and remembered. Ash. In her bed, spooning with her, wrapping her with his arms as if she were a small, priceless gift.

They lay on the same pillow, he breathing slow and steady against her hair and neck.

Her eyes fluttered open. The room held the night, though the clock on the bedside table read 5:06.

The morning after.

A first.

Floyd had not stayed. In more ways than one.

She cherished the moment, this Ash-moment, tracking the spots their bodies fastened with heat and sweat.

His chest, planed and solid and dusted in black hair that trailed like a kite's string to below his navel before winnowing around his groin.

His left leg, muscular and tough, was clasped between her smooth ones, her feet tucked under his muscled calf. Beneath the pillow, his right arm, keeping them close, inseparable. His left arm around her waist, his hand against her breasts. Gently, she eased that hand upward, ran her tongue over the chapped, work-worn knuckles.

He had told her things last night. Let her glimpse his fears. And like a weed in a high wind, she'd tumbled into a cosmos of love. Another first. She wanted to cry.

"What're you thinking?" His sleep-hoarse voice against her hair.

"You're awake."

"Been for a while."

She lay motionless, wishing for another hour, a day, a year. Eternity.

Behind her, his groin twitched, strengthened. She smiled.

There would be a fourth time, if she counted mouths and tongues.

"Rach?"

"Yes?"

Silence. As if he were contemplating his next sentence, his next word. She turned her head, and he moved, caught her lips in a nomadic kiss. When he finished, when he had prepared himself, he said, "I don't sleep around. Just so you know."

A butterfly touched her stomach. "Ditto."

"This is my first time since—"

Her fingers stayed the words. "I know."

So fierce, his eyes. "You?"

"Four years ago. He cheated."

He set his forehead to hers. "I..."

She whispered it for him. "Love you."

"Rachel."

"Kiss me again, Ash." One last time before life interfered.

He did, then pressed into her from behind, meshing their bodies, melding their hearts.

On the porch, with the sun's rays seeping around his achy bones, Tom watched Charlie come around the house, humming a tuneless melody, dragging a stick through the March mud and spots of leftover snow.

Lost in daydreams, Tom thought, as the boy stopped again to draw some sort of trance imagery into the wet earth.

Jinx trailed his heels. Three years older than Pedro, the female collie had become Charlie's guardian.

Tom knew the boy's destination this Sunday morning. Ash was in the barns. Ash, whom the boy had adopted as surrogate daddy material.

Tom wondered if Ash recognized the similarities from twenty-five years ago. At Charlie's age, Ash had been Tom's shadow, dogging his wheelchair through the barns, asking everything there was to know about cows and horses, birthing and branding, seeding and harvesting.

Hardest to explain was death: stillborn calves or calves defeated by scours, cows in difficult labor, horses with colic.

Ash hadn't understood the needless suffering of animals, had shouldered it like a backpack for days.

Just as he had shouldered his mother's passing—and still carried Susie's unexpected crash.

An honorable son with strong hands, capable of owning a ranch, of owning the Flying Bar T. *Yes,* Tom thought, it was long past time to give over the ranch and let go of the fear of losing part of his soul again.

He smiled as Charlie tossed the stick before slipping inside the barn with Jinx. Would Ash recognize the full-circle gift the boy held in *his* hands?

Cocking an ear, Ash listened.

There…again. A soft, high keening.

Leaving the heifer penned in the farthest stall, he walked across the expanse of the calving barn. As he closed the distance to the Dutch door leading to the corridor, he identified the voice. Charlie. Muttering through tears.

Suddenly the sound ceased and Ash lost the location.

Where was the boy? Beside him, Pedro looked up. "Go," Ash told the collie.

The animal trotted down the alleyway, past the office, the tack room, left around the corner by the main doors. Ash followed fast as his bum leg allowed. Reaching the hall corner, he saw Pedro trot along the narrow thoroughfare to the horse stables. The adjoining door stood open and Charlie sat, head buried in his knees, in front of Areo's stall.

Beside the boy, Jinx wagged a hello to her comrade.

Charlie lifted teary eyes to Ash.

"What happened, britches?"

"Nuthin'." A backhanded swipe across the nose.

Okay. The boy would come around in his own time. Favoring his thigh with a groan, Ash slid down the wall and sat next to Charlie. Kid shot him a sideways glance. "Are you mad?"

"Mad? Why would I be mad?"

"At me crying."

"If a man's gotta cry, then he does. No shame in that, Charlie."

"My grandpa says guys don't cry. If they do, they're wimps."

Ash would like to meet this grandpa one day, give him a piece of his mind for putting such bull on a kid. On his own flesh and blood, no less.

"Some guys think that way," he said carefully. He looked down at Rachel's son, with Rachel's eyes. "Do you think I'm a wimp?"

"No way!"

"Good. 'Cause I cried. A lot just a few years back."

"You did? Um, when your wife died?"

"Yeah."

"Do you still cry?"

"No."

"Are you sad?"

"For Daisy. She's growing up without her mom."

Behind them, Areo blew dust from his nostrils.

Charlie sniffed, dug a knuckle in his eye. "I got no dad. I mean, I got a dad, but I don't think he likes me."

Ash flinched. The night he spent in Rachel's bed, she had told him about Floyd Stephens, deadbeat dad. She'd told him about Bill Brant, the infamous wimp-hating grandpa. She had trembled over her mother's death.

A night of trading facts among pheromones.

You know damn well it was more than that, Ash.

But damned if he knew where it all would end. The notion had him shifting on the floor.

Charlie hiccuped. "Mom said we're gonna leave soon an' I don't want to leave. I like it here." He stared up at Ash. A tear clung to a bottom lash. In a tiny voice he said, "Can I stay with you even if my mom leaves?"

Ash's gut took a dive. The kid was desperate to have a dad figure. "Ah, britches. It isn't all that simple. Your mom and I... Well, there's a lot of stuff you don't know about."

"Don't you like her? She likes you."

Love you. He heard the whisper again, and his heart hurried. "I like her." *Hell, admit it. You more than like her.*

But how much more? Enough to take a chance? Enough to make a home with her? Make a family with her?

He imagined the place empty. Her bed empty. Her *gone.*

And he knew.

He did not want her leaving. Did not want her gone forever. And letting her go back to Virginia, well, that *would* be the end.

Charlie's lip quivered.

"Come here, boy." Ash lifted him onto his lap; Charlie's thin arms stole around his neck and Ash forgot his worries. He forgot that he hadn't told Rachel of his dyslexia, that Daisy wanted to be a journalist, that Rachel was helping his daughter rediscover her mother. That routinely Tom spilled his guts for a story, yet would not discuss his long-term plans for the ranch with Ash. And now the kid wanted a father figure.

Unresolved issues.

Against Ash's neck, Charlie's face was warm and sticky with tears. He patted the kid's hair. "It'll all work out, boy." Though God only knew how.

"Promise?" came the muffled query.

"With all my heart."

"And hope to die?"

"Or stick a needle in my eye." A small giggle, another loud sniff. "Here." Ash dug in his hip pocket. He handed Charlie a tissue. "Wipe your eyes and blow your snozz."

Charlie gave him a shy smile. "You don't really need to stick a needle in your eye."

Ash ruffled the boy's hair, and knew then that whatever happened between him and Rachel, he'd do his damnedest to somehow keep connected to her son.

Rachel was not having a good day.

This morning, she put her foot down on Charlie's nagging about living on the ranch forever, telling him they *would* be moving back east in July, and that was that. Angry, he'd slammed out of the house, yelling, "I hate you."

At that moment, she hadn't liked herself much, either. She'd been disappointed. Angry. She wanted Ash to acknowledge what they shared two nights ago. She wanted him to care.

For who? You? For Charlie? Get real, Rachel. You were a distraction he couldn't resist.

That was wrong. He had cared. She saw his secrets, when he'd come into her, when he'd held her as if he could not breathe without her, could not live without her.

She was crazy in love, her heart brimming for him, with him, but the fact remained he hadn't sought her out yesterday. Nor today. Nor had he picked up the phone in the night when the land and houses lay still.

And that was the crux, of course. He would let her leave. He would stand by as she packed, as she said her goodbyes, as she drove from the ranch one last time.

From the porch of the main house, where she sat with Daisy and Tom, she looked across the yard at the buildings and corrals, to the thick-haired horses and cattle, the snow-crowned Rockies nudging the skyline—and a foreign peace settled in her bones.

"We're done for today." Tom's voice. Bringing her back, back to earth before her mind whirled with Ash.

They stood at an impasse, she and Tom. They'd come to the horror of Hells Field.

"Tom," she said kindly. "Can't we get through this?"

In the last session, he had explained the purpose of the recon mission, to discover the hideout of the enemy, feed the information back to the combat base.

Today he had led her through the jungle, the vines. Led her, gasping dank air thick enough to cut, smelling the fecund earth, with sweat-soaked armpits, crotches, spines. Step by step, right to the second his platoon spotted the VC in the trees, spotted the Americans, on their knees, hands behind their heads. Twenty-year-olds bowing to the jungle floor for execution.

Tom shook his head. They would not get anywhere today and his eyes said *not ever.*

"Grandpa." Daisy leaned forward. "Please. This will be the last of it." She took his hand. "If we finish today, it's over."

Tom rubbed his chest. Daisy glanced at Rachel.

She set aside her notebook. "We'll finish another time, Tom. No worries."

Stepping behind his chair, she wheeled the old soldier into the house and gave him up to Inez's capable hands.

Monday morning, before she woke Charlie for school, Rachel wrote a letter to an editor of a New York publishing house, outlining her completed portion of the Vietnam series. *American Pie,* she knew, could fall through. Having all her ducks in a row when the time came and Tom finally disclosed why twelve of nineteen men died at Hells Field allowed her control of the work.

She would drop the letter at Sweet Creek post office during her lunch break.

How would Tom react, knowing his story could be read around the world? And if she received a book offer from a publishing house, would Ash see it as a betrayal of his father? Another sly reporter tactic?

Rachel had yet to see him following his *see you later* kiss as he rolled from her bed at 5:45 Saturday morning.

She needed to outline her plans. *Damage control,* her daddy called it. In this, he was right.

Still the questions—Was it a betrayal? Or not? Would he think it a trick? Or not?—railed at her throughout the day while she wrote two short stories for the Women's Circuit page, then drove to the Half-Diamond ranch to interview Jake Easton's wife, Lisa, about her Native American paintings.

She arrived home exhausted. It wasn't until she fed Charlie and cleaned up the supper dishes that she picked up the phone on the counter, punched her father's number, hoping to *connect.* Just this once when she needed him most.

He answered on the fourth ring. "Bill Brant here."

"Hi, Daddy."

"Rachel."

Not *Hey, daughter.* Or *Hi, honey.* Or an excited, *Rachel!*

She should know better than to hope every single time. "How are you?" she asked.

He blew a breath in her ear. "Got the stomach flu. Been puking my guts out for two days. Not that anyone gives a damn. This apartment is driving me batty. I need to get back to work. The place is going down the tubes."

She doubted that. The *Post* had incredible editors, some far better than Bill Brant. People who weren't anal retentive, dictatorial or self-centered.

"I'm sorry to hear that."

He snorted. "Like you care. When was the last time you called? Two months? I could've died and you wouldn't know it."

The phone rings both ways, Dad. And someone with a heart would've let me know if you'd died. "I'm sorry," she said again. But he was right in the fact she hadn't called after leaving Phoenix. Irony was her father worked in communication, but with his daughter it vanished. "There was a fire at the ranch. It destroyed part of the place where we were staying."

"Charlie?"

She'd acquired his attention. "No one was hurt, thank God. It happened during the day while he was at school." She glanced over her shoulder. Her son sat cross-legged on the living room floor, ramming his cars around the furniture. "We stayed with friends while the guesthouse was being repaired," she said, filling in airtime.

"What friends?" As if she had none.

"Tom McKee and his son. They have a guest room."

"You're on the Flying Bar T?" A calm question, without surprise.

"How did you know?"

"Tom McKee's ranch in Montana?" he asked.

"Yes. Do you know him?" She was confused. Bill had put her on to the series, claiming she should set aright the rumors about Hells Field. But this was personal. What was he up to?

"We've crossed paths," he muttered.

She straightened away from the counter. "When?"

"Doesn't matter."

"Of course it matters." More quietly so Charlie wouldn't hear, she said, "Why didn't you tell me you knew Tom? It would've made things much easier."

"That's easy come, easy go. On the other hand, when you gotta work for something, you put your heart into it."

She sighed. "I've always put my heart into my writing, Dad."

"Is the series done?"

"Not yet."

"I rest my case."

She could've said, *You're missing the point.* Instead, she clamped her lips, breathed long and slow.

"Let me know when you've got copy," he said and hung up. No goodbye, no good luck, no put Charlie on, no I've missed you so much I could die.

Nada.

Gently, she replaced the receiver. *Thanks, Dad. You've been such a supportive parent. Wish everyone could have one like you.*

Oh, stop whining, Rachel. Consider yourself fortunate. There are parents who maim, even kill their kids.

She'd interviewed them. Written their stories.

"Was that Grandpa?" In front of the fireplace, Charlie climbed to his feet, ready to dash to the phone.

"It was, baby." She walked over and stroked his hair. "But he was in a hurry and couldn't stop to chat. He did say hug the big guy for me." A white lie for the good.

"I'm not a big guy," he said, scowling as she cupped his face, kissed his forehead.

"You are to Grandpa."

"Will I be big like Ash one day?"

"Maybe." Height genes ran on her side of the family; Floyd had been five-ten. "But if you're not, you'll still grow up to be a man."

"And a cowboy."

"Yes," she said, lending a quick hug. "And a cowboy."

She would not smash his heart.

She would not be her father.

At eight o'clock, Rachel lay on her son's bed to read the next chapter of the novel they were reading together.

Fifteen minutes later, his eyes drooped and she closed the book, shut off the bedside lamp. "I need to talk to Ash for a minute, honey. Will you be all right while I go to the main house? I won't be gone long."

"Unnnhmm…" Sleepy mumbles into the pillow.

Rachel nuzzled his hair, smelled her child. Before she got downstairs, he'd be asleep. Tucking the quilt around his little chin, she kissed his brow. "Love you, champ," she whispered.

"'ove oo…."

His mouth opened on a faint snore; he was gone.

Outside, she tightened her coat against the frosty March night and headed for the house. Ash, Inez informed her, was checking the cows.

Before her nerve galloped into the hills, Rachel struck off for the building where a faint yellow patch lay on the frozen ruts in front of the half-opened door. She slipped inside and went down the dim corridor toward the cow office.

On its shadowed threshold, she hesitated. Ash and Daisy leaned side by side against a big walnut desk, intent on what Daisy was reading from a magazine.

A thrill ran through Rachel as she recognized the words from her "Riding Into The Sunset" story in *The Rancher*. With all her worry, she'd forgotten about the magazine's arrival today.

Ash gripped the edge of the desk as he stared at the copy. "What's it say under the photo?"

Daisy read, "'Innis Horton runs his outfit with sons Jude and Dakota, sixth and seventh generation ranchers since the Civil War. Independents like Horton have made Montana what it is today: a land of heart and beauty.'"

"Rachel wrote that?" Ash peered down at her photo of Innis, Jude and Dakota on horseback in front of the Horton corrals and barns.

"I told you, Dad. Rachel is a terrific writer."

"Yeah," he agreed, studying another photo of the Horton clan and ranch. "But after listening to you read Grandpa's story, I'd say you're just as good."

"I still have a lot to learn."

"We all do, Daiz."

"You're not mad anymore?"

He continued to browse the photographs. "That you want to be a journalist? No."

"I'll read you every one of my stories. Even if I'm off in some other state, I'll read them over the phone. I promise."

"I know you will, honey. Or Grandpa or Inez will. I'll hear them somehow. Now, where did we leave off?"

Daisy placed her finger on the page. "Here," she said and began again.

Rachel's lungs labored on a gulp of air. Her mind whirled, bits of memories flying, slamming into place, completing the puzzle—

The lunch recipe. Whole tomatoes confused for stewed tomatoes.

Daisy reading the paper to her father and Tom.

Ash, unaware of Daisy's dreams, her writing.

Tom, never Ash, on the computer.

Ash avoiding Charlie's bedtime story.

Ash, backing away from her manuscript Friday night.

Ash, she thought. *Aw, Ash. You can't read.*

She must have made a sound, for his head snapped up.

Daisy slapped the magazine closed. "Rachel!" Face draining of color, she pushed from the desk. "We—We were just reading your article—"

Rachel fled the barn. *Dear God.* The shame, the embarrassment in his eyes! No wonder he was leery of her work.

She ran through the dark, stumbling on ruts, grunting when her boot slipped on a strip of ice.

From under the porch of the house, the collies came, quiet

companions at her side as she rushed down the road. She couldn't go back to her house in the woods. Not yet. She needed to think, *think*.

He wouldn't want to see her again.

His shame would distance him further.

It was over. Over before it started. Over because his embarrassment—and her stunned surprise—would ripple through his memories whenever he saw *The Rancher*.

Gasping from the cold air, she stumbled to the fence along the roadside. There she waited with the dogs at her feet for her heart to calm, her breath to ease.

"I'm sorry," she murmured into the night. "So sorry you saw my expression." Guilt and shame heated her cheeks. "I didn't run from you. I ran from me."

"That's good to know."

Rachel whirled around.

He stood on the road, arms at his sides, blocking the white plate of the moon. "I was about to get Northwind if you'd gone any farther."

"Ash, I…" Tears smudged her vision.

"Daisy's right." He came toward her. "You nailed the heart of ranching. Listening to those words, I would've sworn you'd been raised in Park County."

He cupped her face, thumbed her tears. "I have severe dyslexia, Rachel. Words are a jumble for me. Letters missing, sentences running together. A long time ago, I gave up trying to make sense of print. For a lot longer, I felt downright useless—" He set a finger against her lips. "Just listen, okay? I grew up in an era when reading meant you were smart. And, hell, sometimes I still think that way. Then after Friday night—" he brushed away the hair a breeze pushed into her eyes "—I couldn't look at you without thinking the worst." He sighed. "You've seen me naked, but this—this was…"

"A baring of the soul," she whispered.

"Yeah. Cliché as it is."

She covered his hands warming her temples. If she could take on his pain, grant him her ability. If, if, if. "Not clichéd, truth," she said. "Ash, you live such a strong life. And I am in awe because there are things here I will always stumble over and read incorrectly."

She drank in his rich tea eyes. "I can't," she went on, "read the cows when they're due to calve, or when they're in trouble, or if the weather will change. I can't read if a horse is ornery or gentle, young or old. I can't read if the soil is good to grow grain or grass, or if it should be plowed under. I can't read the night sky or the morning dawn. Or how long a snowstorm will last or why a calf won't make it through the night. And it's taken me seven years to realize my son needs a dependable home, whereas you—you understand your family's needs immediately and you work toward attaining them. I haven't always done that for Charlie.

"And I'm awful at reading people. I misread Charlie's father, believing him a man of honor. He isn't. And I have huge issues that I can't get a read on with my own father." She took a breath. "When I arrived here, I thought you were a man with a grudge when in reality you're a man who's endured a lot of heartache. Ash," she whispered, "teach me to read like you. Teach me to understand your language."

In the distance of night, the horses snuffled the hay while high in the foothills a coyote howled.

When he said nothing the second guesses reared their heads. Hadn't she learned yet? She'd spent a lifetime attempting to understand her father, to read his broken heart.

Gently, she stepped back. *Time to wake up and smell the coffee, Rachel.*

Ash tugged her back against his chest, set his chin on her

hair. "Don't go." Then softly, so softly she almost misheard, "Maybe we can teach each other."

Hope bloomed. "Maybe," she said into his coat where she smelled the night and the barns and she thought he said *love you*, but was afraid to lift her head for fear she'd heard only the wind bringing the season of spring.

They stood an eternity under the gossamer light of ten million stars and the moon's aura sprinkling diamonds across the earth. The dogs watchful at their feet, the horses feeding beyond. At last he asked, "Okay Daisy's with Charlie?"

"He's been asleep for the past half hour."

"Come with me." He guided her down the road, back to the barns and the cow office, where he locked the door, where the cot he used during the cold and bitter nights of calving was pushed against the far wall.

He made up the bed with the blankets and pillow that were stacked at one end while she waited by the door. *This is how it will be if I stay. We'll catch moments whenever and wherever we can, here on the ranch.*

He turned, took her hand. "No one will bother us, don't worry." His eyes smiled. "I'm on the first shift."

Then he kissed her, and she vowed that as of this day she would take the first shift with him. Always.

If he asked her to stay.

Chapter Fourteen

Tom knew this day would come. Rachel had waited patiently while he made the journey to this point.

Today was that day. Excuses no longer worked. She would ask the question. The one to scrape back the scars.

They sat as always in the den. Daisy and Ash called it an office, but Tom liked den. Like a bear hibernating.

He'd hibernated for thirty-six years, Ash for five.

Until Rachel. Until she had them all living and feeling and wanting more again.

Not that she'd done anything unusual. She hadn't—except bring the boy into their home. Charlie, who needed a family and a daddy the way Laura had needed Tom for Ash and Meggie. The way *he'd* needed them.

So, it had come to this. Peeling back the scars, thick and whitened with age.

"What happened that day, Tom?" she'd asked a moment ago. "What caused the army to sweep Hells Field under the carpet?"

He flicked a look across the coffee table to Daisy. His grand-daughter—Laura's granddaughter—held her breath, her eyes fixed on him. *Don't hate me, girl.* And then his mind went back, back to that day, that dawn when they had stumbled across five U.S. Infantry on their knees in front of makeshift graves they dug themselves. Viet Cong holding M16s to the soldiers' heads.

"I had no choice but to order a forward surge," he began. "Anything more would have taken minutes and minutes kill good men."

He told how everybody rushed ahead, screaming, anger on their tongues at the atrocity of what was about to go down.

Gunfire blasted. Three VC crumpled where they stood, bodies riddled.

And then it happened. Men falling through the fragile ground cover over the tunnel under the path where the enemy hid with weapons.

A Recon mission gone wrong.

They saved six of their own platoon and one of the Infantry before the last bullet fired, the last knife slashed, the last grenade exploded, and he lay bleeding into jungle soil, calling for help on a radio strapped to a dead Marine's back, waiting, waiting for the merciful *whop-whop* sound of Hueys above the trees.

Tom stared at the floor. In his head, the choppers flew off, blades whirring, bending trees in their winds.

Him bleeding, bleeding...

A noise to the right brought him home, back to his den.

He lifted his eyes, saw Rachel. "The infantryman we saved? Bobby Brant. Your daddy."

* * *

Rachel jerked. "My dad? I don't understand."

"We've crossed paths."

Mere days ago Bill had dropped the words into the phone. He'd been there in Nam *with* Tom.

Tom. Questioning her that first day when she and Charlie came to rent the guesthouse. She should've known then something was amiss.

He spoke quietly. "Bobby led his men on a mission to massacre a village believed to be harboring VC. They'd killed about half of the people when we caught up to them. It was the wrong village."

"Oh, God."

A soft snort. "Yeah. Bobby claimed misinformation. Who's to say he wasn't right?" Tom stared at the black TV screen. A stillness canopied the room. "Anyway, we parted company after that. My men and I had another rice paddy to check. Two days later the communists caught up to Bobby and his men about ten miles south of the village. He radioed us before they downed his entire platoon." Tom looked away.

"And you went on a rescue mission." Amazing how calm she sounded amidst nausea.

"I ordered it."

"My father is Bill Brant," she insisted. "Your guy was Bobby Brant." *No sympathy, Tom, just the truth.*

Regret tinged the old man's eyes. "Robert William Brant. You have his hair, his mouth. Charlie's the spitting image of Bobby at seven. Freckles and all."

"Tom…" She didn't believe it. Could not. Her father, her precise, efficient father would not be that reckless, that cruel. "There must be some mistake."

"No mistake. I grew up with him. On this ranch."

"What?"

"He was the foreman's kid, Rachel. And my best friend."

Her mind swam. Bill had always maintained their people came from Chicago, that her grandparents were dead, that there had been no aunts or uncles. "I don't understand."

"Me, either, Grandpa," Daisy interjected. "Make sense."

"All right." He hiked his chin toward her purse. "Got a picture of your daddy?"

Rachel dug the photograph from her wallet, the only one remaining after the fire.

Tom studied the picture. "He's gotten heavier."

"He eats at restaurants all the time," she said before realizing she verified Tom's claim.

The old soldier returned the photo to Rachel. "We knew each other in diapers. He was a year older. Went to school together, played football together, did all the silly, goofy things boys do as teenagers. Then we were drafted. We left the same day for training. Standing at the train station in Billings we shook in our skins, but we were also excited as hell. We wouldn't be alone at boot camp, and we were ready to take on the world, *see* the world. Even if it meant going to a hellhole. We'd be strapping on our boots to face the enemy side by side.

"Those days, you were damned lucky to have someone you knew over there. Someone you could talk to about home, who knew exactly what you were saying and thinking."

Rachel sat rigid as stone. It couldn't be. Why hadn't her dad mentioned Tom when he'd sent her on this story? When he knew she would land in Sweet Creek?

Tom continued. "Bobby and I had another friend we always hung out with. Tina Grace Vail."

"My mother's maiden name was Vail." And then another piece of the puzzle clicked. *"Omigod."*

"She was the girl I left behind when I went to Asia."

Rachel shot out of her chair. "My mother never lived in Montana."

"Yes, Rachel," Tom said quietly. "She did. She was the girl I was to marry when I returned." He laughed, the sound bitter. "Trouble was, she hated the fact her groom had gotten a good deal shorter." He shrugged. "So she went AWOL. Along with Bobby."

"That's *not* true." In her ears, her heart boomed. Her mother. Her sweet, *kindhearted* mother. "Mom wouldn't do such a thing to—to—"

"A man like me?" His brow lifted. "But she did. Took one look and—" he sliced the air like a plane "—flew the coop."

Rachel stared at Tom. A man of quiet words, wry humor, uncanny wisdom. A man like Ash.

"Call your dad," Tom said now. Kindly.

Call her dad. *Her dad.* Murderer of innocent people. Betrayer of best friends. Manipulator of daughters.

Breathing hard, Rachel glanced at Daisy on the couch. Such worry between her eyes. *I'll be okay. I'm always okay.*

She turned and walked from the room.

Striding down the lane to the guesthouse, she flipped open her cell phone. He picked up immediately.

"You *know* Tom McKee," she accused.

"So. He's finally told you."

"And what is that?" Her voice rose as anger surged. "What was *he* supposed to tell me that *you* should have told me years ago? Before you sent me on this wild-goose chase?"

"Nothing. We were in Nam together. He lost a few limbs and we were shipped back."

"A few limbs." She stopped ten feet from her door, closed her eyes. "You stole his fiancée."

He barked a laugh. "Tina?" Tina, not Grace. *Tina,* the name of his past. Of Tom's past. "You've seen him. Would you stay with a man like that?"

Yes. Yes, I would. He's an honorable man. She inhaled through her mouth for strength. "Did you know he has a family?" *An honorable son, a sweet granddaughter?*

"He had kids?"

She despised his incredulity. "Stepchildren." *Whose daddy died in a war you desecrated.* "She was a single mother," she said in defense, in loyalty.

"Must have been damned hard up, then."

Had he always been this crass? With the back of her hand, she mopped at her tears. "Who's my father, Bill? You or Tom?"

A snort. "I am. Do the math. You were born three years after Grace and I left Montana." Grace again, not Tina.

Rachel gazed at the late-afternoon light glancing through the pines. *Tom should've been my dad.*

"Just so you know," Bill went on, "it broke your mother's heart to see Tom like that."

So broken she ran away and married his best friend. "Why did she leave then?"

"Because I asked her to come with me. I wanted her with me. McKee was getting the ranch. I wanted the girl."

"I don't understand. What do you mean, Tom was getting the ranch?"

"I mean that my daddy—your grandpappy—was the foreman of the Flying Bar T and he got nothing. *Nothing.*"

Confusion was a vortex. "He didn't get paid?"

"He didn't get the ranch," Bill shouted. "Not one stinking acre."

"Yeah, but he was the foreman, not—"

"He was the illegitimate son—" he spat the word "—of Theodore McKee, Tom's grandfather. *My* grandfather."

A cold stream jetted through her veins.

Bill laughed through her silence. "By blood you're a McKee, Rachel. And Tom knows it. Except you're not his. You're *mine and Tina's*."

She could not speak, could not form a single word. She stared at the phone in her hand, a foreign entity uttering alien news. Slowly, she closed its lid.

She was some sort of second or third generation cousin to Tom?

Her father had it wrong. *Wrong*.

Except deep in her being, Rachel knew he told the cold truth. In front of her stood the guesthouse, reconstructed under Ash's direction, around it the trees, Ash's property, his life, his passion. *His heart*.

Memories surged, crafting two undeniable facts: Bill's emotionless behavior toward her and his love for her mother.

In his eyes, she was a McKee. But outcasted like him. His own daughter, the outcast.

Her father was a sick man.

Dry-eyed, she headed for the horse stable.

"Is that Mom riding Areo so fast way out there?" Charlie asked.

Behind the barns, Ash looked up from the calf he was medicating against scours. Sure enough, Areo trotted down the range road with Rachel bouncing like a basketball in the saddle.

He grinned. "Has your mom ridden much?"

Charlie's shoulders hoisted up to his ears. "Where's she going, Ash?"

"I don't know, buddy." He studied Rachel's direction. No scenic tour on this leg. "Let's find out."

Charlie and the dogs on his heels, Ash headed to the barn office, set the bottle in the refrigerator, then went out across the yard. Pops met him on the front porch.

"She's found out some news," the old man said.

Ash set a boot on the bottom step. "What news?"

"I told her the truth about her parents. Bill Brant," he added.

You're a Brant, right? The question Tom had asked seven weeks ago, that first day. A question alluding to a recognition that Ash had missed because he'd been too caught up in annoyance and anger that she was a reporter.

"What's going on, Pops?" Ash asked calmly, though his heart thrashed.

"You need to go to her. Talk to her." A lifetime of regret and sorrow plaited the old man's face. "Bring her home."

"Is my mom okay?" Charlie asked, eyes exaggerated behind his glasses.

"She'll be all right, son," Tom said gently. "Why don't you come on in the house while Ash has a chat with her?"

The boy peered up at Ash, who said, "Go with Grandpa Tom." The two men exchanged a glance. Tom nodded.

"Okay." Charlie ran up the ramp. "Can I wheel you inside, Grandpa Tom?"

"Wouldn't have it any other way, small fry."

"I'm not a small fry. You're the small fry."

"Ha! You think so, huh?" Tom caught the boy around the waist and tickled him with his prosthesis. "We'll see about that."

Charlie's giggles trailing through the air, Ash headed for the horse stable.

Rachel booted Areo into a lope.

She had lived a lie.

Her mother had lived a lie.

The woman whose pictures and articles, stories and poems Rachel had lovingly set into a scrapbook, was a lie. The woman about whom she'd journaled hundreds of pages—pages she'd shown Daisy so she, too, could treasure *her* mother.

All of it a big, fat lie.

Grace Brant was not kind. Her heart held no compassion. Tom's eyes had grieved the knowledge—for her, Rachel. A man without limbs had felt sorry for *her.*

Sweeping down from the frank and stunning Rockies, the wind stung her face.

Bill Brant had criticized her reporting techniques, then tossed over *this* story for her to tear open. For her to discover a truth she sought in childhood and onward: "What were the names of my grandpa and grandma?" "Why don't I have any relatives?" Then, later, "How did my grandparents make a living?"

Initially, Bill had sidestepped the answers, saying the past wasn't important. Then one day he'd shouted that their families had shunned him and Grace for eloping. And Rachel was never to ask again.

Background checks on the Net turned into reams of ineffective information. Brants littered the U.S. As years passed and Charlie filled her life, Rachel's heritage search waned.

Now, she saw Bill's tactics as cowardice, pure and simple. Cowardice in the jungles of Vietnam. Cowardice in the face of his best friend. But most of all, in the face of his daughter.

And her mother had agreed.

That fact carved a painful groove in Rachel's heart. She had pursued journalism, striving to clone the demeanor of a mother she lost years ago. So Bill Brant would notice. Be proud.

And love his daughter.

Approaching a line of trees, she realized Areo's route was the creek that had trapped Ash in the mud.

Ash… She wanted to cry. Howl. Tear her hair. Go up into the Crazy Mountains like the legend of the Native American woman, mad with grief, searching for the spirits of her lost family.

Ash, Ash. His name doubled her over the saddle. What would he think of her now? How would he feel? He who ached for a partnership in the Flying Bar T, a sorrow he had revealed two nights ago on a cot in the barn. Had her grandfather, that long-past foreman, ached for the same recognition?

Blinded with tears, she reined Areo down the creek slope to the spot where water now gurgled over a bed smooth from spring runoff. Halting the horse, Rachel gazed at the creek. *Sweet Creek.* Right there, smeared with mud and scared beyond reason for his life, she had held Ash's head in her lap.

Stoic cowboy. Reader of life.

He'd given her a chance. And taken a chance. On her.

How could love, that emotion of wonder and joy, hurt so much? She would leave within the week—as soon as she gave notice at the paper, talked to Charlie's principal and teacher.

The series was done. Tom's story would remain the secret he'd maintained for over three decades. Instead, *American Pie* would have to go with six stories. Or not. She no longer cared, no longer wanted to be a journalist—or any writer. She did not want to emulate Bill Brant.

Suddenly, Areo turned his head and whinnied, his round belly quivering under Rachel.

Northwind, with Ash astride, skidded down the treed slope.

"You okay?" he asked, reining the heaving stallion to a halt beside the gelding.

She looked down at the creek, *Sweet Creek,* his community, his home, his land. "You... You could've died here."

"Rachel. Look at me." Beneath the MCA cap, his eyes were grim. "Because of you I didn't die."

Swiping a hand across her nose, she pressed her mouth tight as a saddle cinch. "Anyone would've done the same."

"It wasn't anyone I wanted with me that day—or, for that matter, any other day, now or ever."

His meaning sank into her bones. He wanted her to stay. Oh,

God, she was going to cry, beat her breast against the pain. He didn't understand, wouldn't understand.

Ash dismounted, tied Northwind to a tree, then walked to her side. When he held up his arms, she automatically slid from the saddle. Face in his coat she said, "I'm quitting, Ash. I'm giving my notice at the paper tomorrow."

"Is that what you want?"

She rolled her forehead against his collarbone. "I don't know. But I'm asking myself this—why *did* I pursue journalism? To compete with my mother?"

"You'd lost her as a child, honey. You wanted something tangible to hold that was hers alone."

"Like Daisy with Susie?"

"Yes," he admitted. "Like Daisy with Susie. You've taught me well, Rach."

She looked into his tea eyes—tea with the sunlight shining through—and told of Tom and her father, of Bill Brant's actions before and during the war, of the wiles he used so that she'd unearth her ancestry through the Hells Field story. She spilled the soul of her life, her bloodline to the ground.

He was silent a long while. At last he said, "Listen to me, honey. In the end, the past really doesn't matter. Yes, it can hurt—if we allow it. Hell, it can even haunt us." He huffed a small laugh. "Don't I know it. But we can also stop the hurting. Right here, right now. Together."

"But don't you see?" she cried, voice hoarse. "My whole life's been a mockery. The image I held of my mother. God, my insane need to please my daddy! My career, my relationships." She shook her head. "The only thing that's not a mockery," she whispered, palming away her tears, "is Charlie. He's my truth."

Somewhere deep in the forest, a squirrel chittered. Northwind tossed his big head, clinking metal like small bells.

Ash lifted her chin. "And you're *my* truth, Rachel. That's not a mockery. You're a mother, a writer, a beautiful and talented woman. Tom's story and the ranch article are proof. Charlie is proof. And for it all, I love you." His eyes rooted another truth in her soul. "Stubborn cuss that I am, I know my heart and it's lost without you. So—" he touched her cheeks where the tears tarried "—if you're willing to write as a rancher's wife…Rach… Ah, lady, I'll *always* be proud of you *and* your words. But mostly, I'd be proud if we shared the McKee name. You, me, Daisy and Charlie. What do you say?"

His face, his dear, dear face. "Yes," she whispered, "I say yes and yes and yes."

His grin was a light in her heart. And then he kissed her.

Ash, her man, her cowboy.

Seventeen months later

Ash's jacket pillowing her head, Rachel lay on the Santa Fe blanket she had folded into one of the saddlebags. Above, the noon sun speared light through the leafy trees sheltering the creek's bank.

They were at their favorite spot, the one where she and Ash had saved each other. That's how they liked to delineate this part of Sweet Creek.

"I still can't believe it," she said, holding the book against the filtered August day.

The epitome of ease, Ash lay at a right angle to Rachel, head against her side, fingers linked over his stomach, one denimed knee bent. "Can't believe what?" he asked, eyes closed. "That you put the series together as a book?"

"Yes."

"I knew you had it in you when Daiz read me those pages."

Reading them herself, Rachel had known, too. "I'm glad I quit the paper." A chipmunk scampered across a rotted log several feet away. She watched the little creature pause, fluff its tail, then scurry into the undergrowth. A tiny detail in the vastness that was Montana but, right here, right now, it was their detail. Hers and Ash's.

He said, "Can't wait to hear your next book about the ranch wives of Sweet Creek."

"A strong and valiant breed of woman."

"Hmm. Like you."

She dipped her chin, blinking back the sting. God, she loved his profile, those dreamy long lashes, his glossy black hair.

Tracing the line of his stubbled jaw, she said, "I have a couple ideas for other books."

"Yeah?"

"One, I'd like to write about small-town America. I've lived in enough over the years. And two, I want to do a book about Montana's wild mustangs." The herd he helped through the winter months.

"Huh. Seems I know a guy who can help with that research."

Her ribs ached with the swell of love. "Sometimes," she whispered, "I need to pinch myself to make sure you're real."

A loopy grin. "Oh, I'm real, honey. Just leave the pinching to me and you'll see."

She batted him playfully with the book. "Such an unruly boy."

"Boy? That's not what you thought this morning."

She chuckled. They'd been married nearly a year and still he couldn't get enough of her. Or she of him. In their morning shower, he'd said, "When we're ninety we'll be doing this."

This. Making love. Yes, at ninety *this* would hold a beauty all its own. But today, *this minute,* beneath her skin, inches from his head, their DNA was merging. She was three weeks late and the doctor had confirmed her suspicions an hour ago.

Tonight, when the moon lifted her smile onto the contoured

edges of the Rockies, and far off in the deepening dark, coyotes called to each other, she would tell him.

"Read it again, Rach," he said. "Read the bit just before Pops' part of the book."

She had given each veteran the opportunity to include an introductory paragraph to their section of the series.

Tom had written one sentence. She read it slowly, softly, watching Ash blink open his eyes to the pearls of blue glinting through the leaves.

When she laid the book aside, he reached up, entwined their fingers while the words drifted around them like sunlit fairy dust.

This story is for my son, Ashford McKee,
owner of the Flying Bar T.

* * * * * *

Ambience is everything. Imagine eating a foie gras at a luncheonette counter or a side of coleslaw at Le Cirque. It's not a matter of food but one of atmosphere. Remember that when planning your dining room design.

—Tips from *Teddi.com*

"Now that's the kind of man you should be looking for," my mother, the self-appointed keeper of my shelf-life stamp, says. She points with her fork at a man in the corner of the Steak-Out Restaurant, a dive I've just been hired to redecorate. Making this restaurant look four-star will be hard, but not half as hard as getting through lunch without strangling the woman across the table from me. "He would make a good husband."

"Oh, you can tell that from across the room?" I ask, wondering how it is she can forget that when we had trouble getting rid of my last husband, she shot him. "Besides being ten minutes away from death if he actually eats all that steak, he's twenty years too old for me and—shallow woman that I am—twenty pounds too heavy. Besides, I am *so* not looking for another husband here. I'm looking to design a new image for this place, looking for some sense of ambience, some feeling, something I can build a proposal on for them."

My mother studies the man in the corner, tilting her head, the better to gauge his age, I suppose. I think she's grimacing, but with all the Botox and Restylane injected into that face, it's hard to tell. She takes another bite of her steak, chews slowly so that I don't miss the fact that the steak is a poor cut and tougher than it should be. "You're concentrating on the wrong kind of proposal," she says finally. "Just look at this place, Teddi. It's a dive. There are hardly any other diners. What does *that* tell you about the food?"

"That they cater to a dinner crowd and it's lunchtime," I tell her.

I don't know what I was thinking bringing her here with me. I suppose I thought it would be better than eating alone. There really are days when my common sense goes on vacation. Clearly, this is one of them. I mean, really, did I not resolve less than three weeks ago that I would not let my mother get to me anymore?

What good are New Year's resolutions, anyway?

Mario approaches the man's table and my mother studies him while they converse. Eventually Mario leaves the table with a huff, after which the diner glances up and meets my mother's gaze. I think she's smiling at him. That or she's got indigestion. They size each other up.

I concentrate on making sketches in my notebook and try to ignore the fact that my mother is flirting. At nearly seventy, she's developed an unhealthy interest in members of the opposite sex to whom she isn't married.

According to my father, who has broken the TMI rule and given me Too Much Information, she has no interest in sex with him. Better, I suppose, to be clued in on what they aren't doing in the bedroom than have to hear what they might be doing.

"He's not so old," my mother says, noticing that I have barely touched the Chinese chicken salad she warned me not to get. "He's got about as many years on you as you have on your little cop friend."

She does this to make me crazy. I know it, but it works all the same. "Drew Scoones is not my little 'friend.' He's a detective with whom I—"

"Screwed around," my mother says. I must look shocked, because my mother laughs at me and asks if I think she doesn't know the "lingo."

What I thought she didn't know was that Drew and I actually tangled in the sheets. And, since it's possible she's just fishing, I sidestep the issue and tell her that Drew is just a couple of years younger than me and that I don't need reminding. I dig into my salad with renewed vigor, determined to show my mother that Chinese chicken salad in a steak place was not the stupid choice it's proving to be.

After a few more minutes of my picking at the wilted leaves on my plate, the man my mother has me nearly engaged to pays his bill and heads past us toward the back of the restaurant. I watch my mother take in his shoes, his suit and the diamond pinkie ring that seems to be cutting off the circulation in his little finger.

"Such nice hands," she says after the man is out of sight. "Manicured." She and I both stare at my hands. I have two popped acrylics that are being held on at weird angles by bandages. My cuticles are ragged and there's marker decorating my right hand from measuring carelessly when I did a drawing for a customer.

Twenty minutes later she's disappointed that he managed to leave the restaurant without our noticing. He will join the list of the ones I let get away. I will hear about him twenty years from now when—according to my mother—my children will be grown and I will still be single, living pathetically alone with several dogs and cats.

After my ex, that sounds good to me.

The waitress tells us that our meal has been taken care of by the management and, after thanking Mario, the owner, complimenting him on the wonderful meal and assuring him that once I have redecorated his place people will be flocking here in droves (I actually use those words and ignore my mother when she rolls her eyes), my mother and I head for the restroom.

My father—unfortunately not with us today—has the patience of a saint. He got it over the years of living with my mother. She, perhaps as a result, figures he has the patience for both of them, and feels justified having none. For her, no rules apply, and a little thing like a picture of a man on the door to a public restroom is certainly no barrier to using the john. In all fairness, it does seem silly to stand and wait for the ladies' room if no one is using the men's room.

Still, it's the idea that rules don't apply to her, signs don't apply to her, conventions don't apply to her. She knocks on the door to the men's room. When no one answers she gestures to me to go in ahead. I tell her that I can certainly wait for the ladies' room to be free and she shrugs and goes in herself.

Not a minute later there is a bloodcurdling scream from behind the men's room door.

"Mom!" I yell. "Are you all right?"

Mario comes running over, the waitress on his heels. Two customers head our way while my mother continues to scream.

I try the door, but it is locked. I yell for her to open it and she fumbles with the knob. When she finally manages to unlock and open it, she is white behind her two streaks of blush, but she is on her feet and appears shaken but not stirred.

"What happened?" I ask her. So do Mario and the waitress and the few customers who have migrated to the back of the place.

She points toward the bathroom and I go in, thinking it serves her right for using the men's room. But I see nothing amiss.

She gestures toward the stall, and, like any self-respecting and suspicious woman, I poke the door open with one finger, expecting the worst.

What I find is worse than the worst.

The husband my mother picked out for me is sitting on the toilet. His pants are puddled around his ankles, his hands are hanging at his sides. Pinned to his chest is some sort of Health Department certificate.

Oh, and there is a large, round, bloodless bullet hole between his eyes.

Four Nassau County police officers are securing the area, waiting for the detectives and crime scene personnel to show up. They are trying, though not very hard, to comfort my mother, who in another era would be considered to be suffering from the vapors. Less tactful in the twenty-first century, I'd say she was losing it. That is, if I didn't know her better, know she was milking it for everything it was worth.

My mother loves attention. As it begins to flag, she swoons and claims to feel faint. Despite four No Smoking signs, my mother insists it's all right for her to light up because, after all, she's in shock. Not to mention that signs, as we know, don't apply to her.

When asked not to smoke, she collapses mournfully in a chair and lets her head loll to the side, all without mussing her hair.

Eventually, the detectives show up to find the four patrolmen all circled around her, debating whether to administer CPR, smelling salts or simply call the paramedics. I, however, know just what will snap her to attention.

"Detective Scoones," I say loudly. My mother parts the sea of cops.

"We have to stop meeting like this," he says lightly to me, but I can feel him checking me over with his eyes, making sure I'm all right while pretending not to care.

"What have you got in those pants?" my mother asks him, coming to her feet and staring at his crotch accusingly. "*Baydar?* Everywhere we Bayers are, you turn up. You don't expect me to buy that this is a coincidence, I hope."

Drew tells my mother that it's nice to see her, too, and asks if it's his fault that her daughter seems to attract disasters.

Charming to be made to feel like the bearer of a plague.

He asks how I am.

"Just peachy," I tell him. "I seem to be making a habit of finding dead bodies, my mother is driving me crazy and the catering hall I booked two freakin' years ago for Dana's bat mitzvah has just been shut down by the Board of Health!"

"Glad to see your luck's finally changing," he says, giving me a quick squeeze around the shoulders before turning his attention to the patrolmen, asking what they've got, whether they've taken any statements, moved anything, all the sort of stuff you see on TV, without any of the drama. That is, if you don't count my mother's threats to faint every few minutes when she senses no one's paying attention to her.

Mario tells his waitstaff to bring everyone espresso, which I decline because I'm wired enough. Drew pulls him aside and a minute later I'm handed a cup of coffee that smells divinely of Kahlúa.

The man knows me well. Too well.

His partner, whom I've met once or twice, says he'll interview the kitchen staff. Drew asks Mario if he minds if he takes statements from the patrons first and gets to him and the wait-staff afterward.

"No, no," Mario tells him. "Do the patrons first." Drew raises his eyebrow at me like he wants to know if I get the double entendre. I try to look bored.

"What is it with you and murder victims?" he asks me when we sit down at a table in the corner.

I search them out so that I can see you again, I almost say, but I'm afraid it will sound desperate instead of sarcastic.

My mother, lighting up and daring him with a look to tell her not to, reminds him that *she* was the one to find the body.

Drew asks what happened *this time.* My mother tells him how the man in the john was "taken" with me, couldn't take his eyes off me and blatantly flirted with both of us. To his credit, Drew doesn't laugh, but his smirk is undeniable to the trained eye. And I've had my eye trained on him for nearly a year now.

"While he was noticing you," he asks me, "did *you* notice anything about him? Was he waiting for anyone? Watching for anything?"

I tell him that he didn't appear to be waiting or watching. That he made no phone calls, was fairly intent on eating and did, indeed, flirt with my mother. This last bit Drew takes with a grain of salt, which was the way it was intended.

"And he had a short conversation with Mario," I tell him. "I think he might have been unhappy with the food, though he didn't send it back."

Drew asks what makes me think he was dissatisfied, and I tell him that the discussion seemed acrimonious and that Mario looked distressed when he left the table. Drew makes a note and says he'll look into it and asks about anyone else in the restaurant. Did I see anyone who didn't seem to belong, anyone who was watching the victim, anyone looking suspicious?

"Besides my mother?" I ask him, and Mom huffs and blows her cigarette smoke in my direction.

I tell him that there were several deliveries, the kitchen staff going in and out the back door to grab a smoke. He stops me and asks what I was doing checking out the back door of the restaurant.

Proudly—because, while he was off forgetting me, dropping by only once in a while to say hi to Jesse, my son, or drop something by for one of my daughters that he thought they might like, I was getting on with my life—I tell him that I'm decorating the place.

He looks genuinely impressed. "Commercial customers? That's great," he says. Okay, that's what he *ought* to say. What he actually says is "Whatever pays the bills."

"Howard Rosen, the famous restaurant critic, got her the job," my mother says. "You met him—the good-looking, distinguished gentleman with the *real* job, something to be proud of. I guess you've never read his reviews in *Newsday*."

Drew, without missing a beat, tells her that Howard's reviews are on the top of his list, as soon as he learns how to read.

"I only meant—" my mother starts, but both of us assure her that we know just what she meant.

"So," Drew says. "Deliveries?"

I tell him that Mario would know better than I, but that I saw vegetables come in, maybe fish and linens.

"This is the second restaurant job Howard's got her," my mother tells Drew.

"At least she's getting *something* out of the relationship," he says.

"If he were here," my mother says, ignoring the insinuation, "he'd be comforting her instead of interrogating her. He'd be making sure we're both all right after such an ordeal."

"I'm sure he would," Drew agrees, then looks me in the eyes

as if he's measuring my tolerance for shock. Quietly he adds, "But then maybe he doesn't know just what strong stuff your daughter's made of."

It's the closest thing to a tender moment I can expect from Drew Scoones. My mother breaks the spell. "She gets that from me," she says.

Both Drew and I take a minute, probably to pray that's all I inherited from her.

"I'm just trying to save you some time and effort," my mother tells him. "My money's on Howard."

Drew withers her with a look and mutters something that sounds suspiciously like "fool's gold." Then he excuses himself to go back to work.

I catch his sleeve and ask if it's all right for us to leave. He says sure, he knows where we live. I say goodbye to Mario. I assure him that I will have some sketches for him in a few days, all the while hoping that this murder doesn't cancel his redecorating plans. I need the money desperately, the alternative being borrowing from my parents and being strangled by the strings.

My mother is strangely quiet all the way to her house. She doesn't tell me what a loser Drew Scoones is—despite his good looks—and how I was obviously drooling over him. She doesn't ask me where Howard is taking me tonight or warn me not to tell my father about what happened because he will worry about us both and no doubt insist we see our respective psychiatrists.

She fidgets nervously, opening and closing her purse over and over again.

"You okay?" I ask her. After all, she's just found a dead man on the toilet, and tough as she is that's got to be upsetting.

When she doesn't answer me I pull over to the side of the road.

"Mom?" She refuses to meet my eyes. "You want me to take you to see Dr. Cohen?"

She looks out the window as if she's just realized we're on

Broadway in Woodmere. "Aren't we near Marvin's Jewelers?" she asks, pulling something out of her purse.

"What have you got, Mother?" I ask, prying open her fingers to find the murdered man's ring.

"It was on the sink," she says in answer to my dropped jaw. "I was going to get his name and address and have you return it to him so that he could ask you out. I thought it was a sign that the two of you were meant to be together."

"He's dead, Mom. You understand that, right?" I ask. You never can tell when my mother is fine and when she's in la-la land.

"Well, I didn't know that," she shouts at me. "Not at the time."

I ask why she didn't give it to Drew, realize that she wouldn't give Drew the time in a clock shop and add, "...or one of the other policemen?"

"For heaven's sake," she tells me. "The man is dead, Teddi, and I took his ring. How would that look?"

Before I can tell her it looks just the way it is, she pulls out a cigarette and threatens to light it.

"I mean, really," she says, shaking her head like it's my brains that are loose. "What does he need with it now?"

SPECIAL EDITION™

Logan's Legacy Revisited

**THE LOGAN FAMILY IS BACK
WITH SIX NEW STORIES.**

Beginning in January 2007 with

THE COUPLE MOST LIKELY TO

by

LILIAN DARCY

Tragedy drove them apart. Reunited eighteen
years later, their attraction was once again
undeniable. But had time away changed
Jake Logan enough to let him face his fears
and commit to the woman he once loved?

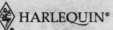

nocturne™

**WAS HE HER SAVIOR
OR HER NIGHTMARE?**

HAUNTED
LISA CHILDS

Years ago, Ariel and her sisters were separated for
their own protection. Now the man who vowed
revenge on her family has resumed the hunt, and
Ariel must warn her sisters before it's too late.
The closer she comes to finding them, the more
secretive her fiancé becomes. Can she trust the man
she plans to spend eternity with? Or has he been
waiting for the perfect moment to destroy her?

On sale December 2006.

In February, expect MORE
from

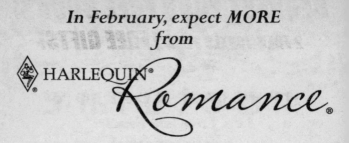

HARLEQUIN® *Romance*®

as it increases to six titles per month.

What's to come...

Rancher and Protector

Part of the
Western Weddings
miniseries

BY JUDY CHRISTENBERRY

The Boss's
Pregnancy Proposal

BY RAYE MORGAN

Don't miss February's
incredible line up of authors!

HRINCREASE

Silhouette®

COMING NEXT MONTH

#1801 THE COUPLE MOST LIKELY TO—Lilian Darcy
Logan's Legacy Revisited

Since their tragic breakup eighteen years ago, Jake Logan had become a successful doctor and seen the world. The farthest high school sweetheart Stacey Handley, divorced mother of his twins, had traveled was in her own heart. With Jake back in town on Logan family business, would the older, wiser couple get a second chance at first love?

#1802 THE RANCHER'S REQUEST—Stella Bagwell
Men of the West

Assigned by her local paper to dig up dirt on an old family scandal at Sandbur Ranch, reporter Juliet Madsen quickly incurred the wrath of wealthy ranch owner Matteo Sanchez. But it wasn't long before their heated words turned to kisses, spurred on by Matt's matchmaking daughter....

#1803 A MAN IN A MILLION—Jessica Bird

Needing backup in her fight to wrest control of her trust fund from a sleazy stepbrother, Madeline Maguire enlisted tough-talking renegade chef Spike Moriarty. Soon things were really cooking between the athletic heiress and the man with a past…until evil stepsister Amelia Maguire arrived on the scene—and tried to steal Maddie's man!

#1804 HOMETOWN CINDERELLA—Victoria Pade
Northbridge Nuptials

Coming home to Northbridge, widow Eden Perry expected peace and quiet. Instead, when she took on a case with police officer Cam Pratt, the forensic artist had to face up to her past as a nerdy, insecure teenager. Cam, the boy she'd preemptively taunted in high school had become an irresistible man—one who stirred up something in Eden's soul.

#1805 HER SISTER'S SECRET LIFE—Pamela Toth
Reunited

Lily Mayfield had left town at eighteen after she was caught kissing her sister's fiancé. Now, thirteen years later, it was time to come home. Judging by his *warm* reception, her ex-boyfriend Steve Lindstrom was letting bygones be bygones…until a question about the paternity of Lily's twelve-year-old child threatened to douse their rekindled affections.

#1806 A PLACE TO CALL HOME—Laurie Paige
Canyon Country

As teenagers, troubled Zia Peters had turned to Jeremy Aquilon for support. Now years later, their paths crossed again—as Zia faced her biggest crisis yet. Ever reliable, Jeremy took her into his home, and Zia did what she should have done long ago—she took this down-to-earth engineer into her heart.

SSECNM1206